THE SPY MASTER'S SCHEME

GLASS AND STEELE, #12

C.J. ARCHER

WWW.CJARCHER.COM

CHAPTER 1

LONDON, WINTER 1891

*I*t was the moment I'd been dreading. The moment I hoped not to experience for some time yet: the arrival of Lady Rycroft and her middle daughter, Charity Glass.

Thankfully, Matt braved their presence alongside me in the drawing room of our Park Street townhouse. Aunt Letitia was there too, although she said very little after the initial stiff greetings. Aunt Letitia had a fractious relationship with her brother and sister-in-law, having been forced to live with the overbearing couple and their entitled daughters for years before Matt arrived in London and set up house.

Bristow bowed out of the drawing room and closed the doors, leaving me to pour the tea and slice the sponge cake. Lady Rycroft didn't even wait to be handed a cup before she got in her first cutting remark of the afternoon.

"We've been back in the city for five days and you have not called on us, India."

"I've been busy."

That was rather an understatement. A mere week ago, I'd been investigating the murder of a toymaker magician, researching gypsy curses, stopping an automaton from running

1

amok, and trying to get answers from a government spy. There was also the rather significant occasion of Matt almost dying after being shot. If it hadn't been for his magical watch, he would not be sitting in the armchair with a frustrated expression on his handsome face. I think the frustration came from being closeted inside the house this past week rather than a result of his aunt and cousin's presence. For an active man like Matt, being cooped up here was tantamount to being imprisoned.

Lady Rycroft accepted the cup and plate from me. "I know you're not used to the way things are done in polite society, so I hope you'll take this as helpful advice, which is how it's intended. It's the duty of the junior members of the family to call upon the more superior members when they return to London." She lifted the cup to her lips and gave her sister-in-law a sideways glare. "I expected Letitia to guide you in this, as in other things."

"She did," I assured her before Aunt Letitia retorted that she didn't want to see her. "I would have called on you before now, but as I said, I've been very busy."

"And what is more important than welcoming family back to the city?" The icy undercurrent of her tone left me in no doubt that she could think of nothing more important.

I sipped and let my gaze drift from her censorial one, hoping my silence would put an end to it.

Matt was in no mood to give in, however. "Murder," he said simply.

Lady Rycroft gasped.

I threw Matt a sharp look. "He means investigating a murder, not committing one."

He returned my look with a tight smile, and I could almost hear his unspoken "Yet."

Charity looked up from her slice of cake, showing some spark for the first time since she'd sat down. "How thrilling. Was it that toymaker? I read about it in the newspaper. Was he really murdered by his own toy, that Medieval knight automaton?"

"His wife killed him," Matt said.

"But the device did the actual strangling."

Lady Rycroft made a sound of disgust in the back of her throat and Aunt Letitia went a little pale. Although she sometimes overheard our conversations during an investigation, we tried to keep the worst of the details from her.

Matt ignored Lady Rycroft and focused his attention on his cousin. There was a rigidity in his shoulders and an intensity in his eyes, both signs of his frustration over the misinformation about magic that circulated among the public. "The automaton no more killed him than a knife can stab someone of its own accord. Mrs. Trentham wielded the automaton like a weapon."

Charity met Matt's gaze with her own, but where his was dark with simmering anger, hers was bright with enthusiasm. "One could say that *magic* was the weapon."

Matt's jaw hardened. "No, one could *not* say that."

Before Charity further stirred the pot she'd inadvertently placed over the coals, I cut her off. "Let's not get into a philosophical discussion now."

"Speaking of magic," Lady Rycroft went on, "India, do you know where I can find a fur magician? My fool of a maid didn't pack my fox stole properly and the moths got to it. I thought if I have to get another, I might as well get the best." At my open-mouthed stare, she added, "I'm willing to pay handsomely, of course."

This must explain the reason for her visit. To have my magic accepted by her was surprising, but to be actively courted for it was astounding. "No, I don't know any fur magicians."

"Pity." She sipped her tea and looked away. The silence stretched thin.

3

"How is the country at this time of year, Aunt Beatrice?" Matt asked.

"Cold and miserable. The house is drafty, none of my friends live close by, and your uncle is out all day checking on the tenant farms or shooting. With only Charity for company, I couldn't wait to come back here."

If Charity felt slighted by her mother's comment, she didn't show it. Indeed, I wasn't even sure she heard a word her mother said. She stared at the door, her eyes dulled again. While I was thankful she no longer wanted to talk about magic or murder, I worried that she was hoping Cyclops would enter. Fortunately he was at work, having been assigned to duty at Shoreditch Police Station after recently becoming a constable.

Lady Rycroft sighed heavily. "How I do miss Hope."

"Has she not called on you either?" Aunt Letitia asked.

Lady Rycroft lifted the cup to her lips. "She has been busy."

"We've seen her. She calls on Matthew and India from time to time. Matthew and India have called on Hope and Lord Coyle too."

That wasn't quite the whole truth. While Hope and her husband, Lord Coyle, had visited us, and we'd visited their house too, it was only as part of the investigation, and our meetings were fraught with tension. Indeed, I'd rather endure a hundred afternoon teas with Lady Rycroft and Charity than a single one with Lord and Lady Coyle.

Lady Rycroft met this news with a pursing of her lips and a flaring of her nostrils. "Clearly Hope is not herself. I blame her husband."

"You *wanted* them to marry!" Charity cried, proving she was listening after all.

"And I am proud of her for securing an earl. But he doesn't realize that a young bride still needs to know that she is as attractive to her husband as she was before they married." She put up her hand to stay our comments, even though no one was about to offer any. "She is still a beauty, of course. The prettiest of all my girls, without a doubt, and the most accomplished, the most agreeable."

Charity pulled a face.

"But he must show her that he appreciates all that she brings to the marriage."

"What *does* she bring to the marriage?" Aunt Letitia asked with a sardonic edge.

Lady Rycroft bristled. "Did you not just hear me? Beauty, accomplishments and agreeableness."

"None of which are important for a successful marriage."

"What would you know?" Lady Rycroft shot back.

Oh lord, this meeting was deteriorating faster than I anticipated. "Have you heard from Patience?" I asked in an attempt to salvage it.

"No." The curt reply invited no more conversation on the topic of her eldest daughter whose husband's title had been stripped from him.

Lady Rycroft set down her teacup, a troubled frown appearing on a forehead pulled tight by the turban wrapped around her hair. The frown was not for her eldest daughter, however, but for her youngest. She didn't want to leave the topic of the Coyles yet. "I'm afraid marriage is not turning out the way Hope would have liked."

"Why do you say that?" Aunt Letitia asked.

"Her letters imply he limits her spending, among other things."

"Other things?" I echoed.

"He doesn't like her visiting her friends. He says they're beneath her, now. But he doesn't allow her to invite new, more appropriate friends to dinner, either. He says they talk too much and he just wants a quiet evening."

"He is old," Matt pointed out.

5

Both of his aunts turned frosty glares onto him. "He's the same age as us," Aunt Letitia said.

"Speak for yourself," Lady Rycroft snipped off.

Matt rarely made such a social misstep and apologized profusely.

I pressed my lips together to hide my smile.

Charity drained her teacup and placed it on the saucer with a loud clatter to gain our attention. "So what if he does control her spending and who comes to dinner? It's his house and his money. He can do what he wants."

"I know, dear, but I am disappointed in Hope for not using her wit and wiles to get her way," Lady Rycroft said. "She should not allow him to manipulate her the way he is. It's simply not like her."

"Marriage isn't about who can manipulate whom," Matt said.

"Theirs is." Aunt Letitia said exactly what I was thinking.

Lady Rycroft continued as if she hadn't heard them. "She used to have him wrapped around her little finger. When they were courting, he gave her whatever she asked for, and more. But now..." She shook her head. "What changed?" She lifted her gaze to Matt's. "You've seen them more than me, these last few weeks, and Lord Coyle is a close acquaintance of yours. What do you think?"

"He's not an acquaintance whose company we enjoy," Matt told her.

Aunt Letitia leaned toward her sister-in-law. "Matt and India are not on good terms with the Coyles."

"He's not a nice man." I could have told them Hope wasn't nice either but refrained. Her mother would leap to her defense, although she was probably the only one in the room who would. Not even Charity liked her sister.

Lady Rycroft stretched her fingers out on her lap and studied them. "Yes. Well. I wrote to her and told her she must learn to control him and not be controlled by him."

"He won't be controlled by anyone," Matt said.

"Pish posh. She must find a way. If there's something my youngest is very good at, it's getting others to do what she wants."

Charity snorted.

Lady Rycroft presented Charity with her shoulder to cut her out of the conversation. "Hope is a clever girl. She'll learn how to do it."

"And if she doesn't, he's an old man and will likely die before too long." The smug look on Charity's face left me in no doubt that she wanted to shock her mother and aunt, both of whom looked at her aghast. "Be honest, Mother. You know that's why she married him. You say it yourself—Hope is no fool. Coyle might be difficult to manage, but it will all be worth it when she becomes his widow."

Her mother clicked her tongue. "Honestly, Charity. You do say the oddest things."

The door opened and Bristow entered. "Lord Farnsworth is here," he intoned.

Matt glanced at me. His expression said it all—this could either be a disaster or a welcome amusement.

"Show him in," I said.

Lord Farnsworth must have been lingering outside the door, waiting. He appeared before Bristow had even straightened from his shallow bow. He was like a burst of sunshine on a cloudy day with his red-gold hair, bright smile and exuberance. Sometimes that exuberance was a little too much, but today I welcomed it. I think Matt did too. He certainly shook Lord Farnsworth's hand heartily.

"Good afternoon, dear friends! How pleasant to see you here, Lady Rycroft, Miss Glass." He beamed at Charity. "I am fortunate to be in the presence of so many lovely ladies. And you too, Glass, of course, although you're not lovely. At least, I don't find you to be so, although I'm sure the ladies do." He laughed.

7

Charity shifted aside on the sofa and patted the cushion. "Come and sit with me, my lord."

"Don't mind if I do."

Bristow returned with another cup and saucer, and I poured tea for Lord Farnsworth. "Are you looking for Willie?"

"Not in particular." Lord Farnsworth accepted the cup from me. "Is she in?"

Matt shook his head. "She went for a walk."

Willie and Duke had left the house when Lady Rycroft and Charity arrived, not wanting to endure an afternoon tea with them. Indeed, Willie hadn't been home very much of late. If she wasn't spending time with Lord Farnsworth or Detective Inspector Brockwell, she was out with Duke or one of her other friends. I suspected she might even have a new lover, but I didn't ask. There was a limit to how much of Willie's private life I wanted to know.

I was still reeling from learning she and Lord Farnsworth had been lovers. After the dust had settled from that bombshell, she admitted it had just been once, at the start of their friendship, and hadn't happened again. They both realized they preferred to simply be friends. I wasn't sure if Brockwell knew. Indeed, I was never sure what Brockwell knew or how he and Willie felt about one another. Their relationship was best left to either ride the turbulent waves or float on the calm surface as they saw fit. It seemed to work for them.

I think.

"Don't mind me," Lord Farnsworth said as he accepted a slice of sponge cake from me. "Please, carry on your conversation as if I weren't here."

Lady Rycroft wasn't going to discuss the marital problems of the Coyles in front of an outsider and quickly changed the subject. "How marvelous to see you again, my lord. Are you well?" She sported an odd smile on her face as she gave him her full attention. Indeed, perhaps it was merely odd because she smiled so rarely and I wasn't used to seeing it.

I exchanged a glance with Matt and the corner of his mouth lifted in a smirk. Clearly he suspected the same as me —Lady Rycroft wanted to grease the wheels, so to speak, in the hope his lordship would notice Charity. So far, he seemed more intent on the cake than on anyone in the room.

"Well enough for someone who didn't get the filly he had his eye on. Duke Something-or-other won her instead."

"How disappointing, but I hear you have a marvelous stable and I'm sure the loss of one horse won't matter."

I suppressed my smile, knowing that Lord Farnsworth wasn't speaking about a horse but a lady he'd hoped to marry. He tended to speak about horses and prospective wives using the same terms.

"True enough," he said. "I have an excellent prospect for the Gold Cup at Royal Ascot this year."

I blinked and shook my head to clear it. Matt tried, and failed, to suppress his smile.

Charity held out her plate and asked me for another slice of cake. Her mother snatched the plate off her and placed it on the table, out of her daughter's reach. "You've had quite enough, my dear."

Charity sat back with a pout.

"My daughter loves horses and racing." Lady Rycroft tapped Charity's knee.

Lord Farnsworth sat up straighter and addressed Charity. "Jumps or flats?"

She hesitated then said, "Both?"

Lord Farnsworth beamed. "Capital!"

"No!" Aunt Letitia cried. "No, this won't do at all. Charity doesn't really like horse racing."

"Of course she does," Lady Rycroft said. "We attend Royal Ascot every year."

"Doesn't everyone?"

9

They all looked to Matt and me.

"I like to go very fast on horseback," Charity said. "I don't mind if it's over flat or jumps. I find riding invigorating. Don't you, my lord?"

"Call me Davide."

Lady Rycroft smiled at Lord Farnsworth then bestowed it upon her daughter. She looked as though her horse had crossed the finish line first.

Aunt Letitia looked like hers had come last, broken a leg, and had to be put down. "Willimena will be back soon. Matthew, go in search of her. Tell her Lord Farnsworth has come to see *her*."

"Oh, but I haven't." Lord Farnsworth picked up his teacup. "I came to see India."

Aunt Letitia seemed to deflate a little, but quickly rallied. "But you would like to see Willie."

"Yes, of course."

She gave her sister-in-law a triumphant smile.

"But I am so glad I had this opportunity to see Lady Rycroft and Miss Glass. They have quite cheered me, and I've been low in spirits lately."

Lady Rycroft perked up. "My middle daughter does tend to have that effect on people." She tapped Charity's knee. "She's quite a...surprising girl."

"I like surprises."

Charity stared at Lord Farnsworth, her face frozen. She seemed unsure how to take him and was rendered speechless.

The same could be said of Aunt Letitia, Matt and me. While it was true that Lord Farnsworth liked unusual experiences, his sudden interest in Charity was out of the blue. He'd previously said she was too odd, even for him.

What was he playing at?

The clock on the mantelpiece chimed the hour softly. Lady Rycroft glanced at it and let out a small gasp. "Charity, we must go. We have another call to make."

Charity wrinkled her nose. "Can't I stay here?"

"We're calling on Lady Burgess."

Charity sighed while Aunt Letitia gave a knowing nod. "How unfortunate that you can't stay longer, but you mustn't keep Lady Burgess waiting. Such an esteemed personage," she said to me. "Once a girl is invited to Lady Burgess's first ball of the spring, it's said she'll be set for a wonderful season. Do try to look happy, Charity."

"I hate balls and parties," Charity muttered.

Her mother laughed, but it rang false. "Don't be silly, child. Of course you love parties and balls." She turned to Lord Farnsworth. "She's just being modest. You know what young girls are like."

"Indeed I do," Lord Farnsworth said.

"Do you like balls and parties, Davide?"

"Depends on who else is there."

"Quite right." Lady Rycroft cleared her throat as she watched me tug on the bell pull. I could see she wanted to say something more to Lord Farnsworth to encourage him in Charity's direction, but she wasn't sure how to do it without coming across as desperate. In the end, she invited him to a musical soiree. "India and Matthew are coming," she finished with a hopeful smile for me.

"We are?" Matt said.

"Yes. It's tomorrow night."

Aunt Letitia's jaw hardened. "I think Davide is going out with Willimena tomorrow night."

"I can do both," he said. "The soiree first then I'll meet up with Willie later."

Lady Rycroft's smile slipped a little. "Nine o'clock, then. It'll just be an intimate occasion, since some of my acquaintances haven't returned to the city." She handed him a card with her address on it. "We're so thrilled you can come, aren't we, Charity? What a wonderful evening it promises to be."

"It does now." Charity beamed at Lord Farnsworth.

His eyes flared for a moment before he smiled too. "I'm looking forward to it already."

I tugged on the bell pull to summon Bristow. He opened the door for Lady Rycroft and Charity, and must have thought Lord Farnsworth was leaving too because he waited. But Lord Farnsworth stopped at the door to wave off the others.

"This is an interesting development," I whispered to Matt. "They both seem keen."

"It suits us well. It means Charity is no longer interested in Cyclops and he's no longer interested in Willie."

"I don't think he was ever interested in Willie."

"Of course he was," Aunt Letitia whispered back. "And he can be again, if Beatrice didn't interfere." She crossed her arms and glared at Lord Farnsworth as he rejoined us.

He stopped upon seeing her frown. "Is something the matter?"

"What are you playing at with my niece?"

"Oh, that. I've just been a little bored of late. She's just a distraction, Letty."

"A distraction!" I cried. "Davide, you can't court a young woman simply because you're bored."

"Never fear. I'll stop it before it gets too far. She doesn't seem like the sort to fall in love anyway."

"One doesn't have to be in love to have one's hopes raised." I looked to Matt.

"Just be careful," he warned. "Your feelings won't matter to Aunt Beatrice. If she can secure you for her daughter, she will."

Lord Farnsworth threw himself onto the sofa as if he lived here. "Don't worry about me. I haven't avoided the institution this long by being an easy target."

I looked to Aunt Letitia, but she seemed rather pleased that Lord Farnsworth wasn't considering Charity seriously. No doubt she still thought Willie was a viable prospect, entirely setting aside her own snobbery that dictated like must marry like when it came to social standing. She was also forgetting both Willie and Lord Farnsworth's disinterest in the other. They might have had one dalliance, but there'd been no sign of it happening again.

Two sets of footsteps loudly clomped up the stairs and headed toward the drawing room. A moment later, Willie and Duke entered.

"You just missed them," Matt said.

"We know," Duke said, eyeing off the cake. "We waited outside until we saw their carriage leave."

Willie cut a slice of cake for herself and took a large bite before sitting down on the sofa. Having her mouth full didn't stop her from talking. "Were you here the whole time, Davide?"

"More or less." He waggled his eyebrows at her. "Lady R invited me to a party tomorrow night. I'm going to flirt with Charity. Won't that be a lark?"

She stopped with the cake halfway to her mouth. "Are you mad? Do you remember what she did to Cyclops? She nearly ruined his life by accusing him of forcing her against her will."

He waved off her concerns. "I can look after myself."

Duke accepted a slice of cake from me. "I agree with Willie. I reckon you're playing a fool's game. If you get caught, you'll be stuck with Charity for life. Her father will make you marry her."

Lord Farnsworth looked offended. "What do you think I'm going to do with her?" He stared at me, aghast. "India, you too?"

I lifted a shoulder, no longer sure what was going on.

"I'm not going to have a dalliance with her. I won't even be alone with her. It'll just be a little flirtation here and there. We'll do what all amusing people do at parties—laugh at what the other guests are wearing, talk about horses, and drink too much Champagne. All in full view of everyone, naturally."

I breathed a sigh of relief and caught Matt smiling at me. The devil knew what Lord Farnsworth had meant all along. Perhaps I shouldn't have been so quick to judge him. He was a good man underneath all the frivolity.

"I still reckon you should be careful," Willie said. "Charity's mad, not simple."

Lord Farnsworth rubbed his hands together. "I'm looking forward to this party more and more."

"I'm not," Matt said. "How did we even get invited to this thing?"

"Beatrice doesn't yet know Davide well enough to invite him without you and India, the intermediaries in this new acquaintance," Aunt Letitia said. "If she wanted him to attend, she had to invite you."

"So can we get out of it now that he has agreed?"

"Certainly not."

"What if I'm ill?"

"You're not ill."

Matt appealed to me. "But I think I need to be careful not to tempt fate. Don't you, India?" He was referring to him being out in public, tempting the killer to shoot him. We hadn't informed Aunt Letitia that someone was trying to kill him, and didn't plan to, hence the cryptic conversation.

"We'll see how you feel tomorrow," I said.

We fell into silence, the only sounds coming from Duke and Willie as they drank tea and ate cake. After several moments, Lord Farnsworth clicked his fingers.

"I almost forgot. I had a reason for coming here." He looked serious, which meant something was very wrong. My heart did a little flip in my chest as I urged him to go on. "I dined at my club yesterday and all the talk was about magic and magicians."

"That talk is everywhere," Duke said. "Ever since Barratt

released that damned book, people haven't stopped talking about magic."

"There aren't merely *people* at my club. There are *influential* people, politicians among them. It seems there is a petition circulating with the intent to submit it to parliament. The petition wants the law changed to make it mandatory for craft guilds to exclude magicians."

"No law can do that!" Willie cried. "Membership is a guild matter. Ain't that right, India?"

I nodded as I crossed my arms, hugging myself. A chill crept down my spine that I couldn't shake.

Matt came to stand behind me, his hand on my shoulder. He gave it a reassuring squeeze. "It won't get through parliament, but guilds will exclude magicians anyway. It'll happen soon, I'm sure."

Without guild membership, magicians couldn't get a license to trade, and without that license, they had to close their shops and factories. If Matt was right, it would have devastating consequences for many families.

Lord Farnsworth wasn't quite so worried, however. "Dearest India, don't fret. The monied class are scouring the city for magical wares. They desire the best things money can buy, and now everyone knows the best is made by a magician. You'll see. People like Lady Rycroft will demand magicians be allowed to sell their goods, and we all know that people like her—and me, of course—run this country, not guild craftsmen."

He was probably right. As long as the wealthy and influential wanted magician-made goods gracing their homes, magicians would be protected. Lady Rycroft had practically begged me for the name of a fur magician. "Magicians will have to go into hiding and trade in secret," I said. "That won't be easy."

Lord Farnsworth looked smug. "Or a law will be passed that allows magicians to trade without a license."

It was a radical idea but a good one. Could it be possible? The guilds would put up a fight. If there was no need for craftsmen to obtain a license, there was no need for the guilds to exist.

"The ridiculous thing is, magic doesn't last," Matt said. "Magician-made goods might be excellent quality for a while, but once the magic deteriorates, they become as ordinary as artless-made ones. The tension between magicians and artless is pointless."

We spent the rest of the afternoon discussing what we could do and how we could influence certain politicians. Lord Farnsworth was very helpful, but I discovered that Matt already knew who would be capable of swaying the opinions of members of parliament.

At six o'clock precisely, Cyclops walked in. Dressed in the smart blue tunic of the constable's uniform, his helmet under his arm, he looked authoritative rather than resembling a menacing pirate. He removed his gloves and stood by the fire, warming his back, his hands clasped behind him. "What a day," he muttered. "You all heard, I s'pose."

"Heard what?" Willie asked.

"About the riot." At our blank looks, he continued. "The riot in Shoreditch."

"Who was rioting and why?" Matt asked.

"They were targeting shops on High Street where the proprietor was a known magician. Windows were smashed, doors broken. No one was injured but there was a lot of damage to property."

"The general public started it?"

Cyclops shook his head. "Artless guild members. And guess who led them." He looked at me as he said it.

I suddenly felt sick. "Abercrombie."

CHAPTER 2

*B*ristow entered but didn't have a chance to inform us that Catherine Mason had arrived before she barreled past him. She ran to Cyclops and threw her arms around him.

"Thank goodness you're all right." She cupped his face and inspected him thoroughly. "We were closing the shop for the day when we heard about the riot in your district. I came here directly. I was so worried." Satisfied that he was unharmed, she embraced him again.

His lips twitched as he tried to contain his smile. "I'm fine. You didn't have to come here. You could have sent a message."

She drew back and tilted her head to the side to regard him critically. "And you could have sent back a reply that said you were fine when you weren't, so that I wouldn't worry. I prefer to see you in person and judge for myself."

"What will your parents think when your brother arrives home without you? Is he going to tell them India invited you to dine here?" He glanced over her head at me.

"Of course you can stay for dinner, Catherine, and I will tell your parents that if they ask."

17

She shook her head. "I told Ronnie to tell them the truth. That I came here to see if you were all right, Nate. But I did say that I would stay to dine if invited."

"Then I'll tell Bristow to set another place at the table."

The butler suddenly appeared at the door again, but not because he heard his name or sensed that I wished to speak to him. He announced the arrival of another uninvited, but no less welcome, guest.

"Detective Inspector Brockwell has arrived. Shall I set another two places for dinner, madam?"

"Thank you, Bristow."

Willie greeted Brockwell with almost as much enthusiasm as Catherine had greeted Cyclops. He seemed surprised by her public display of affection, but not unhappy. He, too, warred with a smile.

"Well, this is nice. Is there a particular reason I'm being greeted with an embrace?"

"Can't a woman hug her man?" Willie asked.

"It's not like you. Not in front of the others."

She lifted a shoulder in a shrug. "Cyclops just told us about the riot and I got worried about you."

"I didn't attend the scene. The uniformed men had it under control."

She patted his chest. "Good." She led him by the hand to the sofa then sat beside him.

We all watched her with curious expressions, including Brockwell, but she failed to notice.

"Cyclops was just telling us about the riot," Matt said.

"News reached us at the Yard some time ago." Brockwell turned to Cyclops. "Did you make any arrests?"

"Five," Cyclops said.

"Including Abercrombie?" Matt asked.

Cyclops shook his head. "He didn't commit any of the violence himself."

I couldn't imagine the aloof and somewhat delicate man

throwing a brick through a window, but I also had trouble envisaging him involving himself with such a violent group, yet Cyclops said he led them. "Couldn't he be arrested for inciting violence?"

Cyclops shook his head. "He claims he wanted the protest to be peaceful. In fact, he called for calm, but it fell on deaf ears. I witnessed his attempts myself."

"He should still be arrested for organizing it," Matt said.

"A detective from my district will make inquiries. If he can prove Abercrombie did organize it, he'll be arrested."

Willie nudged Brockwell with her elbow. "You should be heading up the investigation. It involves magic."

"I think we're past the point of assigning crimes related to magic to me," Brockwell said. "This is just the beginning."

Matt agreed. "It's no longer a secret, best kept to a small group at the Yard."

"Dashed ugly business," Farnsworth muttered. "Why can't everyone just get along?"

"Because people's livelihoods are at stake," I said.

"Money is the root of evil."

Willie snorted. "Says the man who owns two houses, acres of land, and dozens of racing horses and magical objects."

Farnsworth sniffed. "Yes. Well. I'm a generous employer, too. Everybody likes working for me."

Willie and Duke rolled their eyes.

Catherine left Cyclops's side to come and sit with me. She handed me a piece of paper. "Seeing as it's just us, I'll take the opportunity to give you this now rather than wait until your aunt returns."

With Aunt Letitia getting dressed for dinner and only our friends present, we all felt comfortable talking freely. While Lord Farnsworth was a new friend, we trusted him after he'd helped Matt become acquainted with the home secretary. He knew all about Sir Charles Whittaker's position as a spy, our suspicions about Lord Coyle, and the attempts on Matt's life.

While his opinion was usually an unconventional one, his help as a nobleman was invaluable. Matt hadn't made many powerful connections among the nobility yet, but he was starting to, thanks to Lord Farnsworth.

That was why Catherine felt comfortable giving me the piece of paper with names on it for my list of magicians in front of him. I'd begun the list a mere week ago and asked my friends to help contribute to it where possible. While it was still a short list, I hoped to expand it so that it became a definitive catalogue. The trouble we'd experienced with Mrs. Trentham the toymaker magician and Amelia Moreton the fireworks magician proved that we needed to know who wielded magic for those times when it was used as a weapon.

But I would not share the list with the authorities unless and until it became necessary. It would be kept here, locked away in a secret place, with only myself, Matt, Cyclops, Willie and Duke knowing where to find it.

I unfolded the paper and scanned the three names. I recognized one. "Are these all woolen magicians?"

Catherine nodded. "I heard the woolen guild revoked the membership of suspected magicians, effective immediately. I asked a few questions of an acquaintance and discovered these men were identified by their superior workmanship and rumor."

Willie scoffed. "So a person is deemed guilty based on rumor now?"

"This isn't the work of the police," Brockwell reminded her.

She huffed and folded her arms. "It should be a crime to take a person's livelihood away from them without a trial."

"Or a thorough investigation or process of appeal," Cyclops added.

I handed the paper to Matt. "My Pyke's name is on there."

Mr. Pyke was a rug maker who used his woolen magic to make his carpets stronger and last longer. He'd given Fabian and me a spell which I'd changed to include the relevant words for the moving spell. The subsequent new spell had made Fabian's woolen rug fly.

The wool magic didn't work for long, however, so Mr. Pyke rarely used it. Despite that, he'd been correctly identified by his guild as a magician, and now he couldn't trade at all. He'd have to close his shop. It would be utterly devastating for him.

"The woolen guild has gone too far," Lord Farnsworth declared. "They ought to be punished for such a travesty."

"How?" Duke asked.

Lord Farnsworth had no answer.

"There may be public backlash," Cyclops said. "The locals were none too pleased with the riot in High Street today. They'll blame the organizers."

Willie smacked her fist on her knee. "Good. Abercrombie should be made to suffer the consequences. Maybe I'll spread the word myself that he was involved."

"Willie," I warned. "Don't cause trouble."

"He started it."

Bristow sounded the dinner gong at seven-thirty and we set aside grim conversations for more agreeable ones. It was such a companionable evening that I forgot all about the troubles beyond our doorstep, including the attempt on Matt's life. I exchanged glances and smiles with him, seated at the other end of the table. He seemed happy, too. Perhaps the forced confinement wasn't so difficult for him after all.

"I'm jealous." Lord Farnsworth's quiet declaration was intended only for my ears, and not Aunt Letitia, sitting on his other side.

I followed his gaze to Willie and Brockwell, seated next to one another. They looked comfortable, even going so far as to complete one another's sentences. Or, rather, Willie completed Brockwell's when he took too long to finish, which was something of a peculiarity of his.

"I thought you and Willie decided not to pursue anything further," I said.

"I'm not jealous of the inspector, you understand. I'm jealous of their relationship."

I used to think Willie and Duke would make a good couple, but I now knew how wrong that pairing would be. While they were firm friends, they'd make terrible lovers. They seemed to bring out the childishness in each other, and their constant bickering would wear thin. They reminded me of siblings, often arguing yet always there for one another if necessary. Willie and Brockwell were an odd couple on the surface, yet they were actually better suited.

"I want what they have," Lord Farnsworth said in an earnest tone I'd never heard him use before. "

"Companionship?"

"Yes, but something else too."

"Love?"

He wrinkled his nose. "Not necessarily love, no."

Now I was intrigued. "Then what, aside from companionship, do you want in a relationship?"

"The freedom to do as I please."

"Oh. I'm afraid not all relationships are as free as theirs."

"That's why I referenced them only, and not you and Glass, or Cyclops and Miss Mason. I want freedom to…" He waggled his fingers in the air. "To be myself."

I suspected he meant the freedom to be with other women, but I didn't say so. Some things were better left unsaid between friends. "I'm sure you'll find the right girl one day, Davide. She's out there waiting for you to sweep her off her feet."

He picked up his glass and saluted me with it. "And until I find her, I'm going to flirt with Charity Glass."

I sighed.

I wasn't sure whether I ought to be worried for Charity's reputation or not, but I soon forgot about her and Lord

Farnsworth altogether as we moved into the drawing room. We played cards until eleven, when Aunt Letitia retired.

Lord Farnsworth decided it was time to go too. "There's a boxing match in the basement of the George Inn starting at midnight. Anyone want to come? It promises to be a jolly good bout with that American fellow, Sullivan, up against a local contender."

"I'll go," Duke said, throwing in his cards. "Got to support my fellow countryman. Come on, Willie, Brockwell. I won't bother asking you, Cyclops, I know you won't."

"I have to work tomorrow," Cyclops pointed out.

"As do I," Brockwell said. "Besides, if it's in a basement at midnight, I doubt it's legal."

Lord Farnsworth rocked back on his heels and tried to look innocent.

Willie looked disappointed. "Come on, Jasper, you never go out with me."

"Because I don't like gambling or pugilism." He kissed her cheek. "But you enjoy yourself."

Willie nodded, but I could tell she was disappointed.

"May we offer you a ride home, Miss Mason?" Lord Farnsworth asked.

We escorted them to the door where they put on coats and hats to wrap themselves up against the cold February night. I took the opportunity to speak quietly to Catherine away from Cyclops.

"How are things at home?" I asked. "Particularly in regard to your parents accepting Cyclops?"

"It's fine."

I waited but she offered no more. "You mentioned you had a plan that would change your parents' opinions of him. Has that failed?"

She leaned closer. "I haven't set it in motion yet. But I will soon."

"Can you tell me what it is?"

"No."

"Not even a hint?"

She grinned. "It's more fun if you don't know."

"Not for me."

She kissed my cheek. "Thank you for the lovely evening. I always feel so at home here, more than I do in my parents' house."

I hugged her. "Let me know how your plan goes."

"I won't have to tell you. You'll just know."

We waved them off from the entrance hall then Matt closed the door. Cyclops bade us goodnight and disappeared upstairs. Bristow locked up before he too said goodnight.

Matt and I headed up the stairs slowly, hand in hand. "What were you and Farnsworth talking about at dinner?" he asked when we reached the landing. "You had such a strange look on your face."

"He was telling me how much he was looking forward to flirting with Charity."

"That explains why you looked like you'd heard a rude joke. You seemed shocked and yet on the verge of laughter too."

"Should we worry about her? It's not right that he wants to flirt with her. It could ruin her reputation."

"I'm not worried. He's the one who should be careful. He doesn't know what he's dealing with." He suddenly scooped me up in his arms and continued up the stairs. "Enough about other people's relationships. Let's concentrate on ours for the next little while."

I pouted. "*Little* while?"

"That sounds like a challenge and you know I can't resist one."

He took the rest of the stairs two at a time with me in his arms; he wasn't even puffed when we reached our bedroom door.

* * *

BREAKFAST WAS A QUIET AFFAIR. Cyclops left for work early, Willie had spent the night goodness knows where and not come home yet, and Duke was still asleep. Aunt Letitia joined Matt and me in the dining room, and we were soon joined by my grandfather.

Chronos often arrived unannounced these days, and usually at meal times, although rarely this early. He looked as though he hadn't slept.

"Are you unwell?" I asked as he took a seat opposite me with a plate of toast and sausages. "There are dark circles under your eyes and your hair is wilder than usual."

"What little there is of it," Aunt Letitia muttered without looking up from the open magazine beside her plate.

Chronos smoothed a hand over his head but the flimsy white strands refused to be tamed and stuck straight up again. "I'm not sleeping well lately."

"Something troubling you?" Matt asked.

"You mean aside from the riots and magicians being thrown out of their guilds?"

"So you heard about that," I said with a warning tilt of my head in Aunt Letitia's direction. She didn't appear to be listening, however, and continued to read her magazine, teacup in hand.

"What are you going to do about it?" he asked.

"What can we do?"

He waved his fork in the air. "Something! Come on, Glass, you're an important fellow, these days. Stand up for your wife's rights."

"I can stand up for myself, thank you. And Matt is doing everything he can, but he can't work miracles. No one can make these problems go away overnight."

He grunted and cut into the sausage.

Matt sat back, his own breakfast finished. "I seem to recall you wanting magic to be exposed to the world."

"Not like this. It should have been done in a much grander fashion, in a way that would showcase magic in all its splendor." He paused in thought. "Something like the Great Exhibition of fifty-one."

I barked a laugh. "Nothing too modest, then."

"Something as magnificent and important as magic deserves pomp and ceremony. We just need a royal champion to get behind it, as Prince Albert did for the Great Exhibition. Do you know anyone from royalty, Glass?"

Matt regarded him with a sardonic lift of his eyebrow. "We don't move in the same circles."

Chronos didn't leave after breakfast. He'd brought a clock with him that he was having trouble fixing and asked me to take a look at it. We worked in the library and I soon had all the watch parts spread out on the table. Chronos gave no assistance, and instead he sat with a book by the fire, his hand spread over his belly. He looked a little pale.

"Are you all right?" I asked.

"Just a little nausea. It happens after eating."

"Have you seen a doctor?"

"I have. He diagnosed indigestion. I take a tonic but I left it at home."

"Do you want me to send the footman to retrieve it?"

He shook his head. "Don't bother. It doesn't work."

I picked up my tweezers, but my mind wasn't completely on the task. Chronos was in his seventies and was going to get ill from time to time, but he'd always seemed strong and healthy. He'd not even experienced a head cold this winter. I'd never considered that one day he'd have an illness he couldn't recover from.

That thought shook me. Fortunately the clock wasn't a complicated piece, and I put it back together without really thinking about it. "It seems to be working now."

"Well done, India," he said without looking up from the book.

"You could have fixed it yourself."

"Could I?"

I pulled the book from his hands to force him to look at me. "What's going on?"

"Nothing. May I have my book back, please?"

I hid it behind my back. "Not until you tell me why you're pretending to need my help when you don't."

He picked at the seam on the leather chair arm and didn't meet my gaze. "I wanted to spend time with you. I miss your company."

"Oh."

Chronos and I weren't particularly close. Considering I thought he was dead up until last year, it was perhaps understandable. We were also very different people, with opposing views about magic's place in the world. He'd been upset with me for abandoning the spell-making sessions with Fabian.

"Do you want to go for a walk?" I asked.

He glanced at the window. "It's raining."

I sat on the other armchair, angled toward the fire. "Then we'll stay warm in here and talk."

"Or we could just read quietly." He held out his hand and I gave him the book. He opened it and continued reading.

It would seem he didn't particularly want *my* company. Anyone would have done just as well. I suspected it was loneliness that really ailed my grandfather.

I didn't have an opportunity to ask him if that were true. Bristow entered and announced the arrival of Oscar Barratt.

I stood to greet him and asked Bristow to inform Matt who was upstairs in his study. "Oscar, come in and sit by the fire. You look half-drowned."

"Just a little damp." He joined me at the fireplace, stretching out his fingers towards the coals. "How do you do, Mr. Steele?"

"Morning, Barratt," Chronos said, setting aside the book. His demeanor instantly improved upon seeing Oscar. Here was a man who thought like him, who wanted to see magic brought into the open and celebrated. "You must be very pleased with the reception of your book. Excellent title by the way: *The Book of Magic*."

Oscar ran his hand through his dark brown hair, the ends of which were damp. He mustn't have used an umbrella and only the hair covered by his hat had stayed dry. "Thank you. I am happy with how it turned out. Sales are brisk and early reviews are mostly favorable. What more can an author ask for?"

Despite his words, there was an undercurrent of sadness to his tone, although I wasn't sure Chronos detected it. He smiled and congratulated Oscar on his success.

Oscar eased into the armchair and stretched out his legs toward the fire. "It's not all roses. There's a lot of negativity aimed at me, too. I've received threats."

"What sort of threats?" I asked.

"The kind that wish me harm."

Matt entered, hearing Oscar's comment. "How did they find out where you live?"

"The threats were sent to *The Weekly Gazette*, who passed them on to me. Although I no longer work there, my biography mentions I used to be one of their staff writers."

"How horrid for you," I said. "Although you must admit that a negative reception was not unexpected."

I didn't dare look at Matt but I could feel his temper simmering beneath the surface as he came to stand beside me. He'd been against the book from the start.

"The threats don't particularly worry me," Oscar said. "My home address isn't public knowledge." He offered a smile but it was unconvincing. Something certainly bothered him. If it wasn't the threats, then what?

"You heard about the riot yesterday?" Matt asked.

"I did. Nasty business. I hope they arrested the offenders."

"That riot was a direct result of your book and the added exposure it has given magicians."

Oscar put up his hands. "Come, now, Glass, be reasonable. I didn't force anyone to smash windows. I'm not forcing anyone to hate magicians. You can't blame me for that any more than you blame one of those poor victims for being stabbed by the Ripper."

Matt's entire body tensed. He blinked hard at Oscar and, for once, was rendered speechless.

"Steady on," Chronos said with a frown. "That's a little over the top."

Oscar blew out a deep breath. "You're right. Sorry. I know you're just trying to protect India and this business is worrying for you. Don't mind me. I'm a little out of sorts, these days." He cleared his throat. "Louisa and I have ended our engagement."

That explained the glumness. "I am sorry." I did mean it, even though I'd had my doubts about them from the start. Louisa wanted to marry a magician so that she could hopefully have magician children. Her feelings had never been engaged. I had suspected Oscar's might have been in the beginning, but I also suspected Louisa's money played a significant part in keeping them together, particularly after he learned she had asked Fabian to marry her first. Oscar needed that money to fund the printing of his book.

"I ended it, although I'll let everyone think she did. It's the honorable thing to do." He shifted his weight in the chair. "The dismissal was the last straw. I could have put up with her having feelings for another man. I never loved her, you see, so I didn't expect love in return. But I was *devoted* to her. I would never betray my wife, never say a bad word against her. Unfortunately she proved she doesn't have the same devotion to me."

"What dismissal?" Chronos asked.

"She had me fired from *The Weekly Gazette* so that I'd have more time to finish the book."

Chronos's eyes widened. "And I thought *my* wife was out to thwart me."

I gave him a quelling look.

"At least you learned Louisa's true nature before you married," Matt said, finally taking a seat by the table. "Better now than later."

Oscar sighed. "Better never at all."

"How did Louisa take the news?" I asked.

"She accepted it very well." His tone was bitter. "Very well indeed. No doubt she'll make another play for Charbonneau."

"I don't think he'd accept her."

"So what will you do now?" Matt asked.

"I'll see if the *Gazette* will take me back. I have to do something, and I enjoyed working there. If they won't, perhaps I'll go on a speaking tour around the country. Not all of the messages that came to me via the *Gazette's* office were threats. One asked me to speak at a women's institute about magic."

"What have some of the other positive letters said?" I asked.

"I've received quite a number from magicians who've reached out simply to speak to another like-minded individual. It's surprising to think they've never mentioned their magic to anyone, not even to their spouse in some instances. They've lived in fear for so long."

"Your book won't change that," Matt pointed out, somewhat gruffly. "The riots only prove they were right to stay hidden."

"You know my view on that, Glass. It will be hard in the short term as the artless must concede business to those more skilled than themselves, but in the long term, things will settle down. There will be changes, of course. Magicians will come out on top. The market will see to it."

Matt shook his head in disgust, and I thought he was about to protest, but it was Chronos who snorted in derision.

"Acceptance by the artless won't happen in my lifetime, Barratt."

"But perhaps it will in India's."

I thought Oscar a little insensitive for saying so to my grandfather, but Chronos didn't seem to take it that way. He nodded thoughtfully.

"Do you still have the letters those magicians sent to you?" Matt asked.

"I do."

"Can we take a look at them?"

I held my breath. We'd not told Oscar about our list of magicians, nor Chronos, and I didn't think informing them was a good idea. I didn't quite trust either with such valuable information, although I couldn't imagine what they'd do with the names.

"Why?" Oscar asked.

"India might like to write to them and offer some supporting words. As the most powerful magician in the city, some might know of her and look up to her."

I managed not to roll my eyes at him and continued to smile at Oscar.

Oscar agreed it was a good idea. "I'll collect them now, shall I?"

"There's no hurry," I told him.

He pushed himself to his feet. "I might as well. It's not like I have anything better to do."

I invited him to return with the letters at lunchtime and to eat with us. Willie and Duke were awake by then, and Aunt Letitia was in a good mood, having decided on an outfit to wear to Lady Rycroft's soiree that evening.

At the mention of the evening's entertainment, Matt turned to me. "I feel a sore throat coming on." He coughed for good measure.

Considering the danger posed by him leaving the house, I was happy to go along with the ruse. "I'll pass on your regrets."

Aunt Letitia patted his hand. "Do get an early night, dear boy. You'll be missed."

"Thank you, Aunt."

"Only because it means there'll be one less person I can rely on for good conversation. India and Davide being the others, of course."

Duke barked a laugh as he plucked a sandwich off the silver tray balanced on the tips of the footman's fingers. "Farnsworth? Good conversation? Ha!"

As usual, Willie chose the moment she shoved a sandwich into her mouth to speak. "At least you never know what he'll say. Keeps you on your toes."

Oscar gave me the letters after lunch then departed at the same time as Chronos. I got the feeling both would have stayed longer if I hadn't told them Matt and I had to go out. Oscar seemed to want company just as much Chronos.

I spent the next little while seated at Matt's desk, reading the letters and transcribing the names, addresses and a note about each writer's magical craft to our list. He brought me a cup of tea twenty minutes later.

"How many more?" he asked.

"Four. These will double our list." I picked up the teacup but didn't sip. I regarded him over the rim. "I think I should inform Sir Charles today. It's time the government knew of its existence."

Matt sat slowly, rubbing his jawline. "Very well. We'll go when you finish those."

"You're not coming with me, Matt."

"I am."

"I can handle Sir Charles without you. I've done it before."

"It's nothing to do with how wily Sir Charles can be, and everything to do with—" He shut his mouth.

"With what?"

He shrugged as he stared down at the desk.

"With what, Matt?"

He sighed. "With me wanting to get out of this damned house!"

I stood and rounded the desk then sat on his lap. I looped my arms around his neck. "I know you're bored, but you need to stay indoors until the shooter is caught."

He settled his hands on my hips. "And how will we catch him? The police investigation led nowhere. We have no clues. We need to draw him out and that won't happen if I stay in here, hiding away."

He was right, but I wasn't going to admit it. He'd leap at the opportunity to leave the house, and I wasn't ready for him to risk his life again. Not yet. But I knew that day must come. Matt couldn't go on like this.

I stroked my thumb along his cheek. "Is it really worth getting into an argument with me over a simple outing? Save it for something really important. If we're going to have a falling out, it should at least be over something of vital importance."

He tilted his head to the side. "That's the most persuasive case you can come up with?"

"Yes."

He glared at me so I kissed him lightly on the lips. When I pulled away, he sighed.

"Very well, I'll stay here and choose an outfit for you to wear to Aunt Beatrice's soiree." If any more sarcasm dripped from his tone, I would have drowned.

I stood and returned to the other side of the desk. "Thank you. Don't forget jewelry."

He sighed again, for what seemed like the hundredth time. "Take Willie and Duke with you."

"I will."

"And don't let Sir Charles bully you into giving up the

location of the list or who knows of its existence."

"I won't."

"And press upon him that this is for his superiors' ears only, not Coyle's."

"I will."

"Make him promise you and get him to shake on it. He's a gentleman; a handshake still means something to him."

I glanced at him over the rim of my teacup. "Anything else?"

"Make sure he knows I'll come for him if I find out that Coyle knows."

"I will put as much threat into it as possible. Or Willie will."

"And—"

"Matt! I know what I'm doing." I pointed at the door. "Go."

He rose and strode off without uttering another word, although I could practically see steam rising from his ears. He would calm down soon. He was only angry because he was worried about me. Not that either of us considered Sir Charles an enemy, but he wasn't a friend either. We weren't entirely sure if he could be trusted. We were taking a leap of faith in informing him about the list.

But we'd agreed to do it, if for no other reason than it would prove if he was working for Coyle as well as the government. We had suspected he was feeding Coyle secret information ever since we'd overhead them talking in the garden outside Coyle's house.

We would know soon enough. If Coyle came for the list after we informed Sir Charles of its existence, we'd have our answer.

I studied the next letter, written by a carpenter magician. Even though we weren't giving the list to anyone, and never would, I worried that we were putting these people in danger just by adding their names.

CHAPTER 3

$\mathcal{I}$ called on Sir Charles at dusk and was pleased to
see he was at his Hammersmith lodgings. Since I
didn't know where his office was located, or if he even had
one, I was never quite sure whether he'd be at home. He
received Duke, Willie and me in the parlor, located on the first
floor of the building where he rented rooms. He asked the
landlady to bring tea and cake. As she closed the door, he
eyed Willie carefully.

"Are you carrying a gun, Miss Johnson?"

She pulled her jacket aside to show him the revolver
tucked into the waistband of her buckskin trousers. "I'm as
good a shot as Annie Oakley, and just as quick, so don't do
anything stupid."

His eyes widened. "What do you think I'm going to do?"

"Willie is just being cautious," I said. "Don't mind her."

"Unless you do something stupid," she chimed in. "Then
you should mind me."

Duke cracked his knuckles.

Sir Charles fidgeted with his tie and stretched his neck out
of his collar. It was the most ruffled I'd ever seen him. "This
isn't a social call, is it?"

"No." I sat on the sofa. "I have some information for you that I'd like you to pass on to your superiors."

"My superiors?"

"Don't be coy, Sir Charles."

While he had not admitted that he was a spy for the government, he ceased denying it last time we confronted him. He didn't deny it this time, either, and simply sat and flicked imaginary lint off his trousers as he waited for me to continue.

"We established that you are attempting to gather as much information about magicians as you possibly can. To what end, we can only guess since you won't tell us."

"I don't have the authority to tell you."

"Then perhaps it's time you introduce us to someone who does." It wasn't an idea Matt and I had discussed but I liked it, nevertheless.

"That won't be possible," Sir Charles said with a conde-scending tone. "Men like him don't talk to just anyone."

"I'm the most powerful magician in England, and I have some information for him. I think he'll want to meet me."

"What information?"

"I've made a list of known magicians. Known to me, that is. The list can be consulted by either me or Matt when there is a disturbance of the public order created by a magician's magic, such as we experienced with both Amelia Moreton and Mrs. Trentham."

The landlady entered carrying a tray which she set on the table before backing out of the room again. She shut the door and Sir Charles poured the tea.

"Mr. Duke, if you'd be so kind as to wait outside on the landing. My landlady has a tendency to dawdle."

Duke opened the door to see the landlady bent in half, her ear approximately where the keyhole would be when the door was closed. She blushed scarlet and scurried away. Duke exited the room, closing the door behind him.

"Who does she work for?" I asked.

"The government, the same as me," Sir Charles said. "My superior doesn't trust anyone. She tells him who comes and goes from here and listens in when she can." He handed me a cup of tea with a smile. "She knows that I know."

Willie approached the table and helped herself to a slice of fruit cake. "He's right not to trust you, considering you got history with Coyle."

Sir Charles bristled. "I don't work for Coyle."

"We saw you talking to him," I said. "You passed information about me to him."

"Once, India. Just the once."

"Once is enough for me to distrust you when it comes to Coyle."

He handed me a plate with a slice of cake. "Will you never forgive me for that?"

"Let's return to the topic of my list."

He settled back in the chair with his cup of tea, the saucer balancing on his knee. "We're not interested in your list. We have our own."

"Which I doubt is complete and, let's be honest, I'm in a position to add more names at a much more rapid rate than you."

"Aren't you afraid of breaking the trust of your fellow magicians?"

"I am not handing the list over, Sir Charles. Let's be clear about that. The list and all the information contained on it will be for my eyes only. If I deem it necessary for the information to be shared with the police or any other authority, I will pass on only what is relevant, not the entire list."

"I'm not sure that will be acceptable to my superiors."

"It's a non-negotiable condition. I won't have magicians spied upon just because the government deems all of them are a potential threat. Innocent people shouldn't be subjected to invasive scrutiny. Only the details of those who wield magic as a weapon will be shared."

He sipped thoughtfully.

"We know you have been trying to find out who the magicians are," I went on. He didn't deny it, so I continued. "To do that thoroughly, you need my help."

He set the teacup on the saucer and placed them both on the table beside him. "The release of Barratt's book has expedited the issue somewhat. Now that the general public are aware of magicians, and considering they know that Mrs. Trentham used magic to kill her husband, there is growing support to keep them under control."

"Tosh. For starters, they know no such thing. The official stance was that she murdered him of her own accord. Officially, there was no mention of magic."

"If you think the public believe the official stance, then you are naïve, India."

He was probably right about the public's suspicions. "And secondly, I haven't seen a *growing* support to control magicians. The public seems quite enthused about magic. It's the artless members of guilds who are rioting, afraid of losing custom."

"Can you blame them?"

"No," I said heavily. "Believe me, if a happy middle ground could be found, I'd prefer it. If only the guilds would allow magicians to belong so they could continue to trade. Magic doesn't last, and once the public know that, they'll show no preference for magical wares over artless ones."

He tilted his head to the side. "It may not last, but they are naturally of superior quality. India, the guilds won't give up without a fight."

"Then perhaps it's time the guilds were dissolved. The system is an archaic one, anyway."

He picked up his teacup and sipped as he thought. When

he set it down again, his gaze was distant, his voice soft. "I feel as though the city is balanced on a knife's edge."

"As do I."

I stood and signaled to Willie it was time to go. She drained her teacup and stood too. "Good day, Sir Charles," I said. "Please speak to your superior about the list at your earliest convenience, and don't forget my condition." I headed for the door but paused. "And do not inform Lord Coyle."

His nostrils flared. "I don't work for him."

"And yet I feel the need to say it anyway."

He looked away.

I opened the door and strode off, Willie and Duke at my heels.

* * *

MATT HAD CHOSEN an elegant outfit in cream silk that seemed to shimmer in the light, with embroidered black ribbon detail around the hem and clusters of small rosettes. Knowing I preferred a simple style, he'd also chosen a pearl pendant and matching pearl drop earrings. Polly Pickett, the lady's maid I shared with Aunt Letitia, put my hair up in an elegant arrangement with a string of seed pearls twined through it.

I felt elegant and sophisticated as I entered the Rycrofts' drawing room. But my mood quickly sank at the sight of the ladies dressed in bold colors and elaborate jewelry. I suddenly wished I'd pretended to be sick as well. I felt quite out of place. I hardly knew a soul, but thankfully Aunt Letitia remained at my side and introduced me to several people. She was in her element, chatting breezily with no sign of her frailty.

"Ah, there you are, India," Lady Rycroft said as she glided toward me. "Lord Farnsworth isn't here yet, but never mind. We'll do our best to entertain ourselves without him." Even as she said it, she glanced at the doorway, no doubt hoping he'd walk through so she could begin her matrimonial machinations.

"Perhaps he's not coming," Aunt Letitia said with a wicked gleam in her eyes.

"Of course he is. He's very much looking forward to talking to Charity tonight. He made it quite clear yesterday that he found her charming."

I spotted Charity near the potted palm, a brooding scowl on her face. She wore a black dress with a lot of black lace trim, even though she wasn't in mourning, and black jet jewels to match. While she stood with two other people, she didn't appear to be joining in with their conversation. Instead, she glared at the doorway.

Aunt Letitia followed my gaze to her niece. "She looks as cheerful as always."

Lady Rycroft cleared her throat and seemed to become aware that our conversation was being overheard by two other women. "Have you met my nephew's wife?" She all but pushed me toward them. "She's a magician, you know."

I swallowed my gasp before it escaped, but Aunt Letitia did not.

"Beatrice," she scolded.

"Well, it's true." Lady Rycroft beamed at her friends as they regarded me with smiles. "India makes the most marvelous watches and clocks."

"No, I don't," I told them. "Not anymore."

It was quite an odd situation. Lady Rycroft had been such a snob toward me when I'd first entered their lives. She considered Matt far above me. Yet now that magic had become popular among her set, she was happy to parade me before them.

One of the ladies leaned forward and whispered, "But surely you still do commissions for select clients."

I gave her my sweetest smile. "I'm afraid not."

THE SPY MASTER'S SCHEME

The woman's lips pursed. "But—"

"Lord Farnsworth is here!"

His lordship paused in the doorway until as many people as possible had seen him. His timing was immaculate, as was his evening attire of white tie, waistcoat and black tailcoat. He wore his hair in the usual style, parted down the middle and flat to his head. It gleamed with Macassar Oil.

Lady Rycroft swept across the room to collect him. Being a very eligible bachelor, he was immediately swamped by three young women who'd been pushed in his direction by their mothers. Lady Rycroft glared at Charity and jerked her head toward his lordship in a signal to hurry.

Lord Farnsworth relished the attention. He looked like a king surrounded by sycophantic courtiers. I wasn't sure if Charity would continue to be as appealing as she had been. I also doubted that boredom would be a problem this evening.

There was no opportunity to speak to him before the musicians started. I sat with Aunt Letitia on one side of me and a gentleman on the other. I'd been introduced to him earlier in the evening, and immediately liked him when he'd diverted the conversation away from magic. Ever since Lady Rycroft had announced that I was a magician, I'd found myself even more popular than Lord Farnsworth. I did not enjoy my popularity, however, and was grateful when the gentleman urged the other guests not to annoy me as I clearly wasn't interested in using my magic on anyone's watch that night.

During a bold rendition of *Home Sweet Home*, he leaned toward me and whispered, "Mrs. Glass, I have a proposition for you."

My heart sank. So much for my savior.

"My wife is very keen for me to secure you for our magical evening, to be held at the end of the month."

"As I said earlier, I am not selling anything. I no longer make watches."

He flicked his hand, dismissing my objection as if it were nothing. "We don't want to buy anything from you, just have a demonstration of your magic. It'll be an evening with a few of our intimate friends who will bring along their watches or clocks for your performance."

I very much wanted to round on him and talk loudly to embarrass him, but in deference to the musicians, I kept my voice as low as his. "My response to your offer is no different to the others I received tonight: no."

"But it will be an exclusive, tasteful affair, nothing vulgar."

I nodded at the musicians. "Do allow me to listen in peace."

"Well!" he huffed. "An attitude like that won't see magicians accepted into society."

I pressed my lips together and kept my gaze firmly focused forward, but I could not enjoy the rest of the evening. When the musicians finished, refreshments were served and guests were free to mingle. I searched for Lord Farnsworth in the hope of finding a friendly face before I was asked yet again to use my magic on someone's watch.

It took me a moment, but I eventually spotted him by the large potted palm positioned near the door that led to a small room. Charity was with him, standing very close. She stood on her toes and whispered in his ear. Lord Farnsworth's eyes widened and his cheeks flushed.

He glanced around to see if anyone was watching and his gaze settled on me. As Charity leaned in again, he mouthed "Help" at me. Then he suddenly stiffened and blushed scarlet.

I hurried toward them, but Charity hustled him into the anteroom and quickly shut the door. Good lord! If they were discovered and publicly exposed, she would be considered compromised. As I hurried toward the door, I spotted Lady

Rycroft out of the corner of my eye. She'd noticed the exchange—and she was smiling.

She *wanted* this to happen. She wanted them to be discovered alone in a room and have her daughter's reputation ruined. How could a mother desire such a thing?

The answer was simple—to force Lord Farnsworth to do the honorable thing and say they were secretly engaged. It would make their behavior acceptable in the eyes of her friends. It would also secure a wealthy and titled husband for a difficult daughter.

She saw me weaving my way across the floor and realized that I was about to rescue Lord Farnsworth. She gathered up her skirts and strode across the room in the hope of intercepting me. She would do it, too. She would reach me before I reached the door, and there was no way around. Then it was just a matter of drawing the guests' attention to the anteroom. It was so elegantly simple and I could see no way of stopping her scheme.

Poor Lord Farnsworth. He was going to find himself trapped with Charity for the rest of his life.

But I had not anticipated Aunt Letitia. Whether she was driven by her motivation to see him end up with Willie or whether she just wanted to thwart her sister-in-law's plans, it didn't matter. She peeled away from a cluster of guests and forged a path to Lady Rycroft like a bullet. She grabbed her arm, halting her. Despite Lady Rycroft's attempts to shake her off, Aunt Letitia clung on.

Lady Rycroft watched me pass just out of reach, her face twitching with fury and frustration.

I quickly glanced around and, seeing no one else watching, slipped into the anteroom. Lord Farnsworth was backed up against a wingback armchair, his eyes wide. When he saw me, he let out a small yelp.

"Thank God it's you."

Charity swung around and must have loosened the grip

she had on his arms because he managed to jerk free and step to the side. Her brow crashed into a frown as dark as her mother's. "What are you doing in here?"

"I could ask you the same question," I said.

"We want to be alone."

"No, we don't!" Lord Farnsworth gave her a wide berth and joined me. "I think it's time for me to leave."

Charity watched him from beneath half-closed lids. "But you said we were going to have a lark tonight."

"I meant out there, making fun of the outfits and watching everyone get drunk. This is not my idea of a lark. Not with—" He snapped his mouth shut with an audible click of back teeth. I suspected he was going to say, "Not with you."

If Charity suspected that too, she didn't care. She tossed her head, marched past us, and out the door. She left it wide open.

Lord Farnsworth blew out a long breath. "Thank you, India, you saved my life. Imagine if someone else had walked in here? Someone less likely to turn a blind eye."

I smiled. "You looked terrified."

"I was. She is surprisingly strong for such a little chit, and some of the things she said and did were...unexpected from a young lady. She made me blush and that's not easy to do. I've had a French mistress, you know."

"I do know."

He lowered his voice as we headed back to the drawing room. "I don't think Charity is as innocent as she pretends."

I nodded thanks at Aunt Letitia and she smiled back. Lady Rycroft was chatting to friends, no evidence of her disappointment on her face. Charity resumed her place by the potted palm, her arms crossed over her chest. She no longer tried to mingle with the other guests.

The gentleman I'd been seated next to during the performance approached me, a lady dressed in dark blue velvet on his arm. They were all smiles.

"I think it's time I left," I said loudly to Lord Farnsworth.

"Indeed. I have to meet up with Willie soon. God, how she'll laugh when I tell her what Charity said. It might even make her blush too."

"I doubt that." I accepted his arm and smiled at the lady and gentleman as I passed them.

We collected Aunt Letitia then sought out our hostess to thank her for the evening. She regarded me coolly but kept up a polite façade with her friends so near. She wouldn't say anything about what went on in the anteroom. Doing so would be an admission that she had a hand in it.

"I do hope you enjoyed your evening, India," she cooed. "My friends have been thrilled to meet you. I'll be sure to give everyone your address so they can come and discuss magic with you. So many are interested."

As much as I wanted to snap back, I gritted my teeth. "Do send them to my house, although I can't be sure Matt will welcome them. You know how protective he can be. I'm afraid if your friends come and ask me to perform magic on their timepieces, he'll know you sent them."

I didn't elaborate on what Matt might do about it. In truth, I didn't know. But the unspoken threat behind the words was enough for the fake smile to freeze on her face.

Aunt Letitia kissed her sister-in-law's cheek. "An interesting evening, as always, Beatrice. But do keep a tighter leash on that daughter of yours. If you're not careful, she's going to find herself married to a very unsuitable man. And no one would wish that on a poor fellow."

She took my arm and steered me away. Lord Farnsworth hastily said his goodbyes and exited the drawing room with us.

"Good show, Letty! You were marvelous." He took her elbow firmly and helped steady her as she walked down the stairs. "You too, India. Thank you again for saving me from your husband's cousin. I am sorry she's as batty as she is, or I

might consider her a viable prospect. But I'm afraid I can't."
He sighed. "Could you imagine if her blood got mixed with
mine? Disaster!"

"What do you mean?" I asked.

"Charity is as wild as a jungle cat, and my mother thinks
fairies live in the garden. I shudder to think how our children
would turn out."

I pressed my lips together to suppress my smile. I couldn't
wait to tell Matt how the evening had transpired. He was
going to have a good chuckle.

* * *

I RELAYED the events of the night before over breakfast,
delighting everyone except Aunt Letitia. Willie thought it
particularly amusing, since Lord Farnsworth hadn't told her
how he'd been trapped in the anteroom by Charity. Willie
said he'd simply claimed the party had been a pleasant but
dull experience.

After she finished choking on her laughter and a slice a
bacon, she pointed her knife at me. "Are you telling me *she*
cornered *him*? I know he ain't the strongest man, but she's
been brought up to be delicate."

"She ain't delicate," Cyclops muttered. "I reckon if she
caught him by surprise, she'd have the upper hand."

"He was certainly surprised," I said.

Aunt Letitia asked Duke to pour her another cup of coffee
from the pot as he passed her chair. "India and I thwarted
Beatrice's plans. We make a very good team, don't we,
India?"

"We certainly do," I said.

"But I'm glad we left when we did."

Matt frowned at her. "Was it tiring for you?"

"Oh no, it's not for my own sake that I was glad we left.
It's for India's."

Matt's gaze narrowed. "Why? What happened?"

"Beatrice told everyone India is a magician. She was bombarded with requests to use her magic."

"That would have been unpleasant," he said quietly.

"Not to mention vulgar."

Matt tapped his finger on the table, a habit that he'd picked up since becoming confined to the house for his own safety. He usually wasn't aware when he did it, but this time I glared at him then turned that glare onto his finger. He got the message and stopped, tucking his hand into a fist.

"I think I'll go out today," he announced.

Duke, Willie, Cyclops and I stopped what we were doing and stared at him.

Aunt Letitia continued to read her magazine. "Marvelous idea. It'll do you good, although your sore throat seems to have gone away."

"But it could come back," I said, my tone curt. "The air is cold and cold air is not good for sore throats."

She looked up as Duke gave her back the coffee cup and clicked her tongue. "You are much too protective of him, India. A man like Matthew won't let a little sore throat bother him."

"I've heard people get sick and die from sore throats," Willie said.

"Aye," both Cyclops and Duke chimed in.

Matt rose and buttoned up his jacket. "My decision is final. I'm going out."

Willie stood too. "Then I'll come with you."

"Me too." Duke wiped his mouth with his napkin before standing.

Cyclops continued eating. When Willie smacked his shoulder, he looked up, fork paused at his mouth. "Aye, and me."

Matt shook his head. "You're not spending your day off minding me. Call on Catherine as you planned."

Cyclops looked caught as he weighed his options. "I reckon it's best if I come with you. I can visit Catherine later."

"Or Matt can stay indoors," I said pointedly.

He glared at me and I glared back.

"Why does Matthew need escorting when he simply has a sore throat?" Aunt Letitia asked.

The others looked away, shuffling their feet or clearing their throats. She must have known I was the least likely to lie to her because her gaze settled on me.

To my relief, Bristow entered the dining room. "There's a Mrs. Pyke here to see Mrs. Glass."

"Show her through to the drawing room, please," I said.

"Who is Mrs. Pyke?" Aunt Letitia asked.

"Her husband is a wool magician, but I've never met her."

Matt and I entered the drawing room together and greeted Mrs. Pyke warmly. She was a small woman with a round face and rosy cheeks. She wore what I assumed to be her Sunday best, a black, maroon and white checked woolen dress with a dark blue hat. She tried to smile back, but it was unconvincing. She was on the verge of tears.

"How may I help you?" I asked, taking a seat.

She clutched her bag tightly on her lap with both hands. "You remember my husband, Mrs. Glass."

A feeling of dread settled into my stomach. "I do. Is he well?"

"That's the thing. He's missing."

"Missing?" both Matt and I said.

Her bottom lip wobbled. She bit it until she regained her composure. "He didn't come home last night. It's not like him. Not like him at all. He's devoted to me, you see. We've never spent a night apart, not in all our twenty-two years of marriage."

The day he'd used his spell on Fabian's carpet, Mr. Pyke had told us that he and his wife hadn't been blessed with children. He told me that was why he felt so proud of his magical

48

THE SPY MASTER'S SCHEME

carpets; they were his legacy. He'd then demanded I thank him for his help by using my extension spell on his magical rugs. I'd refused and he'd not asked again, but the encounter had left a sour taste.

"We are sorry," Matt said gently, "but what do you expect my wife to do about it? You should go to the police."

"I have." Her face crumpled and tears filled her eyes. She pulled out a handkerchief from her knitted bag before Matt could offer his. She dabbed at her nose. "They told me he hasn't been missing long enough to warrant an investigation. They said to come back tomorrow. But anything could happen to him by then!"

"What do you think has happened?" I asked.

"I think someone has kidnapped him or…" She let out a sob. "Or worse."

I moved to sit beside her on the sofa and put my arm around her shoulders. I comforted her until her tears abated and she seemed able to talk again. "Why would someone want to kidnap him?"

"Because he spoke to a journalist about magic. He told the writer that magic was wonderful, that nobody should be afraid of it. He admitted he was a magician. The article was published the day before yesterday. I think someone took offence and wanted to…to silence him."

"He gave his name?"

She nodded.

I rubbed her shoulder as she cried into her handkerchief. I appealed to Matt to help me comfort her. I was at a loss for what to say next.

He crouched in front of her. "Mrs. Pyke, several articles have been written from the view of magicians. Some have even mentioned their names, although not many. But those magicians have not gone missing. Why do you think that's the reason behind your husband's disappearance?"

She released a shuddery breath and her spirits seemed to

rally a little. "Because yesterday someone called on him at his workshop. I saw a carriage leave as I arrived. I deliver his lunch every day, you see. I asked Mr. Pyke who it was and what they wanted, thinking it was a good commission, but he wouldn't tell me. When I insisted, he almost bit my head off. He never speaks that way to me. Never. He was troubled." She fixed her watery gaze on me. "I think he's been kidnapped because of what was said in that article."

"Did he go to the newspaper before or after his membership was revoked by the wool guild?"

She gasped. "He didn't tell me he'd been thrown out of the guild." She wrung the handles of her woolen bag in her hands. "Will you find him, Mrs. Glass? I have no one else to turn to."

CHAPTER 4

*K*eeping Matt at home now, after I'd agreed to help Mrs. Pyke find her husband, proved to be an impossible task. After an hour of alternately arguing with him and giving him the silent treatment, I gave up. He was not going to let me take on this case alone.

The problem was, where to start our investigation?

Willie was convinced we should confront Lord Coyle first. "He's linked to this. I know he is."

Duke rolled his eyes. "You don't know that. There ain't no link between Coyle and Pyke."

"I'd wager good money he's involved somehow. If I had money."

Cyclops suggested we speak to Detective Inspector Brockwell. "Find out if the police know anything."

"They turned Mrs. Pyke away when she tried to report him missing," Willie pointed out. "Jasper won't be able to help. It's a local matter."

Duke scratched his sideburns. "Maybe he's got a lover and that's why he didn't come home. Maybe he left her."

"An investigation will prove that, one way or another," Matt said. "I think we should begin by searching his work-

51

shop. According to Mrs. Pyke, someone in a carriage visited her husband there. His disappearance may or may not be linked to that visitor, but we have nothing else to go on right now."

It was agreed and Matt ordered the carriage to be brought around. When it arrived, I left the house first, followed by Willie who stood on the pavement and looked up and down the street.

"All clear," she announced.

Matt exited the house, squashed between the hulking figure of Cyclops and the stocky one of Duke. They bundled him into the carriage and climbed in after him.

"This is ridiculous," he muttered.

Nobody answered. It might seem ridiculous, but it was not amusing.

Mrs. Pyke had given us her husband's spare shop key. Once we had the door open, we ushered Matt inside and closed it again. We had made the journey without incident. It was no small feat. I breathed out a measured breath as I leaned back against the door.

It was dim in the shop, and Willie reached for the curtain to open it.

"No," both Matt and I told her.

"We don't want anyone seeing us in here," he said.

The smell of wool fibers was a surprisingly comforting one. It made me think of home. The shop was quite large with rugs of all different colors, thickness and texture spread over the floor, stacked on top of each other, and hung on the walls like tapestries. I touched a green, brown and black Oriental but it held no magical warmth.

Indeed, few did. "Only the most elaborately woven ones have magic," I said after touching a gold and crimson rug that would suit a manor house drawing room. "This one and those two. The rest are just ordinary rugs."

Duke, who'd been caressing a hall runner on the floor,

suddenly lay down on it and spread out his arms. "The pile is luxurious."

"That ain't one of the magic ones," Willie told him.

"It still feels nice. Come down here and see for yourself."

She got down on her hands and knees and fingered the carpet fibers. "It is soft. Cyclops, come and feel it."

Cyclops looked at them as if they were mad. "I'll check the workshop."

He removed a lamp from the hook by the door and lit it. Matt followed him into the rear workshop.

I sat on the chair at the sales desk and rifled through swatches of carpet samples, all of which were infused with magic. Mr. Pyke must want to keep them fresh and strong so they'd look good, despite being touched by numerous hands.

There were some outstanding invoices to be paid from wool merchants and dyers in the desk drawer. Some went back several months and had 'Pay immediately' written in bold on them. Mr. Pyke must have been having some financial difficulty. I flicked through a notepad that appeared to be used to work out floor area and costs, then set it aside to look through the ledger of orders.

I started from the most recent entry, two days ago and worked backwards. I wasn't expecting to find a name I recognized so when I saw it, my heart skipped a beat.

"Look at this," I said to Duke who was still inspecting the carpets. Willie had joined Matt and Cyclops out the back. I showed him the ledger, pointing to the name.

"Lady Coyle! What was Hope doing here?"

"Ordering a rug, of course. Four, in fact."

He squinted and leaned closer to the page. "Is that a mark next to each order?"

I bent my head, but the light was quite poor. "See if the others are finished with the lamp."

He returned a moment later carrying the lamp with Matt,

Cyclops and Willie in tow. He held the lamp closer to the ledger. "It's an asterisk."

I flipped back another page. "Here's another order with an asterisk. Good lord!"

Matt leaned over my shoulder. "What is it?"

"Professor Nash ordered a rug from Mr. Pyke just before Christmas." I tapped my finger on the entry. "And there's an asterisk placed beside the order too."

"It wasn't a very big rug."

I looked further back through the ledger and although there were a few more entries with asterisks, I didn't recognize the customers' names. "It must refer to those carpets where Mr. Pyke used his magic."

"Makes sense," Willie said. "Hope would know he was a magician through Coyle, and Nash knew...how?"

"Through the magic grapevine," I said with a shrug. "He has several contacts, so if he was in the market for a new rug, he must have asked around. That doesn't mean he's a suspect, but the Coyles are."

"Why?" Matt asked.

"Well, because..." In truth, I couldn't think of a reason why they should be suspects and not Professor Nash. "If nothing else, it proves Lord Coyle knew Mr. Pyke was a magician. When Hope suggested she needed a new carpet, her husband would have advised her to come here and get the best." I closed the ledger and returned it to the desk then showed them the invoices. "Most of those are outstanding. Mr. Pyke owed a lot of money to his suppliers."

"That explains why he went to the newspapers," Matt said.

"And gave them his name," Duke added. "Free advertising. He hoped it would bring more customers here."

Mr. Pyke must have noticed how the wealthy were receptive to buying magical goods after Oscar's book was published. He would have hoped to turn that interest to his own advantage, and what better way to advertise his status as a wool magician than through a newspaper that was circulated widely throughout the city.

But he was also risking expulsion from his guild. According to Catherine, they had revoked his membership, but it wasn't clear if that happened as a result of the article or happened before he spoke to the journalist.

"Did you find anything useful in the workshop?" I asked.

Matt sat on the edge of the desk. "Nothing. But what stands out to me is the lack of any signs of a struggle. There's no blood or scratches, nothing overturned. Everything appears to be in its place, as if he tidied up at the end of the day and was about to head home."

If nothing else, it narrowed down the time of his disappearance. It must have happened after he locked up for the day and before he got home. "We should find out what route he usually took between work and his house. Perhaps someone saw him being bundled into a carriage."

It was a chilling thought. My nerves were so frayed by it, that I jumped when the front door suddenly opened. I wasn't the only one.

Willie drew her gun. "Halt! Don't move or I'll shoot."

The elderly fellow put up his hands. "Blimey, don't do that! Take what you want, I won't stop you, but I don't think you'll find any money on the premises."

Matt put a hand to the barrel of Willie's gun and pushed it down. "Put it away."

"He might be trying to kill you!"

"I swear, I'm not going to kill no one!" the man cried. "I saw some movement in here and thought I better look. Mr. Pyke, the owner, would have wanted me to. But I'll pretend I never saw you. Carry on thieving." He backed out.

"Wait!" Matt said. "We're not thieving, we're investigating Mr. Pyke's disappearance."

The man reappeared around the door again. "Oh. Then why is he pointing a gun at me?"

"I'm a she, and I was just being careful," Willie said.

He touched the brim of his cap. "Sorry, ma'am, didn't notice your...um..."

"Please come inside," I said, rising. "My name is India Glass. This is my husband and these are our associates."

He shook the hands of all the men, bobbed his head at me, and looked Willie up and down. He must be contemplating what sort of greeting to give her. "My name's Marr. I have a leather goods store next door."

His arrival would save us a visit. The less wandering around we did outside, in the open, the better. "Mrs. Pyke asked us to help locate her husband," I said. "He has disappeared."

Mr. Marr removed his cap and scratched his bald head. He was a small elderly man with a slight stoop and white whiskers. He wore a leather apron over his clothes and leather gloves of good quality. "So Mrs. Pyke told me this morning when she came here first thing looking for him. She knocked on my door before I opened and asked me when I'd last seen him."

"And when did you last see him?" Matt asked.

"Yesterday. He locked up at five."

"Is that the usual time he leaves?"

"Aye. Five o'clock every day, like clockwork. He likes to be home in time for an early supper at five thirty."

"Does he walk home?" I asked.

Mr. Marr nodded.

"Did you see him go?"

Another nod. "I was standing in the doorway as I often do at that time, to say good evening to my neighbors. It's just a friendly way to end the day, and many who don't live above their shops leave at that time. Me, I live upstairs so I don't close until five-thirty."

"How did he seem?"

He frowned in thought. "Now that you mention it, he was distracted. He's always cheerful, always asks how my day has been. But yesterday he only waved after I called out goodnight."

"And then?" Matt asked.

"And then he went on his way."

"Alone?"

"Aye, and he walked off in the same direction as always, down Courser Street."

That confirmed our theory that he wasn't kidnapped from here, if he was kidnapped at all. "Did Mr. Pyke have a, er, particular friend he might have stayed with last night?" Even as I asked the question, I could hear Aunt Letitia's voice in my head admonishing me. Asking a man if his acquaintance had a lover was terribly vulgar, in anyone's book.

Mr. Marr tucked his hands into his apron pocket and hunched his shoulders. "No, ma'am. He was devoted to Mrs. Pyke."

"Mrs. Pyke said her husband had a visitor yesterday at lunchtime," Matt said. "She saw the carriage leave but not who was in it. She claimed Mr. Pyke was not himself after that encounter. Did you see who it was?"

"No, sir. He gets ladies coming here from time to time in their carriages to look at his carpets. It's not unusual."

"Do you know if he has ever had an encounter with a gentleman or lady that has left him worried?"

Mr. Marr stroked his whiskers. "There was one encounter with a fellow, but he wasn't a gen'leman. The day before yesterday, it was. I remember it because I could hear the man shouting so I came in to see if Mr. Pyke was all right. The man left, thankfully. Don't know what the two of us would have done if he kept on. He was a big fellow and I'm not as young as I used to be."

"What were they arguing about?"

"Magic."

A sense of dread settled like lead in my stomach. "Go on."

"Seems like everyone in the whole city has read that book with the orange cover. Everyone's talking about it and speculating about who might be a magician and who ain't. It never occurred to me that Mr. Pyke is one, but I haven't looked at his rugs lately." He gazed around the shop at the carpets before focusing on me again. "The fellow accused Mr. Pyke of being a magician, and told him he was cheating and taking customers away from honest rug makers like himself."

"Did Mr. Pyke say who he was?" Matt asked.

"No, but I reckon you only have to go to the wool guild and describe the fellow. He was real distinctive. Young, tall and solid." He angled his chin toward Cyclops. "A Goliath, like your friend there, but with ginger hair."

We thanked him and he bobbed his head and left.

Willie returned her gun to the waistband of her trousers. "We'll go to the wool guild and find this fellow. It's got to be him."

Duke disagreed. "We have to follow the same route Pyke walked last night after he left here. Someone might have seen something."

"Walking through the streets is too dangerous for Matt," Cyclops pointed out. "You and Willie can do that. Matt, India and me will go on to the guild."

"Do I get a say in this?" Matt asked.

"No," Cyclops, Duke and Willie said.

"Of course you do," I said. "Go on. What would you like to say?"

Matt strode to the door, catching everyone unawares. We raced after him. "I think it's a good plan."

I smiled to myself.

With Matt safely ensconced in the carriage, Willie asked Woodall for the quickest route to Mr. Pyke's house via Courser Street, then Cyclops asked Woodall if he knew where to find the wool guild. Our coachman was better than a map. According to the man himself, he knew the streets of London better than he knew his own face.

We set off a few moments later leaving Duke and Willie to walk. I peered through the rear window for the entirety of the journey and breathed a sigh of relief when we reached the guild hall. We had not been followed.

According to the sign etched in stone above the lintel, the building belonged to the Worshipful Company of Woolmen. The coat of arms depicted a wool pack on a red shield crested with a gold spinning wheel. The colors had faded and part of the motto had come off completely, but Matt managed to translate the Latin as *Wool is our Hope*.

It was a reminder of how ancient these guilds were. The building looked as though it had stood for hundreds of years. Its solid stonework and elaborate carvings of spinning wheels spoke of wealth, but that wealth must have been from years past. Today, the windows were dark with soot, one had been boarded over, and the building itself was modest compared to its neighbors. Where once it would have been the grandest structure on the street, it was now the smallest, dwarfed by a bank on one side and a theater on the other.

But it wasn't just the building that was old, it was the entire concept. *Why* did a craftsman need to belong to a guild? What was the point? If it was to regulate the industry, then we now had laws to ensure a customer got what they paid for. Where the law failed, the reputation of the cheating tradesman was denounced in the media.

From what I knew of the Watchmaker's Guild, my father paid an annual fee to belong and that gave him a license to trade, but it didn't protect him if a customer refused to pay. Nor did it protect him if he had a dispute with suppliers, or was having financial difficulty. Guild members rallied around a member's family when he died, but friends and family did

C.J. ARCHER

C.J. ARCHER

that too. It was an outdated and somewhat meaningless institution for the modern craftsman.

Our knock was answered by an elderly porter wearing a cap and tweed livery that looked more suited to a hunting party in the country than city living, but at least it would be warm. I wondered if the guild outfitted him with a lighter livery to wear in summer.

He smiled amiably through his wiry gray whiskers. "Good morning. How may I assist?"

Aware of how exposed Matt was on the porch, I strode inside without being invited. Matt followed, and I shut the door myself. Cyclops remained on watch outside. "We are Mr. and Mrs. Gaskell," I said, using the name of one of my favorite authors. We'd decided on the false names in the carriage. India Glass was like poison in the guilds these days. Whenever we called on a guild, we'd discovered Mr. Abercrombie had beaten us and used his influence as a former guild master to blacken my name.

The porter, an elderly, stooped man, had pursed his lips over a set of false teeth too large for his mouth as we pushed past him, and he continued to regard us as uninvited interlopers. "How may I help you?" he asked stiffly.

It was time to turn on the sweetness to make up for our rude entry. "Forgive us for barging in like this, it's just that I'm so thrilled to finally see the inside of the famous London home of the Worshipful Company of Woolmen." I gazed up at the ceiling with its blackened beams that were no higher than Matt's head.

"My wife is the daughter of a rug maker from Bristol," Matt explained. "We're visiting friends in London and she begged me to come here."

The porter beamed, his stiffness thawed by our praise. "How delightful."

"I heard so much about this place from my father. Not that he was a member here, of course," I added, in case he asked

THE SPY MASTER'S SCHEME

for my maiden name. "He was a member of the Bristol branch of the guild. But he came here once and told me what a wonderful building it was, so full of company history."

The porter puffed out his chest a little and he took on a professional air. "It was built in sixteen-oh-nine, but the company itself goes back much further. Indeed, we're one of the oldest livery companies in the city."

"Oh, I know. So much history."

"Would you care to look through our library? We have a fine collection of books about wool, of course, but also antique spinning wheels, looms and rug making tools. The finest in the country."

Matt must have sensed my hesitation. He put his hand on my lower back and said, "We'd love to." So much for getting the information we needed and leaving immediately.

The porter led us along the corridor past walls lined with woolen tapestries, our footfalls deadened by faded carpets with frayed edges. Why did they not replace them? Tradition, I supposed. That desire to keep things as they always have been, sometimes to the detriment of improvement.

Matt and I spent ten minutes studying the objects in the collection and reading the accompanying cards while listening to the porter tell us about the history of the guild and its members, who were a mix of merchants, rug makers, spinners, and weavers, clothiers and tailors specializing in woolen garments.

When a suitable time had passed, I asked him for the name of a tall, solid fellow with ginger hair. "My father asked me to look in on him, but I'm so dreadful with names." I touched my forehead. "My husband suggested we come here and ask if you knew of such a fellow."

"I do indeed. His name is Fuller. James Fuller." He winked and smiled. When Matt and I gave him a blank look, he added, "In the old days, wool was cleaned and thickened by a process called fulling. The modern name of Fuller means that family's origins can be traced back to the wool trade. So James Fuller hasn't fallen far from the tree, so to speak."

Most magicians could trace their family tree through the same single trade, and while it wasn't unusual for the artless to be able to as well, it was less common. Could Mr. Fuller be a magician? If so, why did he argue with Mr. Pyke, accusing him of having an advantage by using his magic on his rugs?

"Fuller was here just yesterday, as it happens," the porter went on.

"Did he look well?" I asked.

"As fine a figure as always. Nothing wrong with his lungs either. I could hear him bellowing all the way down here, and he was on the second floor in the master's office with the door closed."

"That doesn't sound good. Is he often an argumentative fellow? Only, I don't want to turn up on his doorstep if he's something of a bully."

"Nothing like that. He's not a bully, although he does have a temper. It doesn't snap often, but when it does it's like a bomb going off. I assure you, it takes a lot to rile him. You'll be fine, Mrs. Gaskell. I'm sure he'll welcome you and Mr. Gaskell into his home."

"Just so that I know, what set him off yesterday? I'd hate for it to be the same thing that I want to see him about."

He glanced toward the door then leaned forward and whispered. "Magic."

I waited but he didn't elaborate, not even when I prompted him.

Matt knew how to get an answer from him, however. "No doubt Mr. Fuller wanted the guild master to revoke the memberships of those members who are known magicians. It's happening all over London, so I hear. It won't be long until the discontent spreads to Bristol and other cities."

"A handful of members have been expelled already." The porter sighed. "Why can't everyone just get along? We're all in the wool trade. We need to take care of one another, not destroy." He gave me a grim smile. "But that's a debate for another day. Rest assured, ma'am, as long as you don't mention magic in Mr. Fuller's presence, you'll find him a friendly giant of a fellow. And his wife is a delight."

He told us where to find Mr. Fuller's rug shop. It was a mere two streets away from Mr. Pyke's. We drove back the way we'd come and collected Willie and Duke. Unfortunately they had nothing to report.

"Only one person saw him," Willie said. "A woman who was bringing in her washing says he walks past at the same time every night and she saw him last night too. She always nods at him and he nods back. She said he looked fine but distracted, like he didn't really notice her and was just nodding as a matter of course."

That was similar to what the neighbor told us.

"We kept asking everyone we came across," Duke went on. "No one else saw him, and some said that was strange because they always see him going home that way. So we reckon he was kidnapped between the point where he saw the woman hanging out her washing and his home."

"Yet no one noticed a commotion?" Matt asked.

They shook their heads. "It's a busy route after five," Willie said. "Shop keepers and clerks are going home and it's light enough at that time now the days are getting longer. If someone was kidnapped against their will, they'd be seen."

So Mr. Pyke hadn't been kidnapped. I suddenly felt sorry for Mrs. Pyke. It was looking like he left of his own accord, after all.

Matt had another idea, however. "He might have diverted from his course under his own steam, but he might have been waylaid by someone when he reached his destination. It's possible he arranged to meet someone who then detained him."

"It must be the man in the carriage," I said heavily.

"Or woman," Willie pointed out.

"Whoever it was left him worried, according to Mrs. Pyke, then later the same day, he goes missing. That's not a coincidence."

"It's unlikely it was Mr. Fuller, the rival carpet maker, in that carriage," Matt said. "According to the neighbor, their encounter was the day before yesterday and it's unlikely Mr. Fuller arrived in a private conveyance."

Everyone but Duke nodded. "I don't reckon it's Fuller, but I ain't convinced Pyke didn't run off with a lover," he said. "It explains why he never confided in his wife."

Cyclops scoffed. "And leave his shop untouched? He may have his guild membership revoked, and be forced to close his shop, but no craftsman is going to walk away from his livelihood without making other plans."

Particularly a magician. Rug making was in Mr. Pyke's blood. He was an avid enthusiast who saw his rugs as his legacy, his children almost. Cyclops was right; he wouldn't just walk away and leave his rugs behind. He might have taken a detour on his way home, but he'd not intended to be gone long.

I sighed. "If we don't think Mr. Fuller detained him, we're back to the beginning with no clues."

"We'll speak to Fuller anyway," Matt said. "He might be able to give us some insight into anyone else who held a grudge against Pyke and his magic."

We continued on to Mr. Fuller's shop where the shopkeeper welcomed Matt and me with a smile. The others remained in the carriage. She introduced herself as Mrs. Fuller, the wife of the rug maker. The shop wasn't as large as Mr. Pyke's but it was laid out similarly with rugs on the floor and walls, and a desk tucked into the corner. A clacking and low mechanical hum came from the other side of a door which must lead to the workshop. The smell of wool wasn't as strong here as in Mr. Pyke's shop and there was a whiff of oiliness in the air from the machine.

I removed my glove and skimmed my fingers over several carpets as I walked around. None were warm with magic, and their patterns weren't as intricate as Mr. Pyke's. If the Fullers had once been magicians, the magic had not been passed onto the proprietor of this shop.

Matt introduced us using our real names. Mrs. Fuller showed no recognition. "May we speak to your husband?" he asked.

Mrs. Fuller was about my age with warm eyes and apple cheeks that made her seem approachable, particularly when she smiled, as she did now. "He's just out the back. I'll fetch him for you." She headed for the door, turning her head to speak to us as she walked. "Is this about a carpet you purchased from us?"

"No."

She paused but Matt gave no further explanation. He simply smiled back and waited.

She pushed open the door. A moment later, the machine stopped and the workshop fell silent. Upstairs, children's voices could be heard needling each other. Mr. Fuller emerged from the workshop, but his wife did not.

He was as large as Mr. Pyke's neighbor described with a crop of red hair that was beginning to recede at the front. His sleeves were rolled up, revealing forearms as big as legs of ham, and the hands he wiped on a rag were enormous.

"Can I help you?" he asked.

Matt introduced us. "We're looking into the disappearance of Mr. Pyke on behalf of his wife."

Mr. Fuller stopped wiping his hands. "Disappearance?"

"He didn't return home last night after he locked up the shop."

He grunted. "Probably got himself a mistress. Pardon me,

ma'am, but if you're an inquiry agent, I'm supposing you've heard worse."

"You suppose correctly," I said. "But Mr. Pyke was devoted to his wife, so it's unlikely he had a mistress."

"If you say so." He flung the cloth over his shoulder and turned his attention to Matt. He eyed him up and down as if sizing up the likelihood he could win in a fight.

While I had faith in Matt's strength and ability, I doubted he could win in a fair match. Mr. Fuller would be near impossible to knock off his feet. But when he did fall, he'd fall hard. I shook myself. When did I start to assess men as fighters? I blamed Willie's influence.

Mrs. Fuller returned, having quieted the children. The family must live upstairs. It would be cramped, but no worse than where many shopkeepers lived. "Is everything all right?" she asked through a forced smile.

"Fine," Mr. Fuller growled.

"We were just asking your husband about his encounter with Mr. Pyke two days ago," Matt said. "Mr. Pyke is missing."

She blinked rapidly. "So you thought you'd come here and accuse my husband?" She thrust a hand on her hip, her smile gone. "Just because they're both carpet makers with shops near each other doesn't mean they hate each other. They were competitors, that's all. It's not personal."

"'Were?'" I echoed.

"Pardon?"

"You said they 'were competitors'. Why are you speaking in the past tense?"

She lowered her hand to her side. "Just a matter of speech. It doesn't mean anything."

Mr. Fuller moved closer to his wife. The difference in their height was almost comical, but there was nothing amusing about their expressions. The scowls hadn't left their faces from the moment we mentioned Mr. Pyke's name.

"We know you argued with Mr. Pyke," Matt said.

"Who says that?" Mr. Fuller snapped.

"You accused Mr. Pyke of being a magician."

"So?" Mrs. Fuller said. "He is a magician."

"How do you know?" I asked.

"Because I've seen his rugs. No one can make them that luxurious or have the patterns so intricate. It's impossible."

"And it's not fair," Mr. Fuller added. "Why should he be allowed to make such fine rugs when the rest of us can't?"

Matt opened his mouth to say something but I placed a hand on his arm and he closed it again. I was tired of reasoning with people like the Fullers, tired of their whining and calls for a level playing field. What did they want magicians to do? Not make things they'd been making their entire lives? Try to produce poorer quality goods?

"You're right," I said tartly. "Why should a magician get to use their natural talent for craftsmanship when others can't?"

Mr. Fuller looked pleased that I appeared to understand his discontent, but Mrs. Fuller narrowed her gaze warily. She'd heard my tone.

"After all, you shouldn't be allowed to reach higher shelves when your wife can't just because you're taller. Should you?"

He frowned. "What?"

"A nobleman shouldn't be allowed to inherit his father's estate, just because he was born into that family, either. Don't you agree? And why should a pretty girl have her pick of beaus? She has such an unfair advantage over the plainer debutantes. Nor is it fair that some men are paid to play football when others aren't, just because they've got better skills with a ball or can run faster. Indeed, they ought not be allowed to play at all. You're right, Mr. Fuller. It's not fair for the rest."

"I see you've come to mock me," he ground out between a clenched jaw.

His wife placed a warning hand on his arm just as I had done with Matt. "She does make a good point."

He shook her off. "Whose side are you on?"

"Yours, of course. But—" She broke off beneath his withering glare.

"You better go before I lose my temper," Mr. Fuller said to Matt.

"We haven't finished with our questions," Matt said mildly.

"I'm not answering your bloody questions!" He closed his hands into fists.

I tried to tug Matt away, but he stood his ground. I glanced back at the door, calculating how long it would take for me to fetch the others. Cyclops's presence in particular would be welcome. On the other hand, Willie had a gun.

"You were jealous of Mr. Pyke's flourishing business," Matt went on.

I winced, afraid of antagonizing the giant of a man further.

But instead of getting angry, Mr. Fuller laughed. "Flourishing? He was in debt up to his neck. He bought a new loom last year, in the hope of turning things around, but it almost sent him broke."

"Why was he doing so poorly if he made better carpets than his competitors?" I asked.

"Because he didn't have my Janey to sell them." Mr. Fuller rested a hand on his wife's shoulder. "She could convince a man to buy the moon if she put her mind to it."

She smiled up at him. "I do my best."

"If Pyke had someone like my Janey to sell his carpets, he'd be unbeatable. Lucky for me, he doesn't. He works the shop floor himself, and he's not much of a salesman. It takes a certain skill to get a customer to part with his money and my Janey has it."

I couldn't help getting in another sharp dig. "She was born with the knack."

"That's right."

"You could say it's as natural to her as magic is to a magician."

Mr. Fuller pressed his lips together.

His wife cleared her throat. "The thing is, after Mr. Pyke revealed himself to be a magician in that newspaper article, he gained more custom. I saw people coming and going from his shop all day."

"You spied on him?" Matt asked.

She dismissed his question with a shrug. "We were going to lose customers. It's already a struggle, having two rug shops so close to one another, but if it's revealed that one of those makes a superior carpet, we would be finished."

"So what were you planning to do?" Matt asked.

"Not make him disappear!"

"We weren't going to do anything," Mr. Fuller added, looking down at his feet.

"No?" Matt asked idly. "You didn't speak to the guild and have him thrown out?"

"My husband wouldn't do that. He wouldn't ruin another man's life and livelihood."

The problem with a complexion like Mr. Fuller's is its tendency to flush at even the slightest inducement. His entire face pinked. He tried to hide it from his wife, but she saw.

She stamped her hand on her hip. "You told the guild master about Mr. Pyke being a magician?"

"I was too late," Mr. Fuller told her. "He already knew on account of the newspaper article. He and Mr. Abercrombie were drafting some changes to the guild's bylaws that would allow them to remove magicians from the guild."

I gasped. "Abercrombie!"

Matt steadied me with a hand to my lower back. "What

does this have to do with him?" he asked, his voice so calm it was unnerving.

Mr. Fuller glanced uncertainly between us. "He's a consultant advising on the legalities of banning magicians from guilds. He's helping the guilds draft changes to their bylaws, so the master told me."

"You say guilds, plural," Matt said carefully.

Mr. Fuller nodded. "That's right. He's calling on all the London guilds, offering his services. He used to be the master for the Watchmaker's Guild where they've already dealt with this problem."

"He's no longer master there. He was thrown out of the leadership role after using some underhanded tactics." Matt caught my hand and placed it on his arm then, with his hand over mine, steered me away.

I could feel the vibrations of his simmering anger. Or perhaps that was my simmering anger.

I stopped at the door and glanced over my shoulder at the couple, watching us with perplexed expressions on their faces. I lifted my chin, aware that I must seem as snooty as Aunt Letitia could be at times. But I didn't care. "The Watchmaker's Guild have not *dealt* with this *problem* as there is no *problem* to deal with." I marched out of the shop, not bothering to wish them a good day.

CHAPTER 5

I gave Woodall orders to drive to Mr. Abercrombie's shop on Oxford Street, only to have three loud complaints coming from inside the cabin. Matt had quickly dived inside to join the others, leaving me to give Woodall instructions. The complaints were not about visiting a man we all loathed. It was about something even more important to Willie, Cyclops and Duke—food.

"It's past lunch time!" Cyclops whined. "I'm half starved."

"That's because you're so big breakfast only half fills you," Willie said. "But I agree, India. I'm hungry too."

"Can we stop at a chop house or tea shop?" Duke asked.

"Tea shop!" Cyclops scoffed. "I ain't going to find something there that'll satisfy."

Willie agreed. "We ain't going to a tea shop. They'll take one look at us and catch a case of the vapors."

Duke rolled his eyes. "You can't catch the vapors."

"Anyway," Willie went on, "Matt can't eat in public. He's too exposed."

It would seem we were going to have to eat somewhere if we were going to get any peace. I gave Woodall instructions to drive home. Mrs. Potter's sandwiches would have to do.

I climbed into the cabin and squeezed between Duke and Willie. Matt sported a curious smile as he watched me. I didn't think the encounter with the Fullers warranted such a happy countenance and told him so.

"Why's that?" Willie asked.

"They were selfish people who want to ban magicians from the guild," I said. "Mrs. Fuller spied on Mr. Pyke, and Mr. Fuller complained about Mr. Pyke to the master of the woolen guild. He learned that Mr. Abercrombie was there, offering advice on how to change the guild's bylaws so that magicians could be excluded."

Willie pulled a face. "So why do you look so happy, Matt?"

"This isn't happiness, this is pride. India was marvelous. She put the Fullers back in their place while giving them something to think about. She may have even made them change their opinion on magicians."

His words had me blushing, which only made his smile widen. "Perhaps Mrs. Fuller, but not her husband."

"Don't underestimate the influence of a wife on her husband. He may change his opinion yet." He leaned forward and clasped my hand. He drew it to his lips and kissed the knuckles lightly before letting go.

My heart swelled. I'd always known that I mattered to Matt, but this was more. He made me feel like I could make a difference. I *had* influenced Mrs. Fuller to a degree and she could, in turn, influence her husband. Perhaps they could both go on to influence others.

* * *

ABERCROMBIE'S Fine Watches and Clocks occupied the same prominent corner on Oxford Street that it had for decades. The family business had been established by the current proprietor's forebear, who counted princes and peers among his customers. Being artless had not stopped the family business from flourishing, yet my own family's shop had remained small by comparison. Being ousted from the position of Master of the Worshipful Company of Watchmakers had not harmed Mr. Abercrombie's business in any way. The shop was as busy as always.

The closest Woodall could get to the door was to stop alongside another parked carriage. Matt darted past it and across the pavement to the door with Cyclops flanking his right side and Willie on the left, her hand tucked inside her jacket so she could quickly whip out her gun if necessary.

"Move on!" shouted the coachman stuck behind our carriage.

I instructed Woodall to find somewhere to stop safely or drive in a loop if he couldn't. I waited until Duke disappeared around the corner of the side street on another errand before entering the shop.

It was a wonderland to this watchmaker, and I paused to take in the walls covered with clocks and the glass cabinets housing the more expensive items decorated in gold and other precious metals. Watches hung by their chains from stands on the long counter or were nestled into luxurious velvet pillows inside open boxes. The ticking of dozens upon dozens of clocks were as harmonious to me as a symphony. The two grandfather clocks set the base rhythm that vibrated through to my bones, while the higher pitch of the smaller ones soared to the heights of the ceiling.

Matt touched my hand. "Ready?"

I nodded and searched for Mr. Abercrombie, finding him at the same time he spotted us. He'd been standing behind his four shop assistants, scrutinizing their every move as they interacted with customers, but now came striding toward us.

"Get out of my shop," he hissed.

"Not until you tell us about your interactions with the wool guild," Matt said, not bothering to lower his voice.

"That's none of your business."

"It is when a member of that guild goes missing."

Mr. Abercrombie's *pince nez* fell off his nose where it had been precariously perched since he joined us. He left it to dangle by its chain around his neck. "Are you accusing me of something?"

"Shall we discuss this in your workshop or would you like to remain out here?" Matt smiled and held the door open for a customer as she left carrying a small parcel.

Mr. Abercrombie clicked his tongue and marched off toward the door leading to the workshop. We'd been in the back room before, but I took a moment to take it all in again. It wasn't often I had the opportunity to step inside a workshop of this size. It was twice as big as my father's and Mr. Mason's. Many of the instruments looked in new condition, and the pleasant smell of metal and wood polish hung in the air.

Mr. Abercrombie sent his three workers outside via the rear door then turned to me. "I had nothing to do with the disappearance of anyone from the wool company. Where is your proof? Well? I want evidence." He stamped the end of his forefinger on the workbench. "Show me the facts."

Matt picked up a small gold carriage clock with a mother-of-pearl face. "You've been going to all the guilds and advising them how to change their bylaws to exclude magicians."

Mr. Abercrombie snatched the clock off Matt. "So? They require a service and I am offering it."

"You were seen at the wool guild's hall on the day the member went missing."

"Again, so? That's merely a coincidence. It doesn't mean I had a hand in Mr. Pyke's disappearance."

Matt's gaze sharpened. "How do you know it was him? I didn't mention his name."

Mr. Abercrombie sniffed. "I heard about it. The master of

the wool guild informed me. And anyway, Mr. Pyke is no longer a member of the guild."

"Mr. Pyke was reported missing only this morning by his wife," I pointed out. "The guild would not have even been aware of his disappearance."

His pencil-thin moustache twitched with his indignation. "Someone must have informed them."

"That may be true." Matt picked up another timepiece, this time an elaborately engraved watch. He tossed it from one hand to the next, which set off Mr. Abercrombie's moustache twitching again. "But why would the guild master inform you of Mr. Pyke's disappearance? As you say, it's nothing to do with you."

Mr. Abercrombie grabbed at the watch, but Matt didn't immediately release it. He eyed Mr. Abercrombie from beneath lowered lashes. Mr. Abercrombie's throat moved with his hard swallow, and Matt finally let the watch go.

"Did you meet Mr. Pyke?" he asked.

"No."

"Did you know he was a magician?"

Mr. Abercrombie straightened his shoulders. "I don't have to answer your questions. You are not the police. I'd like you to leave my premises immediately." He pointed at the rear door that led to the lane. "The back way so as not to frighten my customers."

Willie picked up the first clock Matt had set down. It was clearly the most expensive timepiece in the workshop that I could see. She held it up, ready to smash it on the ground. "Answer the question."

Mr. Abercrombie paled. To be honest, the sight was making me feel somewhat ill too. "Don't you dare," he growled at her.

She simply smiled. "Your face is distinctive. It's got a rat-like quality that's easy to remember. I reckon if we describe you to Mr. Pyke's neighbors, they'll know who we mean."

Mr. Abercrombie swallowed heavily again.

"You lied," I said. "You did meet Mr. Pyke. I assume it was after he was revealed as a magician in the newspaper."

Mr. Abercrombie's jaw set. "This is harassment."

"Did you call on him at his shop?" Matt pressed. "Or did you meet him as he walked home alone and coerce him into going with you?"

Mr. Abercrombie bristled. "I am not responsible for that man's disappearance. Now get out before I summon the constables." He pointed at the back door leading outside.

Matt opened the main door that led through to the shop. Cyclops led the way and we followed with Willie bringing up the rear. She stopped to inspect a display of watches.

"They look so elegant," she said loudly. "Shame they don't keep accurate time."

I didn't want Matt to leave until we'd located our carriage, but he didn't want to stay in the shop.

"It's fine," he protested as he followed me outside. "There are too many people about for the shooter to take such a risk."

"There were lots of people around last time," Willie pointed out.

A loud noise had us all leaping in Matt's direction to shield him. My heart jumped into my throat and the too-familiar chill of fear washed over my skin.

"Matt!" Willie cried. "Are you hurt? Did it get you?"

"I'm fine," he growled.

Duke came sprinting toward us from the side street. "I heard a gunshot!"

"It wasn't a gunshot." Cyclops nodded at the intersection where two vehicles had collided. One of the horses stamped the ground while the others looked frightened. The coachmen attempted to calm them while throwing accusations at each other. The occupants of both vehicles had alighted. They seemed dazed but unharmed.

I let out a shuddery breath and clasped Matt's forearms. "You're all right. Nobody is harmed. Everything is well."

"Not for those vehicles," Duke said.

Woodall brought the carriage around and we quickly clambered inside. As we drove away from the chaotic scene of the accident and Mr. Abercrombie's shop, I felt the tension finally leave my shoulders. I was able to give Duke my full attention as he informed us of what he'd learned.

"Abercrombie does keep a carriage, so one of his staff told me," he said. "It wasn't there today as his wife and mother needed it, but sometimes it's parked in the lane if he's going to use it that day. It was there yesterday, but not the entire time."

"So it could conceivably have been he who called on Pyke at lunchtime," Matt said.

"We can't dismiss him as a suspect," I agreed. Even though we couldn't come up with a specific motivation for Mr. Abercrombie to kidnap Mr. Pyke—or worse—it didn't mean he hadn't done it simply because he disliked magicians.

Woodall had been given instructions earlier and drove us to our next destination. If I'd been dreading confronting Mr. Abercrombie, I was even more worried about entering the lair of Lord and Lady Coyle.

Duke and Cyclops remained in the carriage for this meeting, while Willie insisted on coming inside. "It's afternoon tea time," she said when Matt told her he didn't need an escort. "And Hope's a good hostess."

"Her husband isn't," I said as the footman opened the door on our knock.

Lord Coyle was not at home. I sent up a silent prayer of thanks for our good fortune. While I disliked Hope, she was not the threat that the earl was. Her danger to me had ended when Matt and I married. Lord Coyle's danger was ongoing, never far away.

Hope offered us afternoon tea and Willie quickly accepted,

rubbing her hands together as she sat. "Ain't this pleasant. All of us cousins together, enjoying tea."

The corners of Hope's eyes tightened. "You and I are not cousins, Miss Johnson."

"Call me Willie. So, Hope, what sort of cake is your cook serving up?"

"I have no idea." She turned to Matt and smiled. "To what do I owe this pleasure?"

"It's not a social call," he said.

"Sadly, I know that all too well. I do wish you'd come here occasionally to see me rather than my husband."

"We *have* come to see you this time, but it's still not a social call."

"Now I am intrigued. Am I a suspect in some investigation or other?"

"What makes you think we're investigating something?" he asked.

"You always are, and you certainly never come here unless it's to interrogate my husband."

A footman entered carrying a tray of tea things and cake. He deposited it on the table and left, closing the door.

Hope poured the tea. "Help yourself to cake, Miss Johnson."

Willie reached for a plate. "Don't mind if I do, Cousin Hope."

Hope passed out teacups and saucers. When she came to Matt, he said, "Are you all right?"

"Of course. Why wouldn't I be?" Her tone was challenging, accusatory almost.

"Because you're married to—"

"One of the wealthiest, most influential peers of the realm?" She sat beside him and touched his knee. "Darling Matt. You're always so protective of your loved ones."

He took her hand and removed it from his knee. "He's not an easy man to manage."

She picked up her cup. Her eyes were cold as they stared back at him over the rim. "He cannot be managed at all."

"That must be difficult for you," I said.

"Don't pity me, India."

"I don't."

She sipped slowly. "I have much to be thankful for. Even now."

"Now?" Matt echoed.

She waved a hand, the movement elegantly languid. "With magic out in the open after the release of Mr. Barratt's book, my husband has been more irritable than usual. He's angry about it. Very angry indeed."

"With Barratt?"

"Yes, and with Louisa. In fact, he sees her as the driving force behind the book. He thinks Mr. Barratt would never have finished it if not for her."

That was true, considering Louisa had cost Oscar his job to allow him more time to complete the book.

"What's Coyle doing about it?" Matt asked.

"What can he do? The book is released. People are aware of magic. Indeed, the entire city is obsessed with it. He can't do anything about that obsession except guard his information about magicians even as they come out into the open and announce themselves to the entire world."

"He must find it frustrating that they don't appreciate he kept their secret all this time."

She smiled a nasty little smile into her teacup.

"I worry that he's taking that frustration out on you," Matt went on.

She put down the cup and regarded him with fondness. "Thank you, Matt, you're so thoughtful. But I want to assure you, I may not be able to manage my husband—yet—but I do know when to avoid him. The situation may be stormy now, but I can see a way to calmer waters ahead."

"How?" Matt asked.

"Patience." She laughed softly. "It may be my sister's name, but I think it's more suited to me these days. She ought to be Hope as it's all she has left."

"You must come to me if you need my help."

"Dearest Matt, thank you. But all will be well, in time. You'll see."

She spoke soothingly, as if speaking to children who'd awoken in fright in the middle of the night. There was something unnerving about it, particularly when coupled with her promise that all would be well. Perhaps the madness that touched Charity was a family trait after all, but it had taken longer to manifest in Hope. But where Charity was wild, Hope was calculating.

"Is that why you've come here today while my husband is absent?" she asked. "To check up on me?"

"We didn't know he wouldn't be here," Matt pointed out.

"I thought perhaps you'd been waiting for his departure."

Willie snorted. "We weren't spying on your house. We ain't got time for that." She frowned and tapped her fingertip on the side of the cup. She looked as though she was giving the idea some serious thought.

"We're here because a magician has gone missing," I said. "According to his order book, you were one of his customers."

"No wonder you consider me a suspect, knowing what you do about my husband's interest in magic. What sort of magician is the missing man? I've bought so many new things lately, it could be anyone." She indicated the drawing room which had taken on a more feminine appearance since she moved in, with delicate furniture, lighter drapes, and prettier colors.

I shifted my feet, wondering if the rug was one of Mr. Pyke's. If it was, had he infused his magic into it? I would know for sure if I removed my glove and touched it, but I sat as stiff as a board on the chair, and concentrated on Hope.

"Mr. Pyke, the rug maker, is a wool magician," Matt told her.

"Ah, yes. I did know that. My husband gave me his name when I said I wanted new carpets."

I sat forward. "Coyle knew he was a magician?"

"Yes." She pointed at the sofa that Willie and I sat on. "The furniture maker is also a woodwork magician, and the woman who does the piece work on my clothing is a silk magician, so I'm told."

I removed my glove and bent to touch the wooden leg of the sofa. "There's no magic in this."

Her eyes narrowed as she watched me. "I know. Having magic in the items wasn't important, as it doesn't last. But the items themselves are exquisitely made anyway, magic or no."

The carved lion claw feet of the sofa were incredibly lifelike, and the embroidery work on the sleeves of her dress was very fine for a simple day dress.

"What did your husband tell you about Pyke?" Matt asked.

"That he is a wool magician and makes the best rugs in the city. He gave me the address of his shop."

"Did he say how long he has known Mr. Pyke was a magician?"

"No. Why?"

Had Coyle known Pyke was a magician from before he assisted Fabian and me with the creation of our new spell? Or did Coyle go looking for a wool magician only after he learned we'd made the carpet fly? I tried to remember the dates of her orders, but I couldn't.

"When did you first call on Mr. Pyke?" I asked.

"It was just after we returned from our honeymoon, some three weeks ago."

That was *before* we asked Mr. Pyke to help us. "And what about the final time?"

"I can't recall. Several days ago, I think. Why all these

questions? Do you actually believe I'm the reason that man has gone missing?"

"We must look at all possibilities," Matt said.

"Perhaps he left his wife."

"It's unlikely."

"Why? Because he's a good man and they seem happy?" She scoffed. "Come now, Matt, you know that appearances can be deceptive and that good men stray all the time." She held out the plate with slices of cake to Matt. "Would you like some?"

Matt refused. "I don't like that flavor."

I bit back my smile.

Hope was about to return the plate to the table but Willie grabbed it. "I like this flavor. In fact, I like all flavors. I ain't too partic'lar."

I had to bite down on my lower lip even harder to keep my smile in check.

Matt had far more composure than me. "One more thing before we go. Have you seen Louisa lately?"

"No. My husband detests her and has forbidden me from becoming friends with her. That's quite all right with me. She doesn't seem like someone I'd get along with."

"Oh?" I asked. "But you're so similar."

She blinked at me as if trying to determine if I was being insulting or not.

"Does he let you be friends with other members of the collector's club?" Matt asked.

"You make him sound like a tyrant, controlling my every move. He may have forbidden me from becoming friends with Louisa, but I am quite free to be friends with whomever else I like. The thing is, nobody in that ridiculous club interests me. They're either vulgar, dull or foolish. Mrs. Delancey is all three."

"Aye," Willie agreed. "She's even worse when she's trying to get me to sign that damned temperance agreement."

"What about your husband?" Matt asked. "Does he invite any of the collector's club here for dinner or a social evening?" His persistence with this line of questioning was curious, but it only took me a moment to realize what he was trying to find out.

"My husband loathes social events so no, he doesn't invite anyone here. Nobody calls on us in a social capacity. The only people who do come are here to conduct business. Is there someone in particular you want to ask about or do you want to dance around the name for a little longer?"

She was no fool. For that very reason, I didn't think we should mention the name.

Matt had no such qualms. "Sir Charles Whittaker."

"Ah. The debonair public servant. He doesn't come to the house unless it's a collector's club function."

Matt rose and held out his hand to assist me to my feet.

But Hope hadn't finished. "My husband does meet him, however."

Matt sat again. "Go on."

Hope's lips lifted in a smug smile. "I saw them together in the garden." She indicated the window that overlooked the street and private garden of Belgrave Square. The garden was available for the exclusive use of the occupants of the mansions surrounding it.

"When was the last time you saw them meet there?" Matt asked.

"Three nights ago."

That was more recently than Whittaker led us to believe. Indeed, he said there'd only been that one meeting, several weeks ago.

"It would have been dark at night," Matt pointed out. "How did you see them?"

"I saw my husband leave the house, but he did not get into the conveyance. He crossed the street and entered the garden. I thought it odd, so I followed him."

"You're spying on your husband?" I asked.

"I was concerned for his health. He isn't well and the cold night air isn't good for his chest. I didn't confront him, however, when I saw him meet Sir Charles. I thought it best to leave them be." She smoothed her hands slowly over her lap then clasped them, the picture of a demure wife. "Does that help with your investigation, Matt?"

Matt stood. "Thank you for the tea."

She rang for the butler who saw us out. Once we were inside the carriage, Willie huffed out a breath and adjusted her hat on her head. "That was strange."

"Ain't it always?" Duke asked.

"This time was stranger. Hope told us Coyle met Whittaker in the park at night."

"Whittaker lied to us," Matt said. "But more importantly, who initiated the meeting? And why?"

"I don't think that's the most important question," I said. "I think we ought to be asking ourselves why Hope told us. She wouldn't tell us just because we asked. So the question is, what does she gain from it?"

It was a question no one could answer.

CHAPTER 6

Sir Charles Whittaker's landlady informed us that he had not yet returned home from work. We waited in the carriage for over thirty minutes until his new conveyance finally drew up outside the row of houses. He alighted with a newspaper in one hand and a walking stick in the other. We were quite sure no one had followed us so I wasn't too concerned that Sir Charles didn't immediately invite us inside when we approached. He looked content to have this conversation on the pavement.

Cyclops had other ideas. "Mind if we come in? It's exposed out here."

"Is your life still in danger?" Sir Charles asked Matt.

"The shooter hasn't been caught," Matt said.

Sir Charles tucked the newspaper under his arm and led the way up the steps using his walking stick. He didn't need the stick. It was purely an affectation. It was a common accessory for men these days, but I was glad Matt never took to the trend.

Sir Charles asked the landlady to bring tea up to his parlor, but Matt declined. "We won't be staying long."

Upstairs, Duke remained on the landing where he could

make sure the landlady didn't listen in, while Cyclops and Willie joined us in the parlor. Sir Charles deposited the newspaper he'd been carrying and leaned his walking stick against the chair.

"Is this about the missing wool magician?" he asked as he indicated we should sit.

"How do you know about him?" I asked.

"It's my job to know."

I waited but he gave nothing away with his smooth countenance and level gaze. "Do you know what happened to him?"

He hesitated before shaking his head. "No."

I was satisfied with that, but Matt wasn't. "Do you have an opinion?"

Sir Charles's smile returned. "Yes, but I prefer to keep it to myself for now. As it's only an opinion, it might serve to lead you down the wrong path in your investigation. Nobody wants that."

"If I find out you had anything to do with his disappearance, or withheld vital information, I'll see to it that your life is made uncomfortable."

Willie parted her jacket to reveal her gun. "Very uncomfortable."

Sir Charles put up his hands in surrender. "Noted. So, how may I help you?"

"You lied to us about meeting Coyle," Matt said. "You claimed you've only shared information with him one time. We happen to know you've met him more than that. Quite recently, in fact."

Sir Charles blinked rapidly, the only sign that he was caught off-guard. "Why do you say that?"

"You were seen."

"By whom?"

"It doesn't matter. Why did you lie to us?"

Sir Charles kept silent.

"What information have you been exchanging with him?" Matt pressed.

Sir Charles didn't respond.

"Do you work for him?"

"No!"

"Then tell us why you've been meeting with him in the dark in secret?"

Sir Charles stroked his top lip with the side of his forefinger and looked away.

Cyclops slammed his fist down on the table, splintering the polished wooden surface.

Sir Charles leapt to his feet. When he realized Cyclops wasn't going to slam his fist into his face, he sat again.

"Sorry," Cyclops muttered. "But I'm tired of the secrets. We want direct answers, and we know you can give them."

Willie clapped him on the shoulder. "Don't push him," she told Sir Charles. "You don't want to see him when he gets angry."

Cyclops eyed her sideways.

Poor Cyclops must be frustrated that he'd spent the day with us when he could have been with Catherine. Indeed, the situation with Catherine must be getting to him more than we realized. He never lashed out like this.

His frustration was understandable. Unless the Masons accepted him, his future with Catherine was uncertain. Cyclops wouldn't want her to be estranged from her family, and he could very well walk away from the relationship thinking he was doing what was best for her. Perhaps I should talk to him, or warn her.

Matt leaned forward. "I'll ask again, and this time I expect an answer. If not, Willie will shoot you in the foot."

I swallowed my gasp.

Willie withdrew her gun and rested it on her knee.

Sir Charles tugged on his collar and stretched out his neck. "Very well, I'll tell you. But it goes no further than this room. My superior must not know. Do you understand?"

Matt settled back in the chair. "Understood."

"You already know that I work for the Home Office in a surveillance capacity. I am told who to watch and report back my findings. For some years, I've been assigned to watch magicians and the people who support them."

"The collector's club," I said on a breath. "That's why you joined them."

"I infiltrated the club's inner sanctum, yes. But Coyle must have investigated me. He either discovered that I'm a spy for the Home Office or guessed. For some time, he has been forcing me to pass on information I learn about certain magicians to him."

"Forcing you how?" Matt asked.

"With threats to harm my mother. She lives alone in Basingstoke."

This was the first time he'd mentioned family. We'd wondered why he kept no photographs or private letters in his rooms. He must have wanted to keep his mother's existence a secret for this very reason—to keep her safe from people like Coyle.

"What information have you passed on to Coyle recently?" Matt asked. He showed no sign that Sir Charles's plight worried him, but I knew he wasn't unfeeling.

"I told him Pyke called on Mr. Charbonneau's residence."

I blew out a breath. Shortly after that visit, Coyle had seen us flying off on a carpet. He must have made the connection. "You could be responsible for Mr. Pyke's abduction!"

Sir Charles stiffened. "I am no more responsible than you, India."

My stomach rolled. He was right. If I hadn't made that spell, Mr. Pyke would not have come to any harm, if Coyle was indeed his kidnapper.

THE SPY MASTER'S SCHEME

Matt rested his hand over mine. "That isn't fair," he growled.

"The point I'm trying to make is that if Coyle abducted him, *he* is responsible," Sir Charles said. "No one else. All you have to do is prove it was him and he will be in trouble with the law."

Willie snorted. "Sure. Let's prove it, shall we?" She snapped her fingers. "Just like that."

Sir Charles gripped the chair arm so hard his knuckles whitened. "The only reason I'm telling you this is because you can help me. Help get Coyle off my back."

"How?" Cyclops asked.

"Use the information I just gave you to have him arrested. You have contacts on the police force, Glass. Go to them and tell them what you know about Coyle."

Matt shook his head. "Coyle can't be touched without solid proof."

"Then get the proof!" Sir Charles scrubbed a hand over his mouth. It shook. "I'm sorry. Forgive my outburst. But I can't go on like this. The more information I pass on to Coyle, the more likely it is that my superiors will discover my betrayal. I'll be...removed from my position." He swallowed heavily and tugged on his collar again. "And if I refuse to give Coyle information, he'll hurt my mother. I am in a no-win situation. You're my only hope. I see that now."

"There's nothing we can do," Matt said.

"You have to try!"

"Why?" Matt snarled. "Why should we help you after you betrayed my wife to Coyle?"

"Because it's the right thing to do," I said quietly.

Sir Charles shot me a look of heartfelt gratitude as he released a shaky breath.

Matt, however, looked like a tower of pent-up energy. His finger tapped on his thigh and his chest rose and fell with his deep breaths. "We'll think about what we can do to help, but don't get your hopes up. I can see no way out of your predicament yet."

"Thank you, Glass. You're a man of honor and integrity."

"Don't thank me yet. Tell us what you know about India's secret spell."

Sir Charles blinked rapidly at the change of topic. "Considering Pyke was seen leaving Charbonneau's house, I assume they were working on a spell involving a carpet since rugs are his specialty. Is that correct, India?"

I hesitated, unsure how much to tell him.

Matt didn't hold back, however. "It was a flying spell. She made a carpet fly from here to Brighton, carrying four passengers."

Sir Charles's eyes widened. "Bloody hell."

"The spell was then stolen by Mrs. Trentham from Charbonneau's residence. Do you know if Coyle manipulated her into stealing it?"

Sir Charles shook his head. "We weren't watching her. We didn't even know she was a magician. That's something Coyle discovered on his own." He frowned. "If he has the new spell, and now also has Pyke, can he make another carpet fly?"

"It's doubtful," I said. "I don't think Pyke's magic is strong enough. He certainly couldn't make a rug fly with something heavy on it, like passengers. The rug needs solid supports to hold the extra weight and the spell must also be used in the supports by the relevant magician." I didn't tell him that I could do it without the assistance of Fabian or another magician. He didn't need to know how strong my magic was.

"That's a relief. I worried Coyle would use it as a flying device to…" He lifted his shoulders in a graceful shrug.

"To do what?"

"I don't know. What does one need flight for? Traveling quickly from one place to another, I suppose."

It would certainly prove lucrative for Coyle if he could commercialize the spell somehow. But there was also a more dangerous idea. The flying carpet could be used to drop a bomb on buildings below. I couldn't think why Coyle would want to do that, but I didn't pretend to know his schemes. He might do it simply to see if it could be done.

Or he might do it to gain himself more power.

* * *

I WAS in need of cheering up after the long and worrying day we'd had, so I was glad when Lord Farnsworth arrived in time for dinner. His irreverent company was just the tonic I needed. It didn't matter what the conversation was about. As long as Lord Farnsworth was involved, I was bound to laugh.

Matt seemed to be in need of distraction too. Although he claimed he found his lordship irritating, I noticed he no longer tried to avoid him. In fact, he sought him out to engage him in conversation.

"I received a letter from your aunt today, Glass," Lord Farnsworth said over dinner.

We all looked to Aunt Letitia. "I don't remember sending you a letter," she said.

"It was from Lady Rycroft," he went on.

Willie made a sound of disgust in the back of her throat. "What did she want?"

"She invited me to dinner next week." He dabbed at the corner of his mouth with his napkin. "I won't be going, of course. I'm terrified of being trapped again."

"Trapped?" Brockwell asked. He had arrived at dinner-time too and we'd made a place for him at the table beside Willie.

"Charity dragged me into a room last night and closed the door. It was frightening. If India hadn't rescued me, I could have woken up this morning an engaged man."

"That doesn't sound like such a bad thing to me," Brockwell said. He was carefully slicing the pastry lid off his pie and did not look up so didn't see the effect his words had on Willie.

Her eyes widened and her cheeks flushed.

Lord Farnsworth signaled to Bristow to pour more wine into his glass. "It depends on the fiancée. Charity Glass is not the sort of girl a fellow wishes to find himself shackled to." He made a small circle at his temple.

Brockwell set the pastry lid to one side on his plate and dug his fork into the pie, scooping meat out as if it were soup. "True enough. You ought to find yourself a girl more suited to your temperament, my lord."

"So I've been told by everyone at this table. Some even suggested a good friend." His amused gaze settled on Willie.

Her eyes widened even more, to the point where I was worried she'd do some damage to them.

Brockwell dipped his fork into the pie again. "A good friend is an excellent choice. A couple ought to be friends above all else. Marriage is for a lifetime, after all, and a lifetime is better spent with someone whose company you enjoy."

Lord Farnsworth nodded along. "You make an excellent point, Inspector. Marriage is for a long time. An awfully long time. One wouldn't want to spend it with a dull wife. I certainly wouldn't. What do you think, Willie?"

She grabbed her wine glass and drained it.

Duke chuckled. "So you'd look for a wife from outside your own rank?"

"Good lord, no." Lord Farnsworth looked horrified. "Glass might be brave enough to go against convention, but I'm not."

"I'm American," Matt said. "Convention doesn't apply to me." He winked at me.

"Quite right," Aunt Letitia said, as if she'd never objected to me marrying Matt.

Willie released a breath and resumed eating.

Brockwell finished with the inside of his pie, leaving just the shell which he proceeded to cut into. "What do you think, Willie? About marrying a good friend?"

"I, um…"

"I think she needs another drink," Duke said, signaling to Bristow.

Willie avoided answering Brockwell for the remainder of dinner, but she couldn't avoid him after it. I saw him take her hand and speak quietly to her before we filed out of the dining room. They did not join us in the drawing room.

Five minutes later, Bristow entered with glasses of brandy on a tray. "The detective inspector asked me to thank you for dinner and inform you that he was feeling unwell. He just left."

"How odd," Aunt Letitia said with a frown.

"And Miss Johnson has retired to her room," Bristow finished.

"Even odder." She waited for him to leave, before turning to me. "What do you think is going on, India?"

"I think we should wait for Willie to tell us in her own time."

Lord Farnsworth pouted. "She was supposed to go out with me tonight." He turned to Duke and Cyclops, standing side by side near the fireplace. "I don't suppose either of you will come? Willie and I found a rough looking place where they play high stakes poker and Baccarat. You'll fit right in."

Cyclops shook his head. "I have to work tomorrow."

"I'll go," Duke said. "I don't often go out without Willie. It'll make a nice change." He clapped Lord Farnsworth on the shoulder. "It'll just be two cowboys out on the town."

Lord Farnsworth plucked Duke's hand off his shoulder. "I am not a cowboy and this is not a town. But you're right. It will make a nice change to go out without Willie. She's rather a bad influence on me. She makes me spend far too much money."

"You should give your money to me to look after. I'll take good care of it for you."

"How odd. That's what she says."

They left and the rest of us retired for the evening. I yawned as I climbed into bed alongside Matt, snuggling against him for warmth.

He kissed the top of my head. "Are you all right, Mrs. Glass?"

"You mean aside from the fact that my head is spinning after our discussion with Sir Charles today?"

"It was an interesting conversation. Do you think we can trust him?"

"You're better off answering that than me. You're an excellent judge of character, Matt."

"So are you." He tilted my chin to make me look at him. "Don't doubt yourself, India. You've been marvelous today. This entire investigation has been driven by you. I'm just along for the ride."

I propped myself up on one elbow and peered down at him. "Don't think that. You're very important to this and to every investigation. And you're very important to me."

"I know that. But it's also good to know that if I wasn't here, you would be strong enough to carry on."

He turned off the lamp's gas, leaving me staring into the darkness, a hollow pit forming in my stomach.

* * *

WITH SO LITTLE TO go on, Matt sent Willie to watch Mr. Abercrombie for the day. If he was involved in the disappearance of Mr. Pyke, he might visit the place where the rug maker was being held. It was a slim chance, but it was something.

Matt and I called on Mrs. Pyke at her home. She directed us to the parlor at the front of the small house with its exquisite Oriental carpet. I wanted to remove my glove and run my fingers through its lush pile, but refrained and managed a gentle smile for Mrs. Pyke.

The poor woman looked as though she hadn't slept all night and her eyes were red from crying. I immediately informed her that we had no news of her husband, so as not to get her hopes up. Her face fell and she searched her apron pocket for a handkerchief.

"We're going to call on the police on your behalf," I said. "We have contacts at Scotland Yard."

She dabbed at the corners of her eyes. "That would be helpful. They'll take more notice of you than me."

"We'd like to look through your husband's things," Matt said. "His private papers, correspondence, diaries..."

"He's not much of a letter writer," she said apologetically. "And he doesn't keep a diary at home, just an appointment book at the shop." She excused herself and returned a few minutes later with a small collection of correspondence. "This is all he has. It's just a few letters from friends, I think. Take them with you. Show them to the police. Hopefully they'll help."

Matt accepted them and we left, promising to keep her informed as soon as we had some news. After checking up and down the street, Matt dashed quickly across the pavement to the waiting carriage. Duke held the door open for him and gave him a helping hand by shoving him in the back as he climbed in.

We read through Mr. Pyke's letters on the way to Scotland Yard. There were very few, only six, but two of them were in the same hand. I opened the first and checked the sender's name before reading the letter itself.

"Well, well, this is interesting. It's from Mrs. Fuller."

Matt leaned closer and peered over my shoulder. "What does it say?"

"Nothing of great importance. She talks about the weather and she wishes him a happy and healthy Christmas. She mentions someone named Harriet who is having trouble with a man named Wilson." The style was friendly. Friendlier than I'd expect from the wife of Mr. Pyke's business rival.

"What about the other letter?" Duke asked.

"It's dated two weeks later, just after Christmas. It gives an update on the Harriet and Mr. Wilson situation, whom it appears she saw on Christmas Day. The rest reads like gossip about mutual friends."

"Does she sign it in an intimate manner?"

"Not particularly. *'Kindest regards, Rosamund Fuller.'*" I wished we'd read these in Mrs. Pyke's presence so we could ask her about them. "I wonder if Mrs. Pyke knew her husband was corresponding with Mrs. Fuller."

Duke scoffed. "I doubt it. What man in his right mind would tell his wife he's friendly with a younger woman?"

I folded up the letter. "What have you two discovered?"

"Nothing of importance," Matt said.

Duke returned the letter he'd been reading to its envelope. "These are from friends who live outside the city. They don't say much about anything."

Woodall dropped us as close to the entrance of Scotland Yard as he could, but we were quite sure we hadn't been followed. The sergeant at the front desk sent a constable to fetch Detective Inspector Brockwell, even though we said we knew the way to his office.

I regretted not speaking to Brockwell about the case last night. I also regretted not speaking to him after he spoke to Willie. I was wildly curious about their conversation, but didn't think it was the right time or place to ask him now, at his place of work.

Brockwell greeted us and led us back to his office. He sat

heavily behind the desk with a loud sigh. Like Mrs. Pyke, he looked tired, as though he'd hardly slept. While he usually looked scruffy, he was even more so today. He hadn't shaved and his tie was crooked and his hair unkempt. It took all my resolve not to lean across the desk and tidy him up.

"Is this about the Pyke case?" he asked.

Matt detailed all we knew about Mr. Pyke's disappearance, including the latest development of his private correspondence with Mrs. Fuller.

Despite his disheveled and tired appearance, Brockwell gave us his full attention. He always put work first, no matter what turmoil his private life was going through. "Do you think he ran off with her?" he asked.

"We saw her only yesterday," Matt said. "She hasn't left her husband, but she might know something, although why she hasn't told us already, I can't quite work out. We'll call on her after we leave here."

"So what can I do?"

"We'll get further if the investigation is official. You can send men to check railway stations and ports."

"And speak to Lord Coyle in an official capacity," I added.

Brockwell gave me an arched look. "Coyle won't answer to the likes of me. Besides, he won't say anything to incriminate himself. He's far too intelligent to make a mistake."

Matt stood. "Just do what you can."

Brockwell shook our hands then indicated the door. Matt and I filed out, but Duke hung back. "So what did you and Willie talk about last night?" he asked.

Brockwell scratched his sideburns. "I, uh, I don't want to talk about it."

Duke looked as though he'd argue, but I pushed past him to re-enter the office. "Leave him be, Duke. It's none of our business." I straightened Brockwell's tie then patted his shoulder. "But if you need to talk to me about anything,

anything at all, Inspector, I am happy to do so. And so are Duke and Matt."

"Aye," Duke said.

Brockwell eyed Matt.

Matt cleared his throat.

"Aren't you?" I prompted.

"Of course," Matt said.

Once we were safely back in the carriage again, I asked him why he'd hesitated.

"Because I don't think I want an in-depth discussion about their romantic life. She's my cousin. Sometimes it's best to remain ignorant."

Duke didn't agree. "I want to know what it is so I can tell Willie she's wrong."

"Why do you think she's in the wrong?" I asked.

He looked at me as though I were a fool.

I sighed. He was right. It was probably Willie's fault. But I'd give her the benefit of the doubt, for now.

We drove to the Fullers' shop and residence, but I entered alone. Not because it was safer for Matt to remain in the carriage, but because this conversation required a woman's touch. I was immeasurably pleased to see Mr. Fuller wasn't present, although I suspected he was out the back in the workshop, as I could hear the whir of the machinery.

I waited for Mrs. Fuller to finish with a customer then approached the desk. She recognized me immediately and greeted me stiffly. If she was worried about the disappearance of her friend, she didn't show it. Indeed, she looked impatient. It was quite at odds with the pleasant way she addressed Mr. Pyke in her letters.

I glanced at the door to the workshop, but it remained closed. "I have a delicate question to ask you, Mrs. Fuller." I produced the two letters and handed them to her. "It's about these."

She turned them over, frowning. "They're addressed to

Mr. Pyke with no return address." She shrugged. "Are you asking me to read the private correspondence of a man I hardly know?" She handed the letters back with a shake of her head. "I won't do it. I'm sorry, Mrs. Glass, but I don't see how it will help you."

I refused to accept the letters. "Don't you recognize them?"

She looked at the envelopes again. "The handwriting is familiar. Oh! I know who these are from."

"Yes. You."

"No, Mrs. Glass. They're from my mother-in-law."

I stared at her. "Your name isn't Rosamund?"

"No, it's Anne." She frowned. "Is that why you're here? Because you thought I was writing to Mr. Pyke? I can assure you, I hardly know him. My mother-in-law does, however, through her late husband. They were in the guild together and were on good terms." She glanced at the door to the workshop and leaned forward. "That all ended when my husband took over the business. Or so I thought."

"Do you know why your mother-in-law was writing to Mr. Pyke?"

"I can hazard a guess," she said carefully. She studied the letters again, looking tempted to read them now.

"When did you or your husband last see her?"

She clutched her throat as her gaze lifted to mine. "Two days ago. My God. Do you think they ran off together? My husband will be livid."

"Can you write down her address, please. We'll call on her now."

She scribbled the address on the bottom of a notepad and tore it off. Her gaze slid to the workshop door again as the machine slowed and finally stopped altogether. "He'll never forgive her."

I thanked her for the address and rose just as the workshop door opened. Mr. Fuller stood there like a sweating giant, his face red from the heat of the machinery and the stuffy room.

I hurried for the front door and stepped outside. The door swung closed, but not before I heard him ask his wife in a loud voice why I was there.

I gave Woodall the address. Thanks to his fast driving and expert knowledge of the city's streets, we arrived at the small house five minutes later. It was almost identical in every way to Mrs. Pyke's home, even down to a similar Oriental carpet in the parlor. This one wasn't as intricately designed, however, nor the pile as thick.

I was relieved to see Mrs. Fuller Senior, until I realized what it meant. She and Mr. Pyke *hadn't* run away together, which in turn meant it was more likely that something dreadful had befallen Mr. Pyke after all. I was glad for Mrs. Pyke's sake, though, in a way. From the beginning, I'd thought him devoted to his wife of twenty-two years and was relieved to see that belief held true. But was it better for her to be an abandoned wife or a widow?

"You and Mr. Pyke are friends," I said, showing her the letters after we introduced ourselves. "You write to one another."

Matt had joined me this time, but Duke remained outside. Matt suggested I do most of the talking, however, in the hope that she'd confide in a woman.

"We do, yes." The senior Mrs. Fuller was a tall, strongly built woman with gray hair pulled back into a tight bun. She had a friendly face, but it was currently creased into a frown, her gaze wary. "What is this about?"

"Mr. Pyke has gone missing."

She covered her gasp with her hand. "Missing! How dreadful. His poor wife. She must be beside herself with worry."

"You didn't know?"

She shook her head as she studied the letters. "Did Mrs. Pyke give you these?"

"Yes. He kept them, although I'm not sure why. Do you know?" I asked gently.

Her frown deepened. "We're just friends. There's nothing more going on, if that's what you're implying. The man is married, for goodness' sake. Mrs. Pyke is a lovely woman, very sweet. She can't read, of course, but that doesn't mean she's a fool. If she doesn't know where her husband is, I don't know why you think I can help."

"We just thought that, uh, he might confide in you more than he did her. Do you have any letters from him?"

"I don't keep them in case..."

"In case of what?"

"In case my son finds them. He doesn't get along with Mr. Pyke and wouldn't understand our friendship. He'd think of it as a betrayal. That's why I never told him that Mr. Pyke and I kept up our correspondence, even after my husband died." She shook her head. "And now he's left, you say. I wouldn't have thought he'd do such a thing, not to his wife."

"We think he might have been kidnapped."

She blinked at me. "Why would anyone kidnap him? He's just a rug maker. He's not important."

Matt spoke for the first time. "Did you talk to him in the days leading up to his disappearance?"

She lifted her chin. "We just correspond by letter."

I was about to say something, but Matt touched my hand. "This is important, Mrs. Fuller. No one need know."

She blinked down at the letters in her lap. Her deep sigh deflated her chest and she sank into the sofa. "I saw him last Thursday at his shop. I rarely visit him, you understand, and nothing goes on there. We just talk. We're merely friends."

"We believe you," I said. "When you saw him, how did he seem?"

"Now that you mention it, he wasn't himself. He was worried about being followed."

"By a man, woman? Someone on foot?"

"It was a man with a touch of gray in his hair. He was in a private conveyance."

"Did he say what sort?" Matt asked. "The number of horses?"

She shook her head.

"What about the man? Was he slim?"

She frowned harder. "I don't know. He didn't say."

If he mentioned the gray hair to her but nothing else, it's possible it was the only distinguishing feature. That ruled out Coyle, but both Sir Charles and Mr. Abercrombie had gray through their hair. So did thousands of other men.

The front door suddenly crashed back on its hinges, making my heart leap into my throat. Matt shot to his feet as a red-faced Mr. Fuller stormed into the parlor, his hands balled into fists. He completely blocked the entrance so I couldn't see Duke.

"Sorry, Matt," came Duke's voice from behind Mr. Fuller. "I tried to stop him."

Mr. Fuller bared his teeth in a snarl, but it was directed at his mother, not Matt or me. "What's this about some letters, Ma? Why've you been writing to Pyke behind my back?"

Mrs. Fuller rose and took a single step toward her son. "It's nothing."

"It's not nothing!"

"Let me explain."

"Explain what? That you betrayed me? Betrayed the memory of my father?"

"That's not—"

"Don't pretend nothing is going on."

"Nothing *is* going on," she said hotly.

"I said don't pretend!"

Mrs. Fuller clutched her throat. She looked close to tears.

Mr. Fuller stepped toward her, but Matt blocked his path. The rug maker's face turned even redder. "Get out of my way!"

"Not until you calm down," Matt said.

"Don't, Matt," I whispered. "This isn't our business."

He turned to me. "India—"

"Look out!"

Mr. Fuller swung a punch at Matt's face.

CHAPTER 7

*M*att ducked beneath Mr. Fuller's fist.

Mr. Fuller lost his balance, and Matt took advantage. He grabbed Mr. Fuller's arm and twisted it behind his back. Duke caught the wrist of Mr. Fuller's left hand before he could swing another punch.

Mr. Fuller tried to shake them off, but between the two of them, they held the seething giant. Mr. Fuller emanated a low, angry growl, directed at his mother.

I pressed a hand to my rapidly beating chest. Thank goodness for Matt's fast reflexes.

"Let me explain," Mrs. Fuller said to her son.

"Explain what? How you've been carrying on with a married man?"

"That's enough!" Mrs. Fuller pinched his ear and dragged him down to her level. "Don't talk to me like that."

He winced. "Ow."

She let him go but continued to glare at him.

The small figure of the younger Mrs. Fuller barreled into the parlor, out of breath. "Thank goodness. I was that worried he'd do something bad when he got here." She went to her mother-in-law. "Are you all right?"

"I will be when my thick-headed son listens."

Mr. Fuller struggled against Matt and Duke, but they were too strong for him.

Mrs. Fuller Senior took the moment of silence to say her piece. "It's true I've been writing to Mr. Pyke for some time. We're friends, nothing more. He was a friend to your father, and I am friends with his wife, and now they're both friends of mine." She waved the letters in front of his face. "Read these. They'll show you that you're being a fool."

Mr. Fuller stopped struggling. "Why did you write to him and not his wife?"

"Because she can't read."

"Oh."

His wife poked him in the chest. "What do you say to your mother?"

"Sorry, Ma," he mumbled.

She cupped her ear. "I can't hear you."

"Sorry, Ma," he said louder.

Mrs. Fuller Senior *humphed* and crossed her arms. "You owe an apology to Mr. and Mrs. Glass and their friend too."

He gave us sheepish apologies, and Matt and Duke released him. He tugged on his waistcoat. He'd left the shop without his jacket, his sleeves still rolled to his elbows.

His wife took his arm. "We have to get back. I left the children in charge of the shop. Are you sure you're all right, Rosamund?"

"I will be when they find poor Mr. Pyke." She fixed her son with a stern glare. "You didn't have anything to do with him going missing, did you?"

"No!" Mr. Fuller cried. "I don't like him, but I wouldn't hurt him."

His mother clicked her tongue. "You and your competitive nature. It's not his fault he makes lovely rugs. If you knew what was good for you, you'd go into business with him, not cause trouble. He could do with a young, strong man like you about the workshop, not to mention an assistant who can read and write." She nodded at her daughter-in-law who nodded back.

Mr. Fuller dipped his head, his bluster and fury having lost steam.

"I do hope he's all right," Mrs. Fuller Senior said. "But what I don't understand is, why would someone kidnap him? Or hurt him, for that matter?"

"Because some in the wool guild fear him," I said, avoiding looking at her son and daughter-in-law. "After he spoke up in the newspapers about being a magician, they fear he'll take customers away from them."

Mrs. Fuller Senior clicked her tongue. "The guild master is a fool. He should be speaking calmly to his members, and urging everyone to sit down and discuss the new developments rationally. But instead, I hear he's joining in with those rioters. And he and Mr. Pyke used to be friends too! He should be ashamed." She shook her head. "I have a mind to march down there and tell him how to run the guild myself. He might listen to me. He used to respect my husband."

"Don't make trouble for me, Ma," Mr. Fuller whined. "I can't afford to get on his bad side." He took his wife's hand and allowed her to lead him out of the parlor.

Mrs. Fuller Senior pinched the bridge of her nose and released a breath. "My son is a good man, Mrs. Glass, but he has a hot head and that stops him using it properly, sometimes. But if you're thinking he did away with Mr. Pyke, I can assure you he's not the sort who'd kidnap or murder anyone. He hasn't got the stomach for it."

"Do you know anyone in the guild who does?" Matt asked.

She nibbled on her lower lip. "I don't like casting aspersions, but you should look to the guild master. Like I said, he and Mr. Pyke used to be friends, but they had a falling out some time ago, and I'd wager Mr. Pyke's revelation in the papers didn't go down too well with him. He also likes to think he's the best wool man in the business, so finding out that Mr. Pyke is the best would have been a blow to his pride."

"Does he make rugs too?" I asked.

"He runs a clothing factory, but you'll find him at the guild hall most of the time. His son mostly runs the mill now."

We thanked her and left, asking Woodall to drive us to the woolen guild's hall.

I took a moment to admire my husband, seated across from me. "That was quite a confrontation. I thought Mr. Fuller had the upper hand, on account of his size, but you both handled him as if wrestling giants was something you did all the time."

"We've dealt with bigger and meaner men that that," Matt said.

"Aye, and Matt did the hard part. I just came in at the end." Duke frowned at him. "Have you been lifting weights?"

"It's the magic in the watch. Ever since I used it after the shooting, I've felt stronger."

"Was the magic in it stronger?"

"I don't know. But I feel as though I could take on two Mr. Fullers."

The gleam in his eyes alarmed me. "Don't you dare try. You may be stronger, but you're not invincible, and I have enough to worry about without you running around saving the city from villains."

We left Duke in the carriage and knocked on the guild hall door. When it opened, we pushed past the porter.

"You two again," he muttered. "Haven't learned any manners yet, I see."

"We do apologize," Matt said amiably. "But it's raining

and we don't have an umbrella. I didn't want my wife to get wet."

Luckily it had begun to rain steadily. The porter dropped his frosty demeanor and welcomed us inside. "It's Mr. and Mrs. Gaskell, isn't it? I never forget a name or a face. Would you like another look at our library again? It's quite popular today. There's another fellow in there reading, but I'm sure you won't disturb one another if you promise to keep quiet." He put a finger to his lips, his eyes twinkling.

"Actually we've come to see the guild master," Matt said.

The porter shuffled to the desk wedged between the door and the coat stand. "Do you have an appointment?"

"I'm afraid not. We'll wait if there's someone with him now."

The porter opened the appointment book and his bony finger traced a line down the page. "He doesn't have any appointments right now. Let me fetch him for you."

We watched as the elderly man shuffled toward the staircase, his gait slow and unsteady. This could take a while.

"Why don't we go up and announce ourselves," I said. "I'm sure you don't want to go all the way only to come back down again. What if the fellow in the library needs you in the meantime?"

He glanced along the corridor to the library door. "Quite right, quite right. Do you mind? His office is on the second floor, first on the right."

"And his name?"

"Mr. Stocker."

We caught Mr. Stocker just as he was leaving his office. He greeted us warmly and re-opened his office door. Of course, as Mr. and Mrs. Gaskell we were welcome. If we'd given our real names, we'd be thrown out before asking our first question.

"What can I do for you?" Mr. Stocker asked as he settled behind the desk.

He was a middle-aged man, which most guild masters seemed to be, in my experience, with steel gray hair and a neatly trimmed beard. He leaned forward, clasping his hands on the desk surface, and blinked expectantly back at us. He seemed very eager to please. Perhaps he rarely had visitors. The untidiness of the office would suggest as much, with several books on the shelves having fallen over and the desk covered in papers and writing implements. An empty cup perched perilously close to the edge of the desk, and the matching saucer was used as an ashtray for a cigar.

Matt began the questioning, using the ruse we'd established on our first visit, with a slight alteration. "My wife's father was a rug maker from Bristol. He recently passed."

"You have my deepest sympathies, Mrs. Gaskell."

"Thank you."

"He was friends with another rug maker in London, and my wife would like to notify him of her father's death in person. We were coming here anyway, for my business. The problem is, we called on him this morning, but his wife informed us that he has disappeared."

Mr. Stocker's knuckles turned white as he clasped his hands harder, but his face didn't change. After a moment, he said, "You must mean Mr. Pyke. Terrible business."

I pressed a hand to my chest. "So it's true? Oh dear. We had hoped it was a domestic issue between Mr. and Mrs. Pyke and that he was merely staying elsewhere." I turned to Matt. "This is dreadful. Just dreadful. We must see what we can do to help."

"Are the police looking for him?" Matt asked.

Mr. Stocker's tongue darted out and licked his lower lip. "I... I don't know."

"People don't just disappear," I said, frowning. "Do you think he left of his own accord, or has something awful befallen him?"

Mr. Stocker looked down at his clasped hands. "I couldn't say."

"But you must have an inkling," Matt said.

Mr. Stocker swallowed.

It seemed he needed some prompting. "His wife suggested it was because he was a magician, and that he recently advertised the fact in a newspaper article," I said. "Is this true? Could someone have taken offence? Has one of his rivals done him in out of jealousy? Or fear that they'll lose business?"

Mr. Stocker's lips pressed firmly together. He was trying very hard not to speak. I suspected there were several emotions battling within him and it took all his composure not to let them out.

Matt recognized Mr. Stocker's difficulty, but more importantly, he knew how to exploit it to our advantage. "It's happening in Bristol, too. The magicians there see how things have transpired here in London and want to add their voices to the movement."

"Movement?" Mr. Stocker bit off. "I'd hardly call it that."

"What would you call it?"

"Business. That's what this is about. It's just business." The bitterness in his voice implied otherwise. Now I began to see what Matt was seeing. Mr. Stocker felt personally slighted by Mr. Pyke.

"Is it?" Matt said, equally bitter. "I have a tannery in Bristol. My closest friends are other tanners in the area. We dine at the guild hall once a week. Mere days ago, our newspapers reported what was happening here in London—the magicians announcing themselves, the subsequent anger and even riots from other craftsmen who aren't magicians." Matt shifted his weight, as if he were reluctant to say the next part. "I spoke about it to my good friend, who then confided in me that he is a magician." He all but spat the word. "I'm still reeling from the news. I'm devastated. It's as if he betrayed me, when I know it's not his fault. He can't help what he is. And yet..."

"You can't help how you feel," Mr. Stocker finished for him. "And now you feel you cannot be his friend."

"I've been grieving for that friendship ever since."

I eyed Mr. Stocker, worried that Matt had laid it on a little thick. But Mr. Stocker nodded sympathetically.

"I, too, lost my friend when he told me he was a magician. That friend was Mr. Pyke."

"Oh. I didn't realize you were close," I said.

"We've known one another since we were children."

"Then his disappearance must be particularly difficult for you."

"I am...conflicted. He told me some weeks ago that he was a magician, and we hadn't spoken since. I became angry with him and told him I never wanted to see him again."

"Did you throw him out of the guild?"

"Nothing like that. Not then, anyway. I was the only one who knew he was a magician at that time. But now, after he gave his name to the newspapers, it's no longer a secret, and I was pressured to expel him from the guild. It was a difficult decision to make."

"Because you knew it would destroy his livelihood," I said quietly. "You didn't want to hurt your dear friend, but other members weren't as considerate and didn't care."

He cleared his throat. "That's why I hesitated, but you're wrong about the source of the pressure. Some of it came from other guild members, that's true, but many are friendly with Mr. Pyke and didn't want to expel him. No, the pressure came from another source. Someone with no stake in the wool guild specifically, but explained to me the broader, longer view of allowing magicians in guilds. All guilds, that is, not just ours."

Matt and I exchanged glances. "Someone wanted you to betray your friend?" Matt asked.

"Not *betray*. That word is so cruel, so final. He said magicians like Mr. Pyke had to be expelled for the greater good. The future of businesses operated by non-magicians depended upon it." He removed a handkerchief from his pocket and wiped his sweaty brow. "It's warm in here," he mumbled.

"Is it fair that this man would ask you to revoke your friend's guild membership when he has no stake?" Matt asked.

"He has a stake, just not in *this* guild. He belongs to the Watchmaker's Guild."

Even though I'd expected it, I still felt ill knowing that Mr. Abercrombie was actively petitioning each guild in the city. Without that influence, Mr. Stocker probably wouldn't have done anything about magician members. Despite his personal falling out with Mr. Pyke, I didn't think he had the heart to punish his friend so thoroughly.

"What is this agitator's name?" Matt asked, somewhat bluntly.

"Abercrombie. Why?"

"Perhaps he had something to do with Mr. Pyke's disappearance."

Mr. Stocker shook his head. "He wouldn't be involved. What does he gain by Mr. Pyke's disappearance?"

"There'd be one less magician in the world," Matt said darkly.

Mr. Stocker focused on Matt. He looked visibly shaken by the implication. "He wouldn't. He's not..." His voice faded and his gaze fell away. "I'm sorry I can't help you. Hopefully Mr. Pyke will show up at home unharmed and we'll all laugh about this." He did not laugh. He scrubbed a hand over his mouth and beard, looking more worried than ever.

Matt and I saw ourselves out and headed down the stairs. The porter looked up from the desk near the door and smiled.

Before he could get a word in, a voice from the corridor behind us called out.

"Mr. Glass? Mrs. Glass, is that you?"

We both spun around, prepared to tell the person that he was mistaken and that we were the Gaskells.

"It *is* you." Professor Nash hurried forward, a leather document wallet under his arm, as he pulled on his gloves. "What a coincidence this is. I never expected to see you both here."

My heart sank. Beside me, Matt had gone still. Even he wasn't sure how to react.

"Glass?" The porter stamped his hands on his hips. "I thought your name was Gaskell."

Matt pressed a hand to my back and ushered me toward the front door. "Thank you for your assistance."

"Are you India Glass?" The porter's brow plunged into a frown. "I was warned about you. I was told not to let you in."

"Oh dear," Professor Nash muttered.

Matt opened the door just as Mr. Stocker came down the stairs. "Is there a problem?"

The porter wagged a finger at us. "These people are not the Gaskells. It's India Glass and her husband."

Matt grabbed my hand and we hurried to our waiting carriage, where Duke stood with the door open. He climbed in after us and was about to close the door when Professor Nash rushed out of the building.

"May I request a ride to Mr. Charbonneau's house?" he asked, pushing his glasses up his nose.

"Of course," I said. "Although you'll be tainted by association." I nodded at the guild hall door where Mr. Stocker and the porter stood together, arms crossed, identical scowls on their faces.

The professor gave Woodall instructions and climbed in. "That's all right with me. They only had one book of interest, and I finished it today. No need to go back." He sat on the seat beside Duke, the document wallet on his lap. "I am sorry for my gaffe. I wasn't thinking. I should have realized you were in disguise."

"False pretenses more than a disguise," I said. "And don't worry. We probably have no need to return either. It doesn't matter that our real identities are exposed."

Professor Nash looked to Matt and swallowed heavily.

"Isn't that right, Matt?" I asked, nudging him sharply in the ribs with my elbow.

"Hmmm," was all he said.

The poor professor looked as though he regretted getting into the carriage now.

"What were you doing there?" I asked to diffuse the tension. "You mentioned a book."

He pushed his spectacles up his nose. Behind the glasses, his eyes gleamed. His research enthused him. "They have an old book about wool magic in their library."

"But the guilds loathe magicians. Why would they keep a text in their own library on the subject?"

"I don't think anyone knows it's there. The book was quite dusty and shelved high up. I'd say it's been undisturbed for years." He smiled. "I told the porter I was researching the history of the guild. I didn't mention magic."

Matt had been lightly stroking his finger across his top lip, but now lowered his hand. "What did you learn from the book?"

"It mentioned a flying carpet."

I inhaled sharply.

"Anything else?" Matt asked idly.

"That's not exciting enough for you? Well then, listen to this." He leaned forward, just as the coach slowed. We were nowhere near Fabian's house yet.

Matt leaned out of the window. "Woodall?"

I couldn't hear the coachman's response, but I didn't need to. With the window open, I could hear the angry shouts up ahead. It sounded like hundreds of voices joined together in a chorus of abuse.

Abuse directed at magicians.

Matt got out, while Duke peered through the other window. He quickly pulled his head back in. "We should turn around," he said.

The road was too narrow for that to be possible. There was just enough space for two vehicles to pass each other, as long as the pedestrians kept to the pavements. We had to go forward through the advancing mob or turn into a side street before reaching it.

I tugged on Matt's jacket. "Get back in. It's not safe for you out there."

"It's not safe for *you*, Mrs. Glass," Professor Nash said. "Some magicians know you."

It wasn't what I meant, but I didn't inform the professor of the attempts on Matt's life.

Matt spoke to Woodall and climbed inside, firmly shutting the door. He closed the curtains. "This could get rough."

We all grasped the nearest strap. Matt also took my hand.

The carriage moved forward at a steady but sedate pace. The shouting grew louder and the cabin rocked with the jittery steps of the horses, but I resisted the urge to lift the curtain and peer out.

Duke watched through the gap in the curtain on the other side. "The police are here."

My heart dove. "Cyclops?"

Matt squeezed my hand. "It's not his jurisdiction."

Thank God. "What else can you see?"

Duke angled his head to get a better look. "They're marching this way."

"Is the road blocked?" Matt asked.

"I think so. Wait." He pressed his cheek to the glass. "There's a lane up ahead. We might make it before the mob blocks it."

"Woodall will take it if he can."

Professor Nash clutched his document wallet to his chest. "Isn't this thrilling." He didn't look thrilled. He looked terrified. "It'll be all right, Mrs. Glass. Don't fret. They don't know you're in here. You're perfectly safe."

I gave him a reassuring smile. "Of course." I squeezed Matt's hand even harder.

Outside, glass smashed. The horses balked at the sound then stopped altogether. I could just make out Woodall's attempts to get them moving again over the shouts of the mob.

Then his voice was drowned out by the crowd, baying for the blood of a magician named Woods.

"They seem focused on a particular shop up ahead," Duke said, peering through the window. "They're crowding around it, banging on the door, throwing whatever they can at the window. The police are making some arrests, but they're outnumbered."

Even as he said it, the crowd erupted into a furious cry.

"They're turning their violence onto the police and the police are responding in kind. This won't end any time soon, and it won't end until someone is badly hurt."

Thankfully Cyclops wasn't there, but would he be called to assist?

The carriage moved forward again, slowly, the horses clearly reluctant. Another shout erupted, louder than the last. It was so close now, mere feet in front of us. The carriage stopped and Matt peered out. Men surged around us. They shook their fists at the furniture shop and brandished tools of their trade—hammers, fire irons, saws, scissors—as well as anything else they could get their hands on. They shouted at the shop, their faces red with the effort and eyes feverishly bright. We were not the focus of their attention but a pack like this didn't need much incentive to turn against us if we got in the way.

One voice rose above them, starting up a chant that the rest repeated. "Stop magic! Down with magicians! Stop magic! No magicians!" His voice was clear above the others and it made the horses shift with fright.

Duke reached for the door handle. "I have to help."

"No!" I cried.

"The horses are too scared. They need to be guided, and Woodall can't do it. If he doesn't stay on the seat with the reins, he'll completely lose control and if those animals rear or bolt, someone will get hurt."

He opened the door and jumped down. On the pavement, the man with a brass speaking trumpet to his mouth stopped shouting. He lowered the trumpet and stared at me.

I gasped. It was Mr. Abercrombie!

His top lip lifted with his sneer. He pointed at the carriage. His mouth moved, forming my name, but no one heard over the chorus of the mob. He hadn't used the speaking trumpet.

Matt slammed the door shut and thumped his fist on the ceiling. "Go!"

Woodall wouldn't have heard him over the crowd noise, but we did move forward, no doubt thanks to Duke comforting the horses and leading them through the mob.

But it was so slow. So very slow.

Matt pulled out the box of pistols from the compartment under the seats. He loaded one and held it out to Nash. The professor sat wide-eyed, clutching the wallet to his chest, his face pale.

"Do you know how to shoot?" Matt asked.

"No!" The professor's voice was a mere squeak.

I took the pistol from Matt. "I do." Willie had taught me, but I was hardly an expert.

Matt loaded the other one and pointed it at the door.

I followed suit, but I didn't want to hurt anyone. We didn't have enough bullets, anyway. There were too many people, and they all wanted to blame someone for their trou-

117

bles. As a figurehead for the magicians of London, I had a very big target on my back. The moment Mr. Abercrombie remembered he held a speaking trumpet, he would alert the crowd to my presence. The carriage would be set upon, and we would have no choice but to shoot our way free.

CHAPTER 8

The carriage inched forward at an excruciatingly slow pace. The crowd now completely surrounded us. I didn't dare lift the curtain to look, but I caught glimpses through the gap as the cabin rocked. Everyone's attention remained focused on a particular shop, now guarded by a wall of policemen.

Abercrombie's shout alerting the mob to my presence never came.

The carriage turned into the narrow lane and the crowd thinned. The chanting shouts receded and our pace picked up. The door suddenly opened and Duke stopped short when faced with the barrels of two pistols.

Matt and I lowered them, and Matt helped Duke in before shutting the door.

Duke slumped onto the seat, knocking his hat askew. He removed it and wiped his forehead with the back of his sleeve. "You won't believe who's leading the mob, getting them all riled up."

"Abercrombie," Matt said. "He saw India and was about to tell the crowd, but must have thought better of it."

Duke smiled as he drew in deep breaths. "That ain't why

he didn't tell them. It was because someone punched him in the stomach before he could. He collapsed to the pavement, too winded to utter anything more than a wheeze."

"Did *you* punch him?" I asked.

His smile widened. "It was Willie."

"Miss Johnson!" the professor cried. "What was she doing there?"

I laughed. I couldn't help it. I felt light-headed with relief. "Following Abercrombie. I'd forgotten we'd set her that task, and I didn't see her there."

"She went in disguise," Matt said. "She left the house in trousers, not buckskins, and wore a cap instead of her usual hat."

Professor Nash loosened his grip on the document wallet and lowered it to his lap. "And she punched Abercrombie, you say. What a remarkable woman your cousin is, Mr. Glass. Truly remarkable."

Duke rolled his eyes and I smiled. It would seem Willie had gained herself another admirer without even trying.

* * *

AFTER THE EXCITEMENT of the journey, it was a relief to sit with a good cup of tea on Fabian's sofa, surrounded by people I knew and trusted. Once my heart resumed its regular rhythm, I was finally able to relax and enjoy the company. Fabian had offered the men a nip of liquor to add to their tea, but only Duke held out his cup.

"Mr. Abercrombie was there, you say," Fabian said with a shake of his head. "That man is a thorn in your side, India."

"More than a thorn. He was agitating the artless crafts-men, encouraging them to commit violence. I suspect he also organized the event."

"You must tell the police."

"We will," Matt said. "But Abercrombie himself wasn't

violent. He'll claim he organized a peaceful protest, but some of the attendees took it upon themselves to damage property. He'll get away with it."

Professor Nash shook his head which made his spectacles slip down his nose. He pushed them up. "He's a disagreeable fellow. I saw him at the wool guild the first time I visited. He was speaking to the master about a particular member who'd admitted to being a magician in the newspaper. He was furious when the master seemed reluctant to revoke the fellow's membership."

I sat up straighter. "That'll be Mr. Pyke."

Fabian frowned. "Pyke? The wool magician who helped us?"

I nodded. "He's gone missing."

"Missing? Has he left of his own accord or been kidnapped?"

"We don't know. He could even be dead."

"*Mon dieu.* This is terrible. Are you investigating? Do the police know?"

"Brockwell is organizing a search," Matt told him. "And we have been making inquiries, but…"

"But you have no hope."

"We haven't got any suspects yet."

Fabian looked shaken by the news. "Do you think it is because he helped us with the wool spell?"

"We don't know," I said. "It could be simply because he spoke about his magic in the newspaper. Perhaps another rug maker became fearful of losing business to him."

Professor Nash lifted the cup to his lips. "Or perhaps an artless wants to rid the city of as many magicians as possible and Pyke is merely the first."

We all turned to stare at him, but he failed to notice as he sipped.

I shuddered as a chill crept through me. If he was right, the kidnapper could be anyone. It may not be just another rug

C.J. ARCHER

maker but any artless craftsman. If that were the case, he'd be almost impossible to find. We had a city full of suspects. The police never caught the killer dubbed Jack the Ripper for that reason.

Professor Nash cleared his throat as he cradled his teacup and saucer on his lap. "I'm afraid this is partly my fault."

"You had a hand in the disappearance of Mr. Pyke?" Duke asked.

"No! I only meant that I contributed a chapter to Mr. Barratt's book. If it weren't for the book, ordinary folk would never know that magicians lived among them."

"Nobody blames you for the book," Matt said. "Barratt must bear responsibility for it."

"And Louisa," Fabian added darkly.

I studied each of the men in turn, their faces glum and their gazes staring into the distance as they considered what to do next. "Nothing can be done about it," I told them. "The book is widely available, and everyone knows about magic now. We must continue the search for Mr. Pyke, of course, but we must also look to the future. We must find a way to make sure magicians are safe, and that means allaying the fears of the artless."

"How do you suggest we do that?" Fabian asked.

"I'm afraid I can see no option except to once again go into hiding. I think the violence and riots will ensure many keep quiet, anyway. We should encourage others to follow suit."

Fabian clicked his tongue. "I disagree, India."

Duke grunted. "You can disagree all you like. India's right."

"If you see another way out of this, Fabian, then please advise me, because I don't," I said. "Now, on another note, I'm glad you're both here. I wish to ask you to do something for me." I set down my teacup and smoothed my hand over my skirt. "Can you write up a list of every magician of your acquaintance."

"My list would be small," Professor Nash said, somewhat apologetically.

"Why do you want this list?" Fabian asked me.

"I'm going to keep a catalogue of every known magician and their craft. It will be stored safely with the location known only by our household. It's the only way we can reassure the government that magicians will not be a threat."

Professor Nash frowned. "A threat? To whom?"

"To national security." I wasn't sure how much to tell them, but Matt had no such qualms.

"After recent incidents involving magicians with murderous intent, the government has become nervous. The only way to ensure magicians aren't rounded up and locked away is to reassure them that a definitive list exists. It will also ensure magicians don't use their magic for nefarious reasons."

"Surely it's unnecessary," Professor Nash said. "They wouldn't imprison someone who has done nothing wrong."

Matt lifted his palm and shrugged. "It makes the government feel better, particularly during this phase of unrest. Hopefully as things calm down, we won't need to continue maintaining the list. But in the meantime, if you could write down the names for India, that would be helpful."

Professor Nash sniffed. "It offends my rights as a citizen of a free country, but I'll do it."

Fabian nodded. "I'll send you a list soon, India, although I do not like to think of magicians being catalogued like books."

"Noted." I looked to Matt, hinting that we should leave, but he didn't get up.

"Professor, you were about to tell us something in the carriage earlier," he said. "Something you discovered in the book at the wool guild."

The professor's spirits lifted and he sat taller. "Yes! It's very exciting. The book mentioned two long-lost spells involving wool magic. One was the flying carpet, as I said earlier."

Fabian glanced at me.

"The other is a spell to make a woolen doll vocalize."

Duke choked on his tea. "Vocalize? As in...talk?"

Professor Nash looked pleased with our shocked expressions. "In a way."

"How is that possible?" Matt asked.

Professor Nash pushed his glasses up his nose. "How is any magic possible? With a spell, of course."

Fabian sat forward, frowning deeply. "What did the doll say?"

"It didn't speak, as such. It made a noise, like crying. You know how little girls like their dolls to represent babies. Well, this particular spell could render it quite lifelike by having it make a sound like a cry." He grinned and waited for our reactions. He looked as though he expected applause. "Isn't it marvelous?"

My thoughts went immediately to the negative ways the spell could be used. A kidnapper could swap it with a real baby in a perambulator, and while it made noise, the mother or nurse might not be aware until too late. Other than that, I couldn't see how the spell would pose a problem.

"Did the book say if the spell could make the doll speak?" Fabian asked. "Or just cry?"

"It only mentioned crying," Professor Nash said.

"If it could be made to speak, then the spell could be used on other, more lifelike, things. That automaton knight from Trentham's shop, for example. If a speaking spell could be combined with the moving spell—"

"Fabian, no." I sliced my hand through the air. "It's not a good idea."

His suggestion opened the floodgates and now I could think of all number of horrid uses for the spell, or a combination of the two spells, spoken by a magician capable of directing a creature that could speak. A lifelike toy could be used as a decoy in a robbery, calling the police away from the scene of a crime. It could be used to frighten the unsuspecting who attempted to engage it in conversation, or be used to deliver anonymous threatening messages. A lifelike wooden soldier could march into an enemy camp and give orders... The list of possibilities was endless. And worrying.

"No, Fabian," I said again. "Don't talk any more of it. I won't help you recreate the speaking spell."

"But only you could control it, India. No one else. And you don't have cruelty in your heart."

I sighed. "We've been through this. I might not be the only magician capable of using it. And what if someone threatens to hurt my family if I don't use the new spell for them? You know I would not stay strong."

"But—"

"India's right," Matt snapped. "The spell could be dangerous."

"Or it could be wonderful!"

I shot to my feet. "That is my decision, Fabian."

"Is it? Or is it your husband's?" It was quietly spoken but the effect was as the aftermath of a thunderclap. It felt as though his words reverberated around the room, rattling the panes of glass and frayed nerves.

A weighty silence descended upon us as Matt placed his teacup on the table in a slow move that was rigid with tension. He stood, rising to his full height, and took a step toward the still seated Fabian. "If you think that, then you don't know my wife at all. She's more than capable of coming to a sensible conclusion on her own."

Fabian and Matt glared at one another. Duke moved to stand by the door, a motion to leave, but it took Professor Nash's audible gulp to break the standoff. Matt came to my side and offered me his arm.

I took it, circling my hand around the taut muscles. "I

can't stop you from attempting to recreate the spell, Fabian, but I won't be a part of it."

"I cannot do it without you."

We said our goodbyes and together with Duke, we left. I wanted to look back to see Fabian's face. Despite everything, I wanted to know that he wasn't offended. I wanted him to know that we were still friends. But I kept my gaze forward.

"Mrs. Glass is right," I heard Professor Nash say. "There are too many unknowns for it to be completely safe. It must be a spell confined to the pages of history books. An extinct rarity to be wondered at by academics and history buffs through the ages. Don't you agree?"

I didn't hear Fabian's response.

CHAPTER 9

*M*att did not remain angry for long. His temper might flare when he was pushed, but it rarely ruled him and he was usually quick to release it. I, however, was still seething at dinnertime. I'd shed a tear when we arrived home, but when my tears abated, I became angry with Fabian.

He'd agreed that we wouldn't make new spells. He'd led me to believe he saw the dangers too, and that he wouldn't pressure me to resume our work. But all of his promises had been forgotten the moment an interesting prospect reared its head. My wishes had been discarded as if they didn't matter, my concerns swept aside.

It felt like a betrayal. I was beginning to wonder if Fabian saw me as a friend at all.

I changed for dinner and met the others in the drawing room before going in. Aunt Letitia wasn't there, but Cyclops had finished work for the day and Willie had returned too.

I threw my arms around her and hugged her fiercely. "Duke told us what you did to stop Abercrombie. You are a true friend, Willie. A true, dear friend."

She drew away and clasped my arms. "Want me to punch Charbonneau for you too?"

"So they told you."

Matt took my hand and kissed my forehead. "Are you all right?"

"I will be, although Willie's offer sounds attractive."

Willie cracked her knuckles.

"She was just telling us how the police interviewed Abercrombie but let him go," Matt said.

I sighed. "That was to be expected, I suppose. He wouldn't do anything against the law."

"Not in front of independent witnesses." Willie stabbed a finger in Cyclops's direction. "But your lot should investigate him. I reckon he's saying one thing in public and another in private to rile up the younger members of the craft guild."

"'My lot' are doing their best," Cyclops said. "We have to operate within the law."

"They should send a spy into his camp, someone in disguise who can listen in to conversations and report back."

Cyclops put up his hands. "Don't look at me. I'm too conspicuous."

"And Abercrombie knows you," Duke added. "He knows all of us."

The dinner gong sounded and we filed through to the dining room where Aunt Letitia joined us. "Why all the long faces?" she asked as the soup course was served.

"We're worried about the missing Mr. Pyke," I reminded her.

"Yes, of course, dreadful business. But I'm sure he'll turn up, having had an adventure. Willemina, you look particularly gloomy this evening. Are you unwell?"

"I'm fine," Willie mumbled.

I tried to catch Aunt Letitia's attention to warn her not to bring up the subject of Brockwell and his abrupt departure after talking to Willie the night before, but she didn't notice.

"You must call on the detective inspector after dinner. He always cheers you up."

"No he doesn't," Willie snapped. "Not always."

"Well, nearly—"

"What have you been doing today, Aunt?" Matt asked. "Did you go out for a walk?"

Her lips pursed at being politely but forcefully diverted from a potential intrigue. "I did, and then I attended to some correspondence. One letter in particular caught my eye. My friend, Lady Sloane, has a niece who'll have her first season this year."

"Season of what?" Duke asked.

"*The* season."

Duke gave her a blank look.

"She'll be presented," Aunt Letitia went on.

"Presented?"

"At court. It means she'll be out."

"Out of what?"

Aunt Letitia returned to her soup. "Honestly, Duke, you're so American. Tell him, Cyclops. But first, take your elbow off the table."

Cyclops sat back and lowered his arms. "When a young lady of good breeding turns eighteen or thereabouts, she comes to London and makes her debut. She's presented at court then spends the spring and summer attending social engagements—balls, dinners, afternoon teas, races, and soirees." He waved a hand in the air to indicate the events went on and on. "It's a way of signaling the young lady is hunting for a husband, and the social occasions give her an opportunity to catch one."

Duke stared at him with his mouth ajar. "Did they teach you this in the police school?"

Cyclops indicated Aunt Letitia. "Miss Glass taught me."

Aunt Letitia patted her mouth with her napkin. "Although I made it sound less like a blood sport."

"So what did your friend say in her letter?" I asked.

"Lady Sloane said her niece is quite pretty and very accomplished, although somewhat unconventional."

Willie passed her empty plate to the footman collecting the dishes. "Is that code for being as mad as a wild hog?"

Aunt Letitia gave Willie a withering glare. "It might be. Or it could simply mean she has opinions."

"God help us," Willie muttered at the ceiling.

Duke kicked her under the table, but it was not at all subtle and we all noticed.

"Lady Sloane has asked if she can call on me when she arrives in London with her niece," Aunt Letitia said. "I thought she could come for afternoon tea."

"I'd be delighted to meet them both," I said. I hoped Mr. Pyke would be found by then so that I could give my full attention to Aunt Letitia's friend. As the wife of the heir to the Rycroft title, I was probably expected to entertain from time to time throughout the season, although I wasn't sure if anyone would particularly care about us. We weren't important people in society.

"If we like the girl, we'll introduce her to Lord Farnsworth," Aunt Letitia said.

Willie *humphed* loudly.

Aunt Letitia pretended not to notice. "If we like her, and she's not *too* unconventional, then we'll arrange a dinner and invite them both."

"Shouldn't the decision of whether she's too unconventional for his taste be made by him?" I asked.

"Oh, India. You know nothing about matchmaking. I'm very good at it, as you well know. Look at you and Matthew."

If it had been left to her, Matt would have married a lady from a good family and I would have been relegated to the staff quarters. Her memory was selective and it was perhaps best not to dredge up the time when she was against me marrying Matt.

Willie *humphed* again.

"Is something the matter?" I asked her.

She crossed her arms. "No."

Something was bothering her, but I waited until Peter the footman finished collecting our empty bowls and left the room. "Are you worried that Lord Farnsworth will fall in love with the girl?" I asked quietly.

"No! I ain't jealous, India. Not like that." She leaned forward, resting both elbows on the table. "Marriage is just so final. And Farnsworth himself said he reckons he's not cut out for it."

Aunt Letitia poked her fork into Willie's arm. "Elbows off the table. As to Lord Farnsworth's opinion of marriage, he will change his mind. He must. It's his duty. Anyway, he just needs to find the right lady. Perhaps this girl will be her."

"Marriage ain't for everyone, Letty."

Aunt Letitia picked up her wine glass and peered at her over the rim. "As a spinster, I am well aware of that. You and I are cut from different cloth to most, however, and neither of us are expected to find husbands. Not at our age."

Willie frowned. "Are you calling me old?"

Peter returned carrying a covered tray. "Lovely! The main course has arrived," Aunt Letitia said with far more enthusiasm than she'd ever greeted a meal before.

"I could get a husband if I wanted."

"Aye," Duke said with a wink for Cyclops. "Two, according to the Romany fortune teller."

"Preferably not at the same time," Aunt Letitia added under her breath.

* * *

WE HAD JUST FINISHED an early breakfast the following morning and were about to discuss what to do next in the search for Mr. Pyke when Bristow entered the library and announced the arrival of Fabian.

"Tell him to go away," Willie said. "He ain't welcome here."

I'd calmed down overnight and although I didn't like how vehement Fabian had been, I didn't want to fall out over our disagreement. But perhaps I was being too generous. "Matt? What do you think?"

He closed the notebook in which he'd been making notes about the case. "I think it's up to you. I won't pretend I like how he spoke to you yesterday, but I won't hold it against him if you want to give him a chance to apologize."

I turned to Bristow. "Send him in."

Willie and Duke shook their heads at my decision.

If Fabian had kept his hat instead of giving it to Bristow at the front door, I suspected he'd be worrying the brim with both hands as he entered the library. He could barely meet my eye as he stopped near the door.

He waited for Bristow to leave then finally lifted his gaze to mine. He swallowed hard, as if there were a lump in his throat, and stuttered through an apology. "It was terrible of me to speak to you that way, India. I hope you can find it in your heart to forgive me, although I do not expect it."

"Good," Willie muttered.

"I won't pretend I wasn't upset by yesterday's encounter," I said. "I thought you agreed with me that we should not create new spells."

"I did agree." He sighed. "I *thought* I agreed."

"But when a new and exciting opportunity rose, you changed your mind."

"I am not strong like you, India. I cannot resist the calling within me." He tapped his fist against his chest. "I ache to perform magic."

"Then perform it. No one is suggesting you stop manipulating iron, just as I have not stopped tinkering with timepieces."

"It is not enough."

"It has to be enough, because creating spells could bring danger to the world. I don't want that on my conscience. Do you?"

He released a breath then finally shook his head. "Do I have your forgiveness?"

I gave him a tentative smile, not yet ready to welcome him into our home with open arms. "You do."

He released a breath. "And yours, Glass?"

"You don't need mine," Matt said.

"But I do! As India's husband, your opinion matters."

"I told you yesterday, India is capable of making her own decisions."

"Nevertheless, I would like your forgiveness too." Fabian put out his hand.

For one long moment, I thought Matt would refuse to shake it, but he eventually took it. They didn't exchange smiles or any other words and both stepped away when they released hands, like pugilists returning to their corner between rounds. Fabian didn't offer his hand to either Duke or Willie, which was probably just as well as I suspected they might snub him, going by their scowls.

"Please take a seat, Fabian," I said. "We were just discussing what we know so far about Mr. Pyke's disappearance."

Fabian hitched up his trouser legs and sat. "Then what I have to say will interest you. I did not come here just to apologize, although that was the most pressing reason. Something troubling has occurred."

"What is it?"

He rubbed a jawline peppered with dark stubble and flicked an anxious glance at Matt. He was worried about

Matt's reaction. Now I was even more intrigued. "The flying rug was stolen last night."

"What?" Matt exploded.

I rested a hand on his arm and I think it stopped him from getting to his feet and standing over Fabian in a threatening manner. But only just, if the vibrations coursing through him were an indication.

Duke swore under his breath. "That ain't good."

"How could it be stolen?" I asked. "It's a large rug and was on your floor with furniture covering it. You would have heard something."

"It was that servant girl, weren't it?" Willie asked. "The one you've been spending your nights with. Was it her? Or was she a decoy?"

Fabian's face flushed. He hadn't known that we knew about his relationship with his maid. "The carpet wasn't in the house. After I retrieved it from the paddock near Brighton, it didn't clean very well. It was in no condition to be in my drawing room, so I stored it in the stables."

Matt groaned and rubbed his forehead. "You stored the most important magical object in the world in an insecure area."

"You idiot!" Willie blurted out.

"The stables are locked at night," Fabian said. "And the stable boy is always there. It was taken in the evening when I was out and the coachman with me."

"And the stable boy?" Matt asked.

Fabian sank into the chair. "Asleep."

Duke and Willie muttered under their breaths.

Matt merely sighed. "Have you questioned him this morning? Are there any clues? Witnesses?"

"The boy says he heard a noise, but did not know the time. I have not asked the outdoor servants from other houses. They always give me odd looks, because I am French. That's why I came here. You are English and experts at asking questions. Also, the theft could be tied to Pyke's disappearance."

I gasped as it dawned on me that he could be right.

Matt had clearly already made the connection. He didn't look at all shocked. "If the two incidents are linked—and I think they are—then there are two scenarios," he said. "Either Coyle kidnapped Pyke then stole the carpet for Pyke to use in some magical way, or, if Pyke was kidnapped by someone else, he told them about the carpet and they subsequently stole it."

"But only India can make the carpet fly," Duke said. "Why bother with Pyke at all?"

"Only I can make it fly *with passengers,*" I pointed out. "With the new moving spell, Mr. Pyke should be able to make the carpet fly but without any weight on it."

Fabian agreed with Matt. "Coyle stole the spell and carpet and kidnapped Pyke. It must be him. Who else?"

"Who else indeed, but we only *think* Coyle has all three. We have no proof."

Willie had been drumming her fingers on the chair arm, but suddenly stopped. "It could be Pyke himself. He could be hiding out somewhere. Maybe he stole it for himself, not for someone else, and has plans to make flying carpets and sell them."

Duke pulled a face. "Why would he do that? His magic won't last and no one can sit on the rugs while it flies. What's the point of a flying rug if you can't ride it?"

"Novelty gift value," Willie said, as if he were a fool. "Corsets or spinning tops don't have a function, but they're sold the world over."

"Some would disagree about them not having a function," I said.

"What about stuffed animals dressed like humans?" She arched her brow at me. "Curiosities sell, especially to fools with too much money."

She did have a point.

Fabian appeared to be slowly warming to the idea. "Pyke wanted a copy of the spell after we made it."

Matt wasn't convinced, however. "You're forgetting a few key clues. By all accounts, Pyke was worried on the afternoon of his disappearance after he was visited by someone in a carriage. He also told Mrs. Fuller that he was being followed by a man with dark hair, streaked with gray."

The more I thought about it, the more I agreed with him. "Mr. Pyke wouldn't abandon his wife. Not so he could secretly sell off magic carpets. Besides, what would he need that particular carpet for? If he stole the spell, he could just use it on any carpet of his own making. Why did he need to steal that one?"

"Because the magic in it is stronger than anything he could do on his own," Matt said slowly. "You're right, India. He doesn't want to just sell magic flying carpets. He needs that particular one. Or somebody does."

Our gazes met. We both thought it was Lord Coyle but didn't say his name. I wanted to keep an open mind at this point, and I suspected Matt did too.

"There is one thing we can be sure about now," Matt said. "Pyke probably wasn't kidnapped by a rival artless rug maker out of jealousy. That eliminates a lot of suspects, including Abercrombie."

Willie wrinkled her nose. "Abercrombie's still guilty of being an ass."

"I think we can also safely say Pyke has not come to harm," Matt went on. "Whoever stole the spell most likely also stolen the rug, and they need Pyke and his magic. As long as they need him, he'll be safe."

But what happened if he couldn't do what his kidnapper wanted? What happened if they thought he could fly the rug with passengers then learned he couldn't?

I pressed a hand to my throat and my eyes unexpectedly

welled with tears. I hardly knew the man, but in a way, I was responsible for his fate. The moment Fabian and I had enlisted his help with the flying wool spell, we'd put him in danger.

Matt crouched beside me and gathered my hands in his. "He's alive, India. We'll do our best to keep it that way."

Duke suddenly got to his feet and stalked to the window. He pulled the curtains closed, plunging the room into near-darkness.

"What'd you do that for?" Willie cried.

"Y'all have forgotten something."

Matt rose but kept hold of one of my hands. "What?"

"If the kidnapper realizes Pyke can't make the carpet fly with passengers on it, and Pyke tells him it's because his magic isn't strong enough, what's to stop Pyke from keeping India's name out of it? Who's to say he won't tell his kidnapper that he needs India?"

"*Mon dieu*," Fabian murmured. "The kidnapper may come for India next."

Matt squeezed my hand and held on tightly. My own hand began to shake.

CHAPTER 10

*M*att sent a message to Scotland Yard asking Brockwell to meet us at Fabian's stables, located in the mews behind his townhouse. We alighted from our carriage at the end of the mews. Duke and Willie remained there so I felt it was safe for Matt to be exposed.

"Hold my hand," he said. "The cobbles are slippery."

I suspected he was as concerned about me being kidnapped just as much as he was concerned about me falling. I could have told him no one would attempt it with him nearby, but I doubted it would change his behavior. Besides, I liked holding his hand.

We dodged horse deposits and puddles until we reached the coach house and stables opposite the rear entrance to Fabian's townhouse. We waited a few minutes for Brockwell to arrive with two constables in tow. He immediately ordered them to interview the outdoor servants of other houses up and down the mews. We then relayed what we knew to Brockwell. It amounted to very little.

He tipped his head back to look up at the servants' quarters above the coach house. "Why did Charbonneau leave the rug here?"

Fabian had agreed not to join us so that his staff felt freer to answer honestly. He'd sent word ahead ordering them to tell us everything they could. The stable hand and the coachman greeted us politely if stiffly in the coach house. The double doors stood open and the natural light made the glossy black paint of the carriage shine. The coachman must polish it often because the smell was almost overwhelming. I couldn't smell the horses at all. Perhaps that was the point.

The first thing Brockwell did was reassure the two staff they were not in trouble. It didn't seem to ease them, however. They remained rigidly standing to attention, their gazes averted.

"Nothing you say to us will be reported back to Mr. Charbonneau," Matt said. "No one is in trouble with the police or your employer. We just want to find the thief."

Some of their tension eased and the coachman relaxed his stance. The stable hand followed his superior's lead although he still looked nervous.

"Tell us when you first noticed the rug was missing," Matt said.

Brockwell put up a finger for silence then reached into his pocket and removed his notepad and pencil. He removed his glove, licked his thumb, and used it to flip the pages until he found a blank one. "Proceed."

The stable lad, Jimmy, spoke first. "It was me. I noticed it was gone when I got up this morning to feed the horses. The rug was stored at the back of the stables with the feed, see."

"Was it there last night?" Brockwell asked.

"Aye. At least it was at about five when I checked the stock."

"It was also there at seven-fifteen," the coachman said. "I had to fetch a whisp on account of Farthing's tail needed currying." He shot the stable boy a sharp glare. "It wasn't done proper, and I can't have an untidy horse pulling the master's brougham."

"You drove Mr. Charbonneau last night," Matt said. "How long were you gone?"

"I drove the master to Knightsbridge, that's correct. I left promptly at five-to-eight, so that I'd be around the front at eight, and returned here to the coach house at twenty minutes past midnight."

Brockwell wrote the times down in his notebook. "You didn't notice the carpet missing at that point?"

"No, sir. I didn't need to go to the back of the stables. The harness is stored over there." He pointed to the straps and other equipment hanging on the wall.

"And where was the rug stored?"

The youth led the way through to the stables, past the two horses in individual stalls, to the back where buckets, brooms, sacks of feed, and other equipment were stored. He pointed to a wooden barrier and a chair without a seat positioned some feet away. "It was rolled up with one end here and the other here. When I came down at six this morning, I saw it was gone. I informed Mr. Ogilvie when he woke up." He nodded at the coachman.

Mr. Ogilvie lifted his chin. "And I informed the inside staff immediately."

"Did you conduct a search first?"

"No, sir. I thought one of the inside staff had fetched it while we were asleep. It wasn't until the butler informed me that they hadn't that we both realized it was stolen. We searched high and low but couldn't find it."

Matt and Brockwell checked the area where the carpet was kept then inspected the floor. There were three possible exit points from the stables and adjoining coach house—the double doors used for the carriage, the single door that also allowed access to the coach house and another door for the stables. There was no sign the rug had been dragged along the floor. Not that the floor was particularly dirty, but it wasn't spotless either. If a large object had been dragged, it would have left a mark.

I inspected the stable door, but the lock looked as it should. It hadn't been tampered with. "When did you fall asleep?" I asked Jimmy while Matt inspected the locks on the other doors.

"About nine or so," he said.

The coachman clicked his tongue. "He usually falls asleep between nine and nine-fifteen. I wasn't here at that time last night, of course, but you can write that down in your book, Inspector."

Brockwell did. "Thank you, Mr. Ogilvie. Accuracy and precision are important in my line of work."

"Mine too, sir."

Jimmy rolled his eyes behind his superior's back.

"And are the doors locked at night?" Brockwell asked.

"Not while the carriage is out, no," Mr. Ogilvie said. "I lock up after I get back and the horses are settled."

Brockwell flipped his notebook closed and pocketed it. "Thank you for your time. We may have more questions for you later."

The coachman tugged on his forelock and the lad touched the brim of his cap. "All this for a dirty old carpet," Jimmy muttered.

"Well?" Brockwell asked once we were outside. "Were the locks tampered with?"

Matt shook his head. "I couldn't see any signs of a break-in."

"The thief must have entered after the boy fell asleep at nine and before Mr. Ogilvie returned at twelve-twenty while the doors were unlocked."

Matt looked one way along the mews then turned to look the other, back toward Duke, Willie and our waiting carriage. That way was a much shorter distance to the end. It was also

C.J. ARCHER

where the constables had begun their inquiries. They now walked toward us.

"Nothing, sir," one of them reported to Brockwell. "None of the staff up that end saw or heard any unusual comings and goings from the Charbonneau outbuildings."

"They were not asked by strangers which stables belonged to Charbonneau?" Matt asked.

"No, sir."

Brockwell indicated the other, longer section of the lane. "Continue down that way."

We watched them go but I, for one, wasn't hopeful they'd discover anything useful. "If the thief didn't ask the location of Fabian's outbuildings, then he already knew which belonged to him. He would have come and gone from that end." I indicated the shorter way.

Matt followed my gaze and looked back at the stable door. "The rug is large and heavy. It wasn't dragged, so there must have been at least two men to carry it then load it onto a vehicle. Someone must have seen something."

We stepped out of the way as a carriage rolled past. A lad sitting on a barrel outside a coach house got to his feet to greet it and offer help to the coachman. Just as he opened the doors, another vehicle emerged from a neighboring coach house and drove off. It didn't go past us but headed in the other direction. It was just as well, because the mews wasn't wide enough for both vehicles to safely pass one another.

"The traffic goes in one direction," I said. "They leave that way and come back this way so that they don't have to pass."

"It would seem so," Brockwell said, watching the carriage drive off. "But I don't see how that matters. Not if our thieves carried the rug between them to a waiting vehicle at the end."

"It's true they could have done that. But with coaches arriving back at all hours of the night, at unpredictable times, it would be less conspicuous to load it onto the back of a wagon that waited here." I indicated Fabian's coach house

142

and stables. "They could carry it out, load it up, and be gone in two or three minutes."

"And they could cover the rug in the back of a wagon so no one would notice it," Matt finished. "You're right, India. If they carried it all the way to the end, they risked being seen and witnesses would remember something as unusual as two men carrying a large rug between them. They would not take particular note of a wagon or other vehicle driving off, however. Not in a mews as busy as this one."

Brockwell stuck up his thumb. "So we can assume they knew which of these outbuildings belonged to Charbonneau." A finger joined the thumb. "Secondly, they used some sort of vehicle to aid their departure." He counted off the other points on his remaining fingers. "Thirdly, there were at least two of them. And fourth, the theft occurred between nine and twelve-twenty."

Matt turned to study the back door that led to the service rooms of Fabian's townhouse, located opposite the stables. "That indicates they knew something of the household routine—what time Charbonneau usually arrives home and what time the stable boy goes to bed."

"A member of staff," I said. Poor Fabian, to be betrayed by his own servants.

"Or a professional," Brockwell said. "One who learned the household routine."

Matt approached the door to the townhouse. "And the quickest way to do that is to make inquiries."

I felt a little better knowing it might not have been Fabian's servants. But if it were professionals, then they must have been employed by someone. Someone with enough money and the right contacts. And the person who was top of our list of suspects had a lot of money and a network of spies.

Coyle.

The maid named Jane answered Matt's knock. I recognized her from the time we'd questioned the staff after the spell had been stolen. She alluded to being in a relationship with Fabian, if that's what a liaison between master and maid could be called.

She recognized us too and bobbed a curtsy. "Do you wish to see Mr. Charbonneau, sir?"

"We want to ask you and the other staff some questions," Matt said. "May we come in?"

She hesitated before stepping aside. "Come this way."

She led us past a larder, store room and kitchen where the cook and a maid were busy at work, slicing and stirring. They didn't look up as we passed through to the small dining room used by the staff. A footman suddenly stood upon seeing us, knocking the newspaper he'd been reading to the floor. He hurriedly gathered it up, clasped it under his arm, and stood to attention.

"Please round up the other servants," Brockwell said to Jane.

"Round up?" Matt muttered.

Brockwell scratched his sideburns. He looked more awkward down here in the service rooms than he did seated at our dining table. This was a domain even more alien to him than upstairs. I knew the sensation well. One assumed that people such as Brockwell and me would be more at home among those who worked for others, but in truth, there was a set of rules among servants in grand households that were as foreign as the rules governing their masters and mistresses. At number sixteen Park Street, I'd always felt more comfortable upstairs than down. Mrs. Potter was mistress of the kitchen, while Bristow and Mrs. Bristow ruled over the rest of the staff. Matt and his friends made me feel more at ease.

Fabian arrived with the servants, which only added to the awkwardness, not to mention the squeeze in the servants' dining room.

Matt began in the same way as he had done with the outdoor staff, by telling them no one was in trouble and we only wanted to find out more about the theft. "It appears as though the thief knew precisely which stables belonged to Mr. Charbonneau, as well as when the stable boy would be asleep and what time Mr. Ogilvie would return."

The butler stiffened. "Are you suggesting one of us did it?"

"No. I'm suggesting the thief may have made inquiries about these things. Perhaps someone answered unwittingly, thinking it wasn't important."

Some of the staff exchanged glances or shrugged.

"It weren't me," Jane said, looking at the housekeeper.

The housekeeper peered down her nose at the girl. "Nobody said it was."

Brockwell cleared his throat. "Might I remind everyone this is a police investigation."

The kitchen maid bit her lip and stared down at her feet.

"What's your name?" I asked her gently.

"Edna."

"Edna, did someone come to the back door and make the sort of inquiries Mr. Glass is suggesting?"

She nodded. She was young, probably no more than seventeen, with milk-white skin and blue-gray shadows beneath her eyes. The poor thing looked exhausted. "There was a delivery yesterday. He came to the back door and handed me a box from Goodes the grocer."

"Oh, aye, the delivery we never ordered," the cook said. "Now it all makes sense. Edna came in with a box from Goodes, but I didn't have an order in with them yet. We just chalked it up to a mistake, and I sent it back. It must have been him. The delivery man."

Jane gasped. "Goodes employs a thief?"

"No, silly girl. He wasn't a delivery man at all, and he doesn't work for Mr. Goodes."

Edna wrung her hands in her apron, on the verge of tears.

"I didn't realize. I thought he was just being friendly when he asked me all them questions."

Matt dismissed the other servants and indicated Fabian should leave too. Once we were alone, he pulled out a chair for the maid. She blinked up at him through damp lashes. She'd probably rarely had a man offer her a seat before, and certainly not a gentleman.

He sat beside her. "It appears you may have been duped."

Edna pressed her apron to her mouth.

Matt touched her arm to encourage her to lower it. "It's not your fault. The man was likely a professional thief and liar. I'll tell Mr. Charbonneau as much. You won't get in trouble for speaking to him."

"What did the delivery man look like?" Brockwell asked.

Edna sniffed and appeared to rally. "He had short dark hair and a beard. He weren't big but he weren't small either." She shrugged. "He just looked normal."

Brockwell wrote that down in his notebook, even though the description was of little use. "And what did he want to know?"

"He told me I looked tired and that I must work long hours. He asked if I have to stay up for the master to return home at night to make hot chocolate for him. I said I don't, the footman does that if he wants something." She bit down hard on her lip. When she released it, an indentation remained. "I think I might have mentioned the time Mr. Charbonneau usually gets in—between twelve and one."

"And did he ask about the stable boy?"

She nodded. "He leaned against the door frame and, all friendly like, told me he reckons house maids, scullery maids and stable boys work the hardest. I told him our Jimmy doesn't, and he made up a joke about them getting to bed earlier than the house staff. That's when I told him Jimmy is in bed by ten at the latest. And I pointed to the coach house across the way." Her face crumpled and she sobbed into her apron.

I rubbed her shoulder while Matt and Brockwell filed out of the servant dining room. "It's all right, Edna," I said gently. "You won't get into trouble."

"But I feel such a fool."

"You're not a fool. You're an innocent girl who has never done anything wrong in her life, that's why you can't see men like that for what they truly are. Now, buck up and enjoy a cup of tea before you go back to work."

"I can't. I've got to prepare a cake for Mr. Charbonneau's afternoon tea."

"That seems like a lot of effort for just one man."

"It's for that professor too. He comes here most days and they read books together." She made a face as if she thought that was the dullest thing in the world. At least she seemed to have cheered up a little.

Instead of leaving by the same door through which we'd entered, we headed upstairs to the main part of the house where Fabian was waiting for us in the entrance hall.

"Did you get the answers you needed?" he asked Matt.

"The maid was tricked by a skilled liar. It's not her fault."

Fabian put up his hands. "I do not blame her. I am told she works hard."

"A little too hard, perhaps," I said. "You might want to employ another kitchen maid to ease her workload."

We promised to keep him apprised of any more developments and left through the front door. We joined Duke and Willie, who quickly bundled Matt into the carriage and urged me in too. Willie gave my bottom a shove when I took too long, and I landed on Matt's lap.

"There's no one about," Matt growled at them.

"And I am not going to be kidnapped with all of you here," I said, taking a seat opposite Matt.

C.J. ARCHER

Duke shut the door but remained on the pavement with Willie.

Matt opened the window to speak to them. "Was that necessary?"

"Aye," Willie said, folding her arms. "Jasper, here's your men."

The two constables joined us but had nothing to report. No one had seen or heard the thieves. Brockwell asked them to wait out of earshot.

"I don't want to confront Coyle yet, even though he is the most likely suspect," he said to us. "He won't admit anything, and we have no proof against him. So the question is, where to now?"

Matt tapped the window frame, that nervous energy manifesting itself again. "While this appears to be a professional theft, we need to rule out the possibility that Mr. Pyke orchestrated his own disappearance as well as the theft of the spell and the rug. We'll start by finding out if he has access to another property where he could be hiding. A warehouse or rented rooms, perhaps."

"I'll see what I can find in official property registers," Brockwell said.

"And we'll ask Mrs. Pyke."

"What if he kept it secret from her?" Willie asked.

"There's nothing we can do about that."

"I'll also look through the records of known perpetrators for someone who looks like the man Edna described, but I doubt it will help. The description she gave could fit almost any man."

Duke opened the door and climbed in, but Brockwell caught Willie's hand. "Can I have word, Willie? In private?"

"I ain't got more to add," she said, as if they'd just been having a conversation.

"I don't expect you to, but I'd like to...clear the air."

She glanced uncertainly at me. I gave her an encouraging nod.

"Make it quick," she said.

They walked a few feet away, Willie with her arms crossed, her gaze lowered to the pavement, and Brockwell scratching his sideburns. He said something to her and lifted a shoulder in a shrug.

"India, give them some privacy," Matt chided.

"I can't hear them."

"Watching them is bad enough."

"It doesn't matter. Willie is returning." I sat back and fidgeted with the hair at the nape of my neck. "Act as if nothing is amiss."

"Nothing *is* amiss," Matt said.

Duke grunted. "*Everything* is amiss. Something's upset her, and she won't tell me what. She's acting like she don't care about him but she does. If she ain't careful, she's going to lose him."

I blinked at him. When did he become so insightful about Willie's love life?

She climbed in and shut the door. The silence invaded the small space like the smell of rotting meat. It was unbearable, and after a few minutes, I had to speak.

"Well? Would you like to tell us what that was about?"

"Nope. I just want to get on with the investigation. Why's Woodall driving so slow?"

"He ain't," Duke said.

She opened the window and shouted up to the coachman. "Go faster! Miss Glass could drive quicker than this."

Woodall could not go faster, thanks to the traffic, and it took some time to reach the Pyke residence. Mrs. Pyke was not alone. Mrs. Fuller Senior was there, having tea. Mrs. Pyke asked Matt and me to join them. Willie and Duke remained outside to keep an eye out.

Mrs. Pyke carried a tray into the parlor and Matt took it from her. He set it on the table while she sat, wringing her hands in her apron. She looked too anxious to even ask if we had news.

I thought it best to get the worst out of the way. "We have no firm information about your husband's whereabouts, I'm sorry to say."

Her face fell. "Oh." She stared at the teacups as if it were just too much effort to pour.

Mrs. Fuller filled our teacups and handed them to Matt and me. "But there is a development? Is that why you're here?"

"We have a theory which could give some hope. A couple of theories, actually." I looked to Matt, unsure which one to begin with. The one where we thought Mr. Pyke was alive, or the one where we assumed he'd taken himself into hiding, deliberately keeping his whereabouts a secret even from his wife?

"Did your husband tell you about the flying carpet?" Matt began.

"The what?" Mrs. Fuller barked. When she saw Matt was serious, she apologized for her outburst.

"He did," Mrs. Pyke said.

"Both the spell and that rug have been stolen. We think the thief has kidnapped your husband to force him to replicate the rug's one and only flight."

She blinked watery eyes. "Oh. I see."

"So there is hope that he's still alive. Indeed, there's a lot of hope. We just need to find him."

"Before the kidnapper discovers he's of no use to them," Mrs. Pyke muttered. "He told me he could never do what Mrs. Glass did. He could never control the rug's flight with any accuracy. And when the kidnapper realizes..." She pressed her lips together but her chin wobbled nevertheless.

Mrs. Fuller patted her friend's hand. "And your second theory?"

THE SPY MASTER'S SCHEME

Matt shuffled his feet and rubbed his jaw. I thought perhaps he'd want me to tell her, but he continued. "Mr. Pyke may have gone into hiding of his own accord. He might be the thief."

"No." Mrs. Pyke's voice was choked with tears and anger. "No, he wouldn't do that. I don't believe it. He's not a thief and he's not greedy. You're wrong, Mr. Glass."

"He told the newspapers he was a magician," I said. "Why do that if he wasn't going to capitalize on the reputation of magicians?"

Mrs. Pyke's lips firmed. "He wouldn't put me through this if he could help it. He is *not* greedy."

I glanced at Mrs. Fuller, but she remained silent. If she had agreed with her friend, I might not have continued with our line of questioning, but her silence was telling. "Mrs. Pyke, does your husband own any other properties?"

"No."

"Does he lease a warehouse or storeroom?"

She shook her head. "I told you. He's not hiding somewhere, Mrs. Glass."

We were getting nowhere and only making her more upset. I indicated to Matt that we should go and we made to leave.

"I'll show you out," Mrs. Fuller said, following us into the corridor.

She did not open the front door, however, but rested her hand on the doorknob. She glanced back toward the parlor. Mrs. Pyke had not emerged. "I know you have to ask those questions," she whispered. "I can see how it looks after Mr. Pyke gave his name in the newspaper. And the truth is, he has become more passionate about his work lately." She glanced again at the parlor then leaned closer. "But I don't think it's the money that drove him to speak to the newspaper. It's his reputation. Well, I suppose the two *are* linked. A good reputation leads to more customers which allows his business to thrive. But...it's something more, too. Something that has little to do with how much he sells his rugs for."

"Is it possible he wants to leave behind a legacy?" I asked, recalling Mr. Pyke's words when we first met.

"Yes, that's more likely the reason behind him going public."

"So you think he might have stolen the rug and gone into hiding?"

"It's possible he plans to use the stolen rug somehow, although I don't see why. To sell it? Make more magical rugs and sell them? It just doesn't ring true. Not for Mr. Pyke."

"Perhaps he has other plans that don't involve selling them," Matt said.

She bit her lip and I suspected she had more to say. Neither Matt nor I hurried her, however. But we didn't leave either.

Our patience was rewarded. "He was very good friends with Mr. Stocker, the guild master."

"I thought they fell out when Mr. Pyke told Mr. Stocker he was a magician," I said.

"They did, but before that, they were close." The sound of china cups being gathered came from the parlor. Mrs. Fuller opened the front door. "Ask Mr. Stocker about rented rooms and the like. If anyone knows whether Mr. Pyke is hiding, it'll be him."

* * *

THE PORTER WOULD NOT ALLOW us entry into the wool guild. Neither Matt nor I were surprised after our last visit, but it was a disappointment. Not even Matt's charms could convince the porter to give Mr. Stocker a message. The porter sent us away with a stern glare then slammed the door in our faces.

I ushered Matt back to the safety of the carriage where we discussed what to do next.

"We'll go to Scotland Yard," Matt said. "Brockwell will have to call on Stocker. The porter can't refuse the police entry."

Willie slouched into the corner, a petulant pout on her lips. "Do we have to see him again?"

"We do," Duke told her. "You better fix whatever's going on between you because we're going to keep seeing him. We can't avoid him to suit you."

"It ain't my fault! It's his!" She kicked the seat opposite. "It's his."

Matt blocked her foot with his own before she kicked the seat again. "It's certainly not the fault of this carriage. Kindly refrain from punishing it."

"What's he done?" I asked her.

She hitched her crossed arms higher up her chest. "I don't want to talk about it. Let's get this over with so I can get back to ignoring him."

I sighed.

Matt took my hand and squeezed. The squeeze was meant to mean something, but I couldn't determine what. He asked Duke to give Woodall orders to drive to New Scotland Yard. Twenty minutes later, Woodall stopped at the front of the grand police headquarters on the Victoria Embankment.

"Willie, stay here," Matt ordered. "Duke, come with us."

"Why?" both Duke and Willie asked.

Matt didn't answer, and Duke trailed behind him as we crossed the pavement and entered the building. Before approaching the sergeant on the front desk, Matt turned to face us.

"The more you press her for an answer, the less likely she is to tell you," he said.

Duke sighed. "I know, but..." He finished the sentence with a shrug.

C.J. ARCHER

"Wishing she could be something other than stubborn is not going to make it so." Matt clapped Duke on the shoulder. "I know you're worried about her ruining things with a good man like Brockwell, but have faith in her. She has a big heart and sometimes she doesn't know what to do with it, but she will do what's best for her in the end. It'll just take longer if we interfere. The more we push her, the more she'll push back."

He was right. Whatever their dispute was about, Willie wanted to keep it to herself for now. She was too proud to hear criticism, too stubborn to take advice, and too independent to be steered. As Matt said, we had to have faith in her.

Duke emitted another sigh. "I'll back away. But you might want to give Brockwell the same advice." He clicked his fingers as an idea struck him. "Maybe he can tell you what they're arguing about."

"Duke," I chided. "We won't interfere."

He reluctantly agreed then left to return to the carriage while Matt and I approached the front desk.

"We *could* ask Brockwell," I said. "Willie would never find out."

He eyed me sideways. "I think we should stick to investigating and leave Willie's private life alone. She won't thank you for meddling."

I didn't argue with him, but I didn't necessarily agree either. Willie's past was littered with discarded lovers of both sexes who didn't truly understand her or accept her. Brockwell did and that was rare. If he'd said something to upset her, she needed to give him the chance to apologize and make amends or she was in danger of losing him forever.

Matt was in the process of asking the sergeant if we could see Brockwell when the detective inspector himself emerged from the corridor that led to his office.

"Good," he said, striding up to us. "I was just on my way

to find you." Something must be wrong. Brockwell never strode anywhere.

"What is it?" Matt asked, sounding wary.

"I just received a telegram." He waved a strip of paper in the air. "An unidentified male was found in Hampstead Heath and taken to the Royal Free Hospital. He's badly injured and unconscious. A description of the victim was sent to all metropolitan stations." He flicked the paper with his finger. "It matches that of Pyke."

CHAPTER 11

*M*rs. Pyke's tears were the confirmation we needed that the bruised and battered man lying in the bed at the Royal Free Hospital was indeed her husband. Given that his entire head was wrapped in bandages, with only his eyes, mouth and nostrils exposed, I didn't recognize him. She knew him by the pattern of freckles on his hands.

Matt handed his handkerchief to Mrs. Pyke and she dabbed at her eyes.

"Will he be all right?" she asked the doctor.

The doctor hesitated. "It's too soon to tell. He regained consciousness briefly an hour ago, but only for a few minutes."

"Did he say anything?" Brockwell asked, pencil hovering over a fresh page of his notebook.

The doctor shook his head. "He was confused. He couldn't remember his name or the events leading up to his accident."

The doctor left to attend to another patient. A nurse offered Mrs. Pyke a cup of tea while she sat with her husband. Brockwell jerked his head, indicating we should

THE SPY MASTER'S SCHEME

discuss the situation out of her hearing. He instructed one of the local policeman who'd accompanied us to stay with Mr. Pyke and to notify us immediately if he regained consciousness.

Brockwell signaled for the other, a sergeant, to join us in the hospital foyer. "It seems he is our missing man," the inspector said with a nod back at the ward. "Tell us everything about his discovery."

The sergeant, a red-faced man with a luxurious black moustache, pushed out his barrel chest. "He was found by myself and Constable Tully on Hampstead Heath at a quarter past one this morning. We immediately brought him here where he has mostly lain unconscious since."

"Was anything found near his body?"

The sergeant frowned. "Nothing out of the ordinary, sir."

"Where in Hampstead Heath was he found exactly?"

The sergeant offered to show us the precise spot.

"Come with us," Matt said as he strode off.

I raced to catch up to him, worried he'd walk into gunfire. He crossed Gray's Inn Road and climbed into our carriage without incident, however.

"You need to be more careful," I said, settling beside him. "The gunman is still out there."

He kissed my temple. "I am being careful. I didn't even wait to give Woodall his instructions." He opened the window to do just that when Brockwell joined us.

"The sergeant suggests we collect a constable to help us search the vicinity where Pyke was found," Brockwell said. "The local station isn't far from the Heath."

"I prefer a man we know and trust," Matt said.

Brockwell gave Woodall instructions to drive to the Shoreditch police station where the detective inspector used his authority to borrow Cyclops for the day. We then headed to Hampstead Heath.

My immediate reaction upon arriving at the open parkland was one of reluctance and dread. It was too exposed. A gunman would have a clear shot at Matt as he crossed it. He would not listen to reason, however, and remain in the carriage.

"No one has followed us," he said as Woodall pulled to the curb. "It's safe."

"It's *not*."

"I'm coming with you, India, and that's final." He jumped out before the coach had come to a complete stop. He put his hand out to assist me, smiling warmly. "You look pretty when you're scowling."

"Your charm won't work on me this time." I accepted his hand and he kissed my knuckles before I alighted.

"Do I need to kiss you on the mouth right here to stop your scowl?"

I gasped. "You wouldn't dare."

He gave me one of his wicked smiles.

I clicked my tongue and walked off, keeping alert to our surroundings.

The sergeant led the way along the muddy path. Brockwell joined me ahead of the others, keeping up with my brisk pace. I seethed in silence until the detective inspector piped up.

"He's right. No one followed us here."

"I know but I still worry. It's so open." My heart quickened as a carriage rumbled past on the road. In warmer weather, this area was much busier, but today the icy winds and dark clouds kept people away. I clutched my coat collar tighter at my throat.

Brockwell waved toward a woodland ahead. "The pond is somewhat sheltered by the trees."

"Not at this time of year."

The bathing pond was quite large with grassy banks rolling to the water's edge on the near side and the bare trees surrounding the rest. A shed for bathers to change had been built on the bank near the short pier off which swimmers would jump in the summertime. There were no intrepid bathers braving the ice-cold water today.

When we caught up to the sergeant further along the path, he was already inspecting the ground. "Mr. Pyke was found here." He indicated the grass near the path before it sloped toward the pond.

Matt crouched to inspect the ground. "If there was any blood, it's been washed away by the rain."

Brockwell clasped his hands behind his back and studied the vicinity. "It's impossible to tell if Mr. Pyke was attacked here or was brought here after being attacked elsewhere."

Matt stood and looked around too, his expression unreadable.

Duke came to stand beside me. He kept his voice low. "If he was going to launch a flying contraption, this would be a good place to do it. Open space, no one about on a winter's night."

"There wasn't much wind last night," I added. "Or rain. That came this morning. But I don't see how we can prove Mr. Pyke attempted to fly the rug here and fell off. There's no sign of it anywhere."

"The kidnapper took it with him and left Mr. Pyke here to die, maybe."

"Perhaps," Matt said, joining us. He didn't look convinced, however. After turning a complete circle on the spot to scan the area, something near the shed caught his attention. "Duke, keep the sergeant here. Cyclops, with me."

I headed to the shed with Matt and Cyclops. As we drew closer, I saw what they'd seen. Being taller, they'd spotted it first.

"The rug!" I picked up my skirts and rushed toward it. It was definitely Fabian's rug, but it was covered in mud and leaf matter. A closer inspection revealed there were even twigs stuck in the pile. "It crashed through the bushes."

Cyclops inspected the bank of bushes nearby and shook his head. "Not these. They're not damaged."

"So it was brought here and dumped? Mr. Pyke too?"

Matt shook his head. "No, it landed here after its flight, but it didn't fall through these bushes. It came through those." He indicated the hedgerow lining the path, past where the body of Mr. Pyke had been found. There was a large gap clear through the hedge. "It crashed into the shrubs, Mr. Pyke fell off, and the rug landed here."

I was impressed he'd managed to get it off the ground, with himself as a passenger. By the look of the damaged bushes, it had not risen very high, however. Mere inches only. That explained why Mr. Pyke had survived. A fall from a great height would have killed him.

Brockwell barked an order at the sergeant to take his attention away from us. A moment later, the sergeant and Duke headed off, back the way we'd come. They progressed slowly, inspecting the ground as they walked. We returned to where the body of Mr. Pyke had been found where the detective inspector met us.

"He was getting curious, asking questions about what you were looking at over there by the shed," he said. "So is it the carpet?"

Matt told him about the rug and the bushes. Brockwell agreed with his assessment of how the flight had transpired, and how it had ended.

"But we're no closer to determining if Pyke was kidnapped and was forced to fly it or if he did it of his own accord," the inspector said. "The ground here is churned up, but it's that way everywhere. We've had so much rain lately, this area is a quagmire. I can't determine any single set of footprints."

Out of the corner of my eye, I spotted Willie waving her arms above her head. She'd gone down the slope to the water's edge when we headed for the shed. We hurried toward her, me holding onto Matt's arm to ensure I didn't slip.

Willie stood a foot from the water, her boots caked in mud. She looked pleased with herself as she pointed to something in the shallows, half submerged. "See that?" She was too excited to wait for us to inspect it or even make a guess. "It's a bomb," she blurted out.

"Get back!" Brockwell shouted, reaching for her.

She shrugged him off. "It ain't going to explode. It's in the water."

Cyclops stepped closer and inspected the device. "She's right. It won't go off."

"Told you. It's too wet."

"It doesn't have any explosive in it."

She frowned. "What do you mean?"

Cyclops pulled the metal contraption out of the water and showed her the housing. Inside were several rods of iron, not explosives. "It's fake."

Brockwell scratched his sideburns. "Why would someone plant a fake bomb here?"

Matt glanced back up the slope. "It wasn't planted here. This is where it landed after it fell off the flying rug. It probably fell off at the same time as Pyke and rolled down here."

"The question is, why a *fake* bomb?" Cyclops asked.

"They were testing the strength of the magic," I said. "They were attempting to see how much the flying rug could carry."

Cyclops cradled the device, estimating its weight. "One man and one bomb."

We all stared at the metal casing with its fake explosives. An oppressive silence fell, as smothering as any of London's fogs. My breathing became ragged, my chest tight. This was no longer a matter of a collector wanting to own the most precious magical artefact. Nor was it about magicians versus the artless. It was serious.

Deadly.

"Thank God Pyke failed," Matt muttered.

"His magic could never hold his weight as well as that of a bomb," I said. "We have no fear on that score. If the plan is to drop bombs from the sky, it will never work. Mr. Pyke's magic simply isn't strong enough."

"But yours is," Brockwell said. "Do I have that correct?"

I swallowed, nodded. "But there needs to be a support beneath the rug—iron or wood, that sort of thing. I can control both but a magician like Mr. Pyke can't. There needs to be two magicians on the rug, each speaking the flying spell for their magical specialty. Mr. Pyke didn't know that, nor does it seem his kidnapper did."

Matt circled his arm around my waist but he offered no words of comfort. He looked troubled, his gaze distant. Perhaps he too was thinking of Pyke lying in the hospital, his body bruised. If I wasn't always surrounded by Matt or one of the others, would I have been kidnapped instead?

"This wasn't Pyke's idea, was it?" Cyclops asked.

"It might have been," Willie said, not sounding convinced.

"But doubtful," Matt countered.

Brockwell nodded, scrubbing his sideburns. "Coyle. It must be."

It was looking more and more like it.

We trudged back to the carriage then returned to the hospital, but Mr. Pyke had not regained consciousness. Matt brooded for the entire journey, his silence throwing a shroud over our group. I knew he was thinking about me being a potential target for the kidnapper next time, but I also knew there was little I could say to lighten his mood.

Brockwell decided to stay at the hospital to be there to question Mr. Pyke when he woke up. He walked with us to the carriage but did not get in. "Return Cyclops to his station then go home and wait. If Pyke wakes, I'll send a message immediately."

I eyed Matt sideways. Waiting was not his strong suit. He sat with a rigid back and didn't even acknowledge Brockwell.

The detective inspector knew Matt well enough to know this was a worrying sign. "Do *not* call on Coyle. Is that understood, Glass? We don't have enough evidence to confront him. If Pyke can point to Coyle as his kidnapper then we will act, but only then." When Matt didn't respond, he rapped his knuckles on the door. "Glass!"

"Understood." Matt closed the door and thumped on the ceiling. He'd already given Woodall his instructions before we climbed into the carriage. I had assumed we would head home, but as we turned into Wilton Terrace, I realized Matt was prepared to defy Brockwell's orders.

We stopped outside Lord Coyle's residence.

Matt did not try to stop me from joining him as he stormed up the front steps, as did Willie and Cyclops. Duke remained on the pavement to keep watch.

The butler answered the door and allowed us to wait in the drawing room while he checked if his master was in. He was at home, and fortunately he was prepared to see us. Or perhaps it was *unfortunately*. I wasn't sure I wanted this confrontation to take place.

We did not sit down in the drawing room, and when Lord Coyle joined us, he did not offer us a seat. He remained standing too, leaning heavily on his walking stick, and I suspected he preferred to sit but would not do so until I did.

I stood by Matt's side, attempting to appear as defiant as I could while my heart hammered against my ribs. Matt didn't look worried at all. He looked furious.

"Mr. Pyke has been found," he began.

Coyle did not seem surprised by the news. "Dead or alive?"

"Alive. He's in hospital under police protection."

"Protection? From what? Me?" Lord Coyle's laugh bellowed from his stomach and ended in a phlegmy rattle.

"You're barking up the wrong tree, as usual. His disappearance had nothing to do with me. What happened to him? Was he beaten by thugs?"

"His body was found near the magic rug where it had crashed through the bushes. A device resembling a bomb was also found nearby."

"Resembling?"

Matt's jaw firmed. "We know it was you who kidnapped him and forced him to fly the carpet with a device of the same weight as a bomb."

Coyle grunted. "You've got it wrong, Glass."

"You failed."

"Pyke failed. It was nothing to do with me."

Matt pointed his finger at him. "You won't succeed with your mad scheme."

"And what scheme is that?" Lord Coyle's tone was as slithery as a snake's.

"Don't come near my family. Is that clear?"

"That will be difficult considering I married your cousin."

"If you come for India, I will destroy you." Matt grabbed my hand and pushed past his lordship. I quickened my pace to keep up with his long strides.

Lord Coyle's throaty chuckle echoed around the room. "How gallant, Glass. What say you, India? Or do you let your husband speak for you, and drag you hither and thither?" He nodded at my hand, linked with Matt's.

Matt's grip loosened, but he didn't let go.

I made a point of placing my other hand on Matt's arm. "My husband and I are as one on this. Whatever you're up to, you won't get away with it." I turned to go, only to stop again. "He *is* gallant, isn't he? And a true gentleman, too. Perhaps you should take a leaf out of his book. Your wife will think better of you."

"I think we both know I'm not the husband she wants." His gaze slid to Matt.

"No, but you're the husband she deserves."

His smile widened. "Well played, India. You've got steely nerves. That's why I like you for more than your magic."

"We are not friends, my lord."

"Ah, but I am on your side nevertheless."

"I don't see how. You want power and wealth, and you think magic can deliver that to you by harming others. My god, you want to bomb your enemies!"

"*My* enemies? My dear lady, my enemies are your enemies." He took a step forward, ramming the end of his walking stick into the floor. "Magic has the power to protect us and advance us if we use it correctly."

"Not *us*, my lord. I want no part in your plans."

He grunted again, but this time it was more of a derisive laugh. "You're an idealistic fool and we all know from our history books how those fare."

I tugged on Matt's arm and marched out of the drawing room.

"It was not I who kidnapped Mr. Pyke," Lord Coyle called after us. "You have my word on that."

Once we were safely ensconced in the carriage and heading to Shoreditch police station, Willie declared she didn't believe a word Coyle had said. "It was him. He kidnapped Pyke, I know it."

Duke scoffed. "How do you know?"

"Woman's intuition."

He gave a pointed look at her buckskin trousers. "What does *your* feminine intuition tell you, India? Was Coyle lying?"

"He's an accomplished liar, so I suppose it's likely. Matt?"

Matt drew in a deep breath as if it were the first proper one he'd breathed since arriving at Coyle's. "He's still at the top of my list of suspects. One thing I'm almost certain of is that Pyke didn't orchestrate this himself. He was put up to it by someone, either through coercion or flattery."

We all agreed with that.

We left Cyclops to complete his day at work while we returned home. With nothing more to do until we heard from Brockwell, we each went about trying to occupy ourselves for the rest of the day. Duke and Willie accompanied Aunt Letitia on a walk while I discussed some household matters with Mrs. Bristow and Mrs. Potter. I joined Matt afterward in his study with the door closed. It was a rare opportunity to be together in the middle of the day.

For one brief but wonderful hour, we blocked out the world and our troubles and simply enjoyed one another's company. After he helped me dress and I straightened his tie, I pushed him onto his office chair and sat on his lap. I smoothed down his hair. "I needed that."

He smiled against my lips. "So did I. More than I can say. Thank you for distracting me with so much enthusiasm."

I laughed and it felt deliciously cathartic after the last few days.

A knock on the door had me jumping to my feet. I stood by Matt, pretending to read something on his desk, as he asked the newcomer to enter.

Bristow opened the door. "I thought you'd like to know that Miss Glass, Mr. Duke and Miss Johnson have returned home."

"Thank you, Bristow." Matt waited for Bristow to leave then stood and kissed me on the mouth. "All good things must come to an end eventually."

I reached up and clasped my hands behind his neck. "I've never liked that saying. Good things don't have to end."

"An adjournment?"

"Better." I kissed him lightly then led the way downstairs.

Cyclops arrived home just before the gong sounded while Aunt Letitia was dressing for dinner. Before he headed up to change too, he wanted to inform us of a development.

"It's about Abercrombie." He glanced at the door. "What I'm about to tell you must not leave this room."

"Letty ain't going to walk in," Willie assured him. "Coming down before the dinner gong sounds is like breaking the law to her."

"What about Abercrombie?" I prompted.

"I convinced my chief inspector to send a spy into the protestors' camp specifically to watch him so if he's heard encouraging violence, he can be arrested."

"Excellent news. Well done, Cyclops."

He put up his hand. "Don't get too enthusiastic yet. The chief inspector has to have approval from his superiors before it can happen."

It was a start and I told him so.

Dinner was a small affair which, in itself, was unusual. There was no Brockwell, Lord Farnsworth or Chronos. I missed their company. Willie did too, going by her frequent heavy sighs, a sure sign she wanted to have a conversation but not start it.

I eventually gave up and confronted her. "Are you missing Brockwell?"

She screwed up her face. "No! I ain't a desperate debutante just out of the school room, and he ain't no prince, neither."

I turned to her squarely. "Missing someone has nothing to do with one's age or station. Nor is there anything wrong with admitting you miss him. He's a wonderful man, quite interesting, and excellent company. Of course you should miss him."

She sniffed. "Sounds like *you* miss him."

"Is there something you want to tell me? Something about the recent conversation you had with him in this very house?"

She shoveled beans into her mouth and shook her head.

"Sometimes discussing a problem makes it seem less dreadful."

"It's private."

"It'll just be between the two of us. No one else need know, not even Matt." The others had continued their conversation around us. Either they were ignoring us on purpose to give me an opportunity to find out from Willie what had happened between her and Brockwell, or they were genuinely oblivious.

"You can't keep a secret, India."

I bristled. "I can."

"Well I ain't telling you and that's final."

"Why not?"

"Because I know what you'll say, and it's the exact opposite of what I want to hear, right now."

"You don't know what I'm going to say."

She rolled her eyes. "You're predictable."

I snatched up my wine glass. "I am not," I muttered before sipping.

Aunt Letitia retired to her room after dinner, while the rest of us adjourned to the drawing room. We were just about to sit down to a game of cards when Bristow entered.

"You have a visitor," the butler announced.

Willie looked up eagerly from the cards she was shuffling. "I hope it's Farnsworth. I need the distraction."

My mind leapt to earlier in the afternoon when Matt had thanked me for distracting him. I shook off the thought. Lord Farnsworth was not *that* kind of distraction for Willie. Well, he had been, just the one time, but not anymore. Brockwell certainly fitted that description.

It was Brockwell himself who entered the drawing room, however. Willie crossed her arms, slumped in the chair, and refused to look at him.

The detective inspector shuffled into the room clutching his hat in both hands. "Good evening, all."

Everyone responded, except for Willie.

Brockwell's cheeks pinked at her slight. He cleared his throat and addressed Matt. "Mr. Pyke has regained full consciousness. You're welcome to join me and question him."

"We'll come now," Matt said, rising.

We all stood, even Willie. "Not me," she said. "I'm meeting up with Farnsworth."

Duke arched a brow at her. "You never mentioned it before now."

"I don't have to tell you everything."

Cyclops picked up the deck of cards and waved them in front of her face. "If you had a previous engagement, why were you about to deal yourself into a game?"

"'Previous engagement?' You're sounding like an English toff lately, Cyclops." She pushed past him, gave Brockwell a wide berth, and disappeared out the door.

Cyclops sighed as he clasped Brockwell's shoulder. "Whatever is going on with you two needs to get fixed. She's even more annoying than usual."

Duke clasped Brockwell's other shoulder. "We know it's her fault, whatever it is, but maybe you should apologize anyway. It can't hurt."

Brockwell looked like he wanted to sink into the floor and out of sight.

I gave him a sympathetic smile as Cyclops and Duke left the room. "Don't mind them. They're simply worried about her. We all are."

"I'm not," Matt said, quite cheerfully, as he followed the others out.

The inspector turned to go too, but I caught his arm. I lowered my voice. "So what *did* you say to Willie the other night?"

"Don't take this the wrong way, India, but if she wants to tell you then she will." He slapped his hat on his head and strode off too.

I frowned at his back, hands on my hips. Matt stopped at the top of the staircase and flashed me a grin. It made me laugh, despite everything. It was good to see him in a cheery mood for once, his other worries set aside for now.

That mood didn't last long, however, as we once again focused on the case. Mr. Pyke's reappearance signaled the end of our involvement in the investigation, but thankfully Brockwell wasn't prepared to exclude us. As far as we were concerned, there was still more to uncover. Much more.

It remained to be seen whether anything would be done—or *could* be done—with whatever information we did uncover. It depended on whom Mr. Pyke implicated.

Mrs. Pyke still sat in the same chair we'd left her in that afternoon. She had been feeding her husband soup from a bowl and now set it aside. Mr. Pyke was propped up in bed against two pillows, bandaged from head to toe like a mummified Egyptian come back to life.

"It's good to see you sitting up," I said, smiling. "We were worried about you."

"Thank you."

"The doctor says he should make a full recovery," Mrs. Pyke said. "But it will take time for the broken bones to heal." Her eyes were full of tears, as they had been when we left her earlier in the day, but they were tears of hope and relief, I suspected.

"I'm sorry my wife troubled you with this, Mrs. Glass. I'm sure you're too busy to worry about me."

Mrs. Pyke's face fell.

"Not at all," I assured them. "I'm glad she came to us. Indeed, she was right to do so. She knew your disappearance was related to magic and that the regular police couldn't help. By coming to us, we were able to bring it to the attention of Detective Inspector Brockwell. He's used to investigating matters involving magic and he frequently engages our assistance. He's artless, you see."

My speech seemed to lift Mrs. Pyke's spirits. "So my husband can speak freely in his presence?"

"He can."

"It won't matter," Mr. Pyke said heavily. "I can't tell you much. I never saw the face of one of the men, the one who I think organized my kidnapping."

"What do you mean?" Matt asked.

"Wait a moment." The detective inspector removed his notepad and pencil from his pocket and found a blank page. "Let's start at the beginning. Were you kidnapped, Mr. Pyke, or did you leave of your own volition?"

"A little of both." He tried to sit up straighter, but gave up, wincing in pain. His wife fussed with the pillows at his back until he gently shooed her away. "A man came to my shop three days ago and asked if I was a wool magician. I said I was. He then asked if I'd ever made one of my carpets fly. I told him I hadn't but I know someone who had."

"You did what?" Matt asked icily.

"I never named names! Anyway, it didn't seem to matter, because I think he already knew about Mrs. Glass. At least, he already knew about a flying carpet. He didn't say he knew *she* was the magician who made it fly."

"Go on," Brockwell said. "What else did he say when he called on you?"

"He demanded I try to make a carpet fly on my own. When I said I didn't have the spell, he told me he had it written down."

"So you went with him," Matt said flatly.

Mr. Pyke glanced at his wife. "I hesitated at first. That's when he said Mrs. Pyke would be harmed if I didn't meet him after I closed up the shop."

I gasped. "He threatened you?"

Mrs. Pyke had been biting her lip as she listened to her husband's story, but she didn't seem shocked. She must have already heard it. "He wouldn't have gone with that man

171

otherwise, Mrs. Glass. He'd never do anything dangerous or wrong."

Mr. Pyke pressed his fingers to the bandages at his temple. "The man collected me in his conveyance on Courser Street after I left the shop and drove me to Hampstead Heath. It was just going dark by the time we arrived, but we waited hours until it was quiet. I memorized the spell he gave me by the light of the carriage lamp. When we were sure no one was about, he took me to an area on the Heath where another man stood with a rug laid out on the ground. The first man told me it was one that had been flown before, so I assumed it was the one you spoke the spell into that day in Mr. Charbonneau's house."

"Go on," Brockwell prompted, pencil poised over the notepad.

"I did as I was ordered and spoke the spell into the carpet. It lifted somewhat. I tried it again and again, dozens of times, and each time it lifted a little more, sometimes flying a short distance. The men became impatient and annoyed with me, and insisted I keep trying. So I did and finally it flew up and about, although I had difficulty controlling it. It went this way and that, up and down, as if it had a mind of its own."

"So you decided to get on it and fly it?" Duke asked, speaking up for the first time. "Seems foolish."

"I had no choice. The first man ordered me to get on it. To be honest, he frightened me more than the other one. He gave me a metal box to hold and told me to make the rug fly. So I attempted it again, but it couldn't carry my weight. It went forward along the ground, however, taking me with it. I kept speaking the spell over and over and it sped up, but never fully lifted off the ground. It crashed through some bushes which is how I got all these scratches." He indicated his bandaged face and hands. "Then I fell off and must have knocked my head. The box fell out of my hands. I don't know where it went."

"He can't remember anything after that," Mrs. Pyke finished.

Her husband nodded. "The next thing I knew, I was in here."

"And what did the men look like?"

"The first one, the one who visited me in the shop and collected me on Courser Street was a big fellow with black hair and beard. A real thuggish character. He was a young fellow with a Cockney accent."

"And the other one?"

"He hardly spoke and I never saw his face. When I arrived at Hampstead Heath, he moved away into the shadows and kept his face averted. But he was clearly the leader. The thug looked to him from time to time before giving me orders."

"Was he large?" Matt asked. "Did he have a distinctive moustache? Did he walk with a limp or the aid of a walking stick?"

"He had a walking stick, but he didn't need it. He was thin, not particularly tall. I know his name."

We all leaned forward as if Mr. Pyke had pulled on strings attached to our necks.

"Just after I fell off the carpet, I was in and out of consciousness. The thug reached me first and I heard him say something to the other man who was out of my line of sight."

"And?" I asked, breathless.

"He called him Sir Charles."

CHAPTER 12

"We should wait," Brockwell said as we gathered in the hospital foyer to discuss Mr. Pyke's explosive statement.

"Wait for what?" Matt asked. "Pyke has implicated Whittaker. We must act now, before he can concoct a story to explain his involvement."

"He will already have a story prepared," Brockwell said.

"I ask again, why wait?"

"For due process to take its course."

"Due process!" Matt echoed. "We're beyond worrying about that, surely."

"I must consult with my superiors, perhaps even the commissioner himself, and—"

"That will get us nowhere. They'll forbid you to speak to him. You know it, Brockwell. We have to confront Whittaker on our own."

The detective inspector rubbed the back of his neck. "So you think Whittaker was acting under orders from his superiors in the government?"

"I do, yes. That's why you shouldn't consult *your* superiors. You'll get nothing but vague responses that explain nothing. They'll protect Whittaker, or at least protect the secrets he keeps. Confronting Whittaker directly gives us a chance."

A nurse approached, a finger to her lips. "Keep your voices down. This is a hospital."

"My apologies." Matt gave her a smile. It vanished as soon as she turned her back.

Brockwell appealed to me. "Please try to convince your husband of the efficacy of waiting until I've spoken to my superiors."

"I agree with Matt," I said. "Commissioner Munro will protect the home secretary, who will protect Sir Charles. Involving them will not only stop us from getting the answers we need, it will also see this investigation stripped from you, Inspector."

Brockwell glanced at Cyclops, perhaps hoping for support from a fellow policeman. But Cyclops crossed his arms over his chest and regarded the inspector coolly.

"Don't you want to know what Sir Charles is up to?" I asked. "I certainly do."

"We will discover his motives for kidnapping Pyke in due course."

"You're a fool if you believe that," Matt growled.

Brockwell looked torn. I did feel sorry for him, despite our difference of opinion. He was a pedant and stickler for following the rules. Confronting Sir Charles now went against his very nature. He'd been fortunate to have been given free rein to investigate magical cases as he saw fit, but he knew this was different. Pyke's evidence against Sir Charles had raised the stakes to a new level that could jeopardize Brockwell's career.

To everyone's surprise, Matt took pity on him. He placed a hand on the inspector's shoulder and softened his tone. "My wife is the one who could be in danger now, with Pyke's failure to make the carpet fly. I will not stand by and let anyone do to her what they did to Pyke, no matter how much you beg me. I'm sorry that troubles you, but the truth is, you can't stop me from confronting Whittaker. You know I'll do it, but you don't have to come if you don't want to. We'll keep your name out of it."

Matt's change of tone worked. Brockwell heaved in a deep breath and let it out slowly. He gave a small nod. "This requires a delicate touch, Glass, and I think I should be there to lend the interrogation some authority. Can you promise me you won't go in with guns blazing?"

Matt patted Brockwell's shoulder and straightened. "I can control myself and fortunately Willie isn't here."

Brockwell gave a wry smile. "She'll be sorry she missed it."

* * *

I FELT no apprehension about confronting Sir Charles. I didn't consider him a physical threat. Suspicious, certainly, but not dangerous with Matt, Cyclops and Duke alongside me, not to mention an officer of the law.

But apprehension arrived with a vengeance when Sir Charles showed no sympathy for Mr. Pyke. If he wasn't sympathetic toward an innocent man lying in hospital, he would have no qualms coming for me.

"The fellow is lying," he said with a tilt of his chin. "I don't know him."

"Then why would he give your name?" Brockwell asked.

"He must have heard it somewhere. Now, if you don't mind, it's getting late."

We made no move to leave, however. In fact, I sat down. The men remained standing until Sir Charles finally gave in and sat too.

Duke and Cyclops were the only ones who didn't sit. Duke stood outside on the landing to discourage the landlady from listening, and Cyclops remained by the door on the inside, his hands clasped loosely in front of him. Sir Charles swallowed heavily, perhaps worried that he was now a prisoner in his own home. It had not come to that, however.

Yet.

"Let's get something clear from the beginning," Matt said with steely command. "We know you orchestrated the kidnapping of Pyke, the wool magician, in the hope he could make a magic carpet fly."

Sir Charles spluttered a humorless laugh. "A flying carpet?"

"Denying it only delays our departure."

Sir Charles smoothed a hand over his oiled hair—his dark hair streaked with gray. According to Mrs. Fuller, that was the description Mr. Pyke had given for the man who'd been following him in a conveyance.

"We know Coyle told you he saw the carpet fly with us on it," Matt went on.

"I don't work for Coyle."

"Whether you do or don't is irrelevant. You clearly share information."

"You presume too much, Glass."

"Let me tell you what else we presume," Matt went on, unperturbed. "After Pyke was mentioned in that newspaper article, you called on him at his shop. Or your colleague did while you waited in the carriage. You gave him an ultimatum —use his magic to make a carpet fly or his wife will come to harm."

Sir Charles pursed his lips in distaste. "I don't make threats."

"Your colleague did on your behalf. It's the same thing."

Sir Charles's nostrils flared as he looked away.

"Your man also collected Pyke after work and drove him to Hampstead Heath, where he was given directions to attempt to make the carpet fly. When he managed to make it lift a little using the new flying spell created by India and

Charbonneau, you ordered Pyke to ride the carpet with an object resembling a bomb in size and weight. You wanted to test the magic to see if the rug could fly while carrying a man and a bomb. But Pyke couldn't manage it. He fell off and the carpet crashed after barely lifting off the ground. Your experiment was a monumental failure that almost cost a man his life."

"Is there a question in this story?"

"Did you steal the rug and spell from Charbonneau or was that Coyle?"

It was something we'd briefly discussed in the carriage on the way. Brockwell had asked Matt not to mention his lordship's name. Matt had given him no promises.

To his credit, the inspector remained still and did not cast a censorial glare at Matt. As far as Sir Charles was concerned, we were a united force.

"They were given to me by an anonymous source," Sir Charles said.

The muscles in Matt's jaw tightened. "Who gave you the orders to undertake the experiment? Your superiors in the home office or Coyle?"

Sir Charles gritted his teeth. "I told you, I don't work for Coyle."

"Then why do your superiors want to fly bombs?"

"If you think I know what my superiors want, you're a fool. I am a small cog in a vast machine. If you want answers to these questions, you have to ask someone higher up than me."

Matt didn't relent. He was determined to get some answers. "What happens now that Pyke failed? Will the scheme be abandoned?"

"Again, I don't know, although I'm flattered that you think I have the ear of the home secretary and prime minister."

"Is that who we should speak to if we want answers?" I asked. "Are they your superiors?"

Sir Charles looked surprised that I'd spoken. He also seemed unsure how to respond at first. "Ultimately, yes, however my immediate superior is the one I answer to directly. His name is Le Grand."

"What's his role?" Matt asked.

"Those of us who work under him call him the spy master. He's the one who inserts spies into situations and gives us our orders. He advises the home secretary and prime minister. You could say he's the brain of the home office while the home secretary is its face. If you want to know what will happen next, ask him. But I'd bet my life savings you won't get a direct answer."

Matt stood and buttoned up his jacket. "I don't need an answer. I just need to make it clear to him that my wife is to be left alone. She can't fly a carpet any more than Pyke. She'll be of no use to you."

A lump formed in my throat that I found difficult to swallow. It wasn't just because of Matt's protective nature. It was also out of grave apprehension. How was Matt going to convince the nation's spy master to do anything he didn't want to do? He operated at the highest level of government. If he wanted to force me to make the rug fly, he could. The police couldn't stop him kidnapping me or hurting my family. No one could.

Brockwell also stood, but I remained seated. "I have one more question," I said. "Is this scheme of dropping bombs from flying carpets a priority for the government? Or is it just one of many schemes they concoct on a daily basis?"

Sir Charles stood and put out his hand to me. I took it and rose, as if he were about to lead me onto the dance floor. "Destroying an enemy's military base or arms factory is the single most decisive action in a war. It can change the course of a battle in an instant. But they're heavily fortified and it's impossible to get into them. Until now. Dropping bombs from flying vehicles that can move swiftly to avoid cannon fire from the ground is not only the winning move, it's the only move necessary. It will put an end to any conflict if the enemy has no comparable vehicle. Put simply, this scheme is paramount."

"If it works," Matt growled. "It seems the flying carpet can't carry weight."

Sir Charles didn't take his gaze off me. His fingers tightened around mine before he released me. He knew I'd already made a carpet fly with passengers.

He knew.

We saw ourselves out, and I was grateful for Matt's steadying hand on my lower back. He gave Woodall instructions to drive Brockwell home then return to Park Street.

Once on our way, Duke wanted to know everything that had transpired in Sir Charles's parlor as he'd not been able to hear it all through the door. Cyclops gave an account of the conversation. Afterward, Duke removed his hat and wiped his brow, as if he'd just completed a day of hard physical labor. Sometimes I felt like that too after these interrogations.

"So you reckon Coyle told Whittaker about seeing you fly away on the carpet to Brighton?" he asked.

Matt nodded. "It had to be him. No one else knew except for us and Charbonneau. Not even Pyke saw the flight."

Brockwell agreed. "Coyle told Whittaker, and Whittaker told his superior, this spy master. I'm sure of that."

"But *why* did Coyle inform Whittaker?" I asked. "What does he gain?"

"Perhaps they paid him," Matt said. "Perhaps Coyle hinted he had something important they'd be interested in and that hint was enough to convince them to buy the information off him. He wouldn't do it for free."

We all agreed with that.

"So what do we do now?" Cyclops asked. "Pyke has been

THE SPY MASTER'S SCHEME

found and should be safe, because he's of no use to Whittaker's superior. We can't confront Coyle because we have no evidence he told Whittaker about the carpet."

"Thank you for pointing that out," Brockwell said with an arched look for Matt, sitting opposite.

"And we have no access to the spy master," Cyclops went on. "Even if we did, what could we do? He ain't going to listen to us about what a bad idea it is to possess a flying vehicle."

"He won't even see it as a bad idea," I said. "You heard Whittaker."

Matt remained silent for the remainder of the journey until we were finally alone in our bedroom. He looked distracted as he undressed, and it took me parading in front of him in my underthings to force him to focus.

The smile he gave me was somewhat sad, however, as he settled his hands on my hips. "You have my attention."

"Good." I looped my arms behind his neck and kissed him lightly on the lips. "Because what I have to say is important. I want you to know it'll be all right, Matt. I've been thinking, and I realize all I have to do is pretend I can't make the carpet fly. They only have Coyle's word for it. If it comes to it, I'll tell them he was mistaken. I don't think anything will come of it now, anyway. Pyke's failure will put an end to their scheme."

He pressed his forehead to mine. "I hope you're right." He didn't sound sure, however. There wasn't much more I could say to convince him, but I could at least distract him for a while to help him fall asleep.

I unbuttoned his shirt, parting the fabric, and kissed a trail down his chest. When I reached the waistband of his trousers, he expelled a deep groan and his body relaxed.

I smiled against his flat stomach and felt myself relax too.

* * *

I HAD the devil of a time convincing Matt not to call on the home secretary the following day. Because he'd made a connection with the head of the home office through Lord Farnsworth, he wanted to take advantage. Duke and I tried to talk him out of it over breakfast, but the deciding argument came from Cyclops.

"If you go there, all guns blazing as Brockwell called it, the home secretary and his spy master will realize India can make the carpet fly. They'll sense it just by looking at you."

That knocked the wind out of Matt's sails. Indeed, the change in him was dramatic as Cyclops's wisdom sank in. "Very well. I'll read books and play cards with all of you today."

"Not me." Cyclops wiped his mouth with the napkin and rose. "I have to work."

"I'll play," Duke said.

Willie sauntered in, yawning. "Play what?"

"Cards."

"Count me in." She headed straight for the sideboard and poured herself a coffee before surveying the offerings under each of the covers. "Glad to see you and Cyclops didn't eat everything this morning, Duke. I'm starving."

"Did you have a late night?" I asked.

"You could say that."

"Would you care to elaborate?"

"I didn't get home until six this morning. The maid let me in."

"Six!"

She slid a poached egg onto her plate and picked up the tongs for the bacon. "But I slept for a few hours before that."

Duke and I exchanged glances. "Slept where?" I asked.

"In the bed of a woman I met. She joined in our party after her show finished. She's a singer, dancer and actress. Real talented she is, too. She showed me some of her dance moves."

"I'm sure she did," Matt muttered from behind his newspaper.

Willie chuckled as she piled bacon onto her plate.

Duke frowned and opened his mouth to speak, but I put up my finger to silence him. For one thing, I didn't want to encourage intimate talk at the breakfast table in case Aunt Letitia walked in, and for another, I was taking a leaf out of Matt's book. The more we protested over Willie's antics, the more she'd continue. If we wanted her to open up about her recent argument with Brockwell, we had to let her do it in her own time. *Not* asking her about her overnight affair was just another way of getting her to talk.

But she wasn't prepared to talk yet and certainly not about Brockwell.

Her cheery mood vanished as soon as she thought we'd all left the dining room. She didn't know I lingered in the doorway, watching her. She threw down her knife and fork, pushed her plate away, and rested her elbows on the table. For Willie to reject breakfast, she must be upset indeed.

My patience was rewarded when she joined me a short time later as I read to Aunt Letitia in the sitting room. She did not immediately take a seat, however, and wandered about, skimming her fingers over framed pictures, picking up knick-knacks only to put them down again after pretending to study them. It was most distracting, and I stumbled over the words in the book.

Aunt Letitia was too interested in Willie to notice. "You're wearing the carpet thin, Willemina. What is it?"

Willie shrugged and feigned innocence. "What's what?"

"Is it Davide? Are you regretting you didn't try to court his interest more?"

Willie looked genuinely shocked. "No! Why would you think that?"

"You went out with him last night so I assumed. Besides, it is a regretful situation you find yourself in."

"No it ain't. I ain't interested in Farnsworth in that way."

"You could be Lady Farnsworth. Imagine that."

"I don't want his money or title."

Aunt Letitia regarded her with sympathy. "You don't have to maintain a façade with us."

Willie flounced onto the chair. "Anyway, he never asked me to marry him. He's got too much respect for me as I am to ask me to be something I'm not."

"Quite right," I said. "Aunt Letitia, leave Willie alone. She's not upset about Lord Farnsworth."

"Then what is the matter?" Aunt Letitia asked. "Is it still Detective Inspector Brockwell? Have you two not made up?"

Willie lifted a shoulder in another shrug. After a moment of strained silence, she gave in. "I wanted to ask India if Jasper said anything last night."

I perused the open book on my lap, feigning disinterest as she had done. "He said a lot of things. Was there something in particular you wanted him to say?"

She stretched out her legs and crossed her arms over her chest. "About me. Us."

Aunt Letitia gripped the chair arm and sat forward. When I pretended to think about my answer, she clicked her tongue. "India! What did he say?"

"He was very busy," I said. "We had an eventful evening and there was no time for him to discuss his romantic intentions."

Willie lowered her arms and looked away. "Right. It doesn't matter, anyway. I was too busy to think about him, too."

"I didn't say he wasn't thinking about you. I'm sure he did from time to time."

Her gaze snapped to mine. "Why do you say that?"

"It's just a feeling."

Her stared at her fingers, stroking the chair arm back and forth.

"Willie, why don't you speak to him?" I said gently. "He misses you, and you miss him."

"It ain't that simple."

"Whatever happened between you the other night can be resolved."

"You don't know that," she snapped.

"I could be more helpful if you'd tell me what you talked about," I snapped back.

She thrust out her chin. "You wouldn't understand my point of view. You'd take his side."

"I might not."

"I'm quite sure *I* would," Aunt Letitia piped up.

Willie gave her a flinty glare.

"Well?" I prompted.

Willie seemed to be considering it when Bristow entered carrying a silver tray. "The mail arrived, Mrs. Glass."

"Thank you, Bristow." There was only one letter addressed to me. It was from Lady Rycroft. I opened it and read. When I reached the end, I sighed. "It's addressed to you too, Aunt. We're invited to dine with them tonight."

Aunt Letitia frowned. "That's odd. I wonder what she wants."

"Perhaps she doesn't want anything, just a nice family dinner."

"After we thwarted her attempt to trap Davide with Charity? Hardly. She either wants revenge or a favor. If it's up to my sister-in-law, it will be the former."

"According to this message, Lord Rycroft has returned to London, so perhaps it isn't up to her. Perhaps the dinner is for his benefit and has nothing to do with that incident at the soiree."

"You're optimism is charming, India."

I wasn't sure whether Lord Farnsworth needed to know about the dinner, but Willie informed him anyway when he arrived mid-afternoon in time for tea in the drawing room.

He was quite convinced he would be the main topic of conversation tonight.

"I am a very eligible bachelor, India." This declaration was accompanied by a flourish of his hand, as if it was an undisputed fact. "Your aunt won't have given up that easily. She will not go down without a fight."

"It's hardly a battle," I said.

"Clearly you're not familiar with the marriage mart. Just wait until you have a son and see how the mothers swarm around him when he grows up."

Matt grunted into his teacup. "Any children we have will be allowed to choose their partner from among all levels of society."

Aunt Letitia set her teacup down with a loud clink of china. "Do be serious, Matthew. It was quaint with you and India, and everyone accepted your egalitarian behavior because you're an American, but your son will be brought up as an English gentleman."

"And everyone knows there's no such thing as an egalitarian English gentleman or lady," Lord Farnsworth added.

I gave my head a quick shake as Matt opened his mouth to protest. Thankfully, he shut it again. There was no point arguing over the future of a child that did not exist.

Willie, however, never backed away from a fight. "With an attitude like that, nothing will change here."

Both Aunt Letitia and Lord Farnsworth eyed her with a mixture of horror and curiosity. "Who says anything ought to change?" he asked.

Fortunately we were saved by Bristow entering and announcing two more visitors in the form of Fabian and Oscar. I invited them in with enthusiasm, welcoming the distraction from the topic at hand.

It quickly became clear, however, that neither of them were in good spirits. No doubt Fabian wanted to ask us about

THE SPY MASTER'S SCHEME

his stolen carpet, and Oscar was still lamenting the ending of his relationship with Louisa.

Thankfully the always jovial Lord Farnsworth came to the rescue. "How are book sales, Barratt?"

"Excellent. My printer wants to send copies overseas to America, and I'm considering having it translated into French and Italian. The reading public can't seem to get enough of it." Oscar turned to me, "India, will you consider writing an introduction for the reprint?"

I scoffed. "Who would care what I have to say? The artless don't know who I am."

"They will after you write the introduction."

"It's the sort of notoriety I'd like to avoid, but thank you for asking." I glanced at Matt who'd been sitting silently since exchanging pleasantries upon Oscar and Fabian's arrival. He merely lifted his teacup in salute to me and sipped.

Oscar cleared his throat. "I came here to tell you I'm working at the *Gazette* again. They've taken me back. After Louisa cost me my job there, I wasn't sure where I stood, but fortunately my editor championed me. He's a good egg."

Fabian frowned at him. "How do you mean, Louisa cost you the job?"

"She saw that I was dismissed. She wanted me to spend more time at home to finish the book."

"Blimey!" Lord Farnsworth said. "That's a little under-handed. But she was quite right in that you shouldn't work. Not if you're going to marry her. She is a lady, after all. It wouldn't be proper. Don't you agree, Letty?"

"I never get involved in the romantic matters of others," she said.

Willie and Duke both snorted into their teacups.

"We are no longer engaged," Oscar told Lord Farnsworth matter-of-factly. "Louisa ended it."

"My dear fellow, that's hard luck! Never mind, another filly will turn up."

"Louisa told me *you* ended the engagement," Fabian said. "Not her."

Oscar gave him a flat smile. "She clearly thinks of you as a close friend to tell you that."

"Ah, I see. You are a gentleman indeed, Barratt. I do not blame you for breaking off the attachment. Louisa is...forceful. When it comes to magic, she is determined. And we are not that close," he finished.

"She idolizes you, Charbonneau. She talks about you quite a lot and when she does, her voice takes on a different timbre."

"She likes my magic, not me. There is a difference."

Oscar sighed. "You may be right on that score."

Lord Farnsworth frowned at Fabian. "You know, you and Louisa have similar opinions when it comes to magic. You both wish to set it free, as it were. You both want it to flourish and become accepted by the world. You both want the bloodlines of magic to continue."

"No, no. That is not true. Louisa and I are not the same. She is prepared to go to great lengths for magic to flourish, but I am not." Fabian indicated me. "India and Matt have convinced me of the dangers if magic falls into the wrong hands. I do not think Louisa would give in as easily as I have done."

It was a pretty speech, but I wasn't convinced Fabian had given up on his hopes and dreams for magic. I expected him to raise the topic of creating spells again in the future, although hopefully it would be some time away yet.

"You've seen her recently?" Oscar asked somewhat shyly. "Is she well?"

Fabian hesitated before answering carefully. "She is as she always is—determined. The first time she came to my house, I was about to leave. The second time, I was not at home. The third, I could not allow her to dine with me, despite the hour. It would not be proper."

"Quite right," Aunt Letitia said. "It sounds to me like she's attempting to trap you. We know all about young ladies like that, don't we, Davide?"

Lord Farnsworth agreed with a rousing, "Hear, hear. One's bachelorhood is precious. We must protect it and not give it away cheaply. Not even to the prettiest, most eligible, most determined girl in the country. Not until we are ready for the life of a married man, that is."

"And we should not marry someone we don't get along with," Oscar added.

Lord Farnsworth chuckled. "How quaint you are."

Oscar arched his brows but didn't get a word in before Fabian spoke up again.

"Glass, is there any word on my stolen carpet?"

"Somebody stole your carpet?" Aunt Letitia asked. Oscar and Lord Farnsworth also turned their attention to Fabian, curious about the theft of a rug.

It would seem the topic couldn't be avoided anymore. Matt gave them a brief explanation of the events so far, leaving out the part where we'd flown on the carpet ourselves. I suspected that was more for Aunt Letitia's benefit.

"Pyke regained consciousness yesterday and informed us that he attempted to make the carpet fly while it carried him, but he fell off," Matt finished.

"Good lord," Lord Farnsworth murmured. "What a brave fellow. A bit mad, but who isn't these days, eh?"

Fabian said something in French under his breath. "He is a fool. He knew he could not fly it on his own. He could have been killed."

"Then why did he attempt it?" Oscar asked.

"He was given no choice," Matt said. "His wife was threatened.

"By Coyle?"

Matt shook his head.

"Then who?"

Matt didn't say. When Oscar appealed to me, I kept my mouth shut.

"And where is my carpet now?" Fabian asked.

"The police burned it," Matt said.

"Burned! But I did not authorize that. It is *my* carpet. The inspector cannot do this!"

"It wasn't Brockwell's idea. It was mine."

The muscles in Fabian's jaw bunched as he clenched his back teeth. He drew in deep breaths as he glared at Matt.

"It was the right thing to do after what happened to Pyke," Matt went on. "It attracted dangerous people; people prepared to use magicians to make the carpet fly again. You must see that it was a magnet for people like Coyle."

Fabian lowered his head. "You are right, of course." He heaved a deep sigh. "And yet, it was a marvel to see it fly. Wonderous."

"Magical," I added with a lopsided smile. "I know, Fabian, and I understand. But the dangers outweigh the beauty of it."

Fabian returned my smile with an unconvincing one of his own.

Oscar reached for a biscuit from the plate and pointed it at Matt as he sat back. "You're fighting a losing battle, you know. Flight *will* happen. Within a few years, I'd wager. Not the flight of carpets, of course, but there's a German engineer who claims to be almost ready to launch a glider. And we already have hot air balloons."

"A balloon is slow and difficult to maneuver," Matt said. "A glider is better but also limited in speed and the level of control the pilot can exert."

Fabian made a sound of derision in his throat. "Glass is right. Nothing the artless make will be as good as a magician's creation."

"That's not what I said."

Oscar gave a small shrug. "I think this is one area where

you will have to eat your words, Charbonneau. If I'm right, then whoever wanted Pyke to fly the carpet will merely need to wait a little longer for the artless inventors to catch up. Aviation will change the world in the way rail once did, mark my words."

I suspected he would be proved right, but that day was years away, and I doubted the government, or Coyle for that matter, were fond of waiting. His words offered me no real comfort.

Our three visitors didn't stay much longer and decided to leave all at once. Lord Farnsworth positioned himself beside Oscar and me as we walked out together, and kept his voice low and his gaze on Fabian up ahead. "Say, Barratt, would you mind terribly if I made a play for your former fiancée?"

Oscar blinked at him. "You wish to court her?"

"Yes, why not. She's the right sort, good breeding and all that. She is a little intense, but that will balance me nicely. Some call me frivolous, but a serious wife will negate my excesses. So what say you? Would it trouble you?"

Oscar looked taken aback and quite unable to answer as he considered the notion.

I came to his rescue. "I thought you said you must protect your bachelorhood and not throw it away, Davide."

Lord Farnsworth winked at me. "Oh, that was just for Charbonneau's benefit. I didn't want him having second thoughts about Louisa when I've suddenly realized how suited we are. I rather think I'd lose to him. The French know how to seduce when they put their mind to it."

Oscar clapped Lord Farnsworth on the shoulder. "If you feel that way, then you're welcome to court her. Although I should warn you that the danger from that quarter doesn't come from him being French or handsome, it's due to him being a magician. She's intent on having magician children, you see."

"Ah, now I understand why she was with you."

191

Oscar took the barb with a good humored chuckle.

Once they were gone, Matt and I walked back up the stairs arm in arm. "Did you really tell Brockwell to destroy the carpet?" I asked.

"No. I would have asked you first before giving such an order. I simply told Charbonneau it was my decision because I didn't want him getting angry with Brockwell. The carpet was burned, though. I received a message from Brockwell to that effect just before our guests arrived. He ordered its destruction last night. While he didn't say why, I suspect he wanted to destroy it before it was removed from the evidence room without his knowledge."

"It's the right thing to do, given the interest in it."

We rejoined Aunt Letitia, Duke and Willie in the drawing room. They'd decided to start a game of cards, although Willie declined to help make up the numbers. I worried that the conversation about Louisa had troubled her. While she claimed not to be interested in Lord Farnsworth in that way, it wouldn't surprise me if she was jealous on some level. Perhaps not in a romantic way, but she might be afraid of losing a friend.

I was forming the right words to ask her when she suddenly piped up. "How do you reckon I'd get the address of that German engineer Oscar mentioned?"

Matt picked up the cards to shuffle them. "There must be an aviation society here in England that could put you in touch with their German counterpart who would then forward a letter to him. Why?"

"I want to offer myself as a volunteer to fly his glider."

CHAPTER 13

J thought my evening gown of emerald green velvet and cream satin was almost too extravagant for an intimate dinner party, but I looked plain next to Matt's aunt in her gold skirt with red embroidered swirls and the contrasting red bodice with gold swirls.

As we took our seats in the drawing room to await the gong, Aunt Letitia leaned toward me and muttered, "She looks like the drapes that used to hang in this room."

Charity wore her usual black lace as if she were in mourning. I expected Aunt Letitia to make another disparaging comment about her niece's choice of clothes, but it never came. She eyed her closely, however, as if trying to gauge her thoughts on this first meeting after that near-disastrous soiree.

Charity seemed unperturbed and even rather content. She hummed softly to herself as she swayed from side to side, until her mother barked at her to be quiet.

Lady Rycroft did not mention the party. Nor did Lord Rycroft, standing by the fireplace. Matt stood on the other side, his elbow resting on the mantelpiece. He seemed unaware that his uncle was watching him from beneath lowered lashes.

C.J. ARCHER

We survived both the pre-dinner conversation and the inane chat throughout each of the seven courses. Although the food was delicious, it became too much for my palate, with cream poured over almost every dish. Even the final course of meringue was covered in custard and cream.

To say it was an awkward dinner was an understatement. Charity rarely talked while Lord Rycroft seemed disinterested in the entire event altogether, giving brief answers only when called upon. Still, he continued to look at Matt as if he were measuring him in some way.

It was almost a relief to be out of his presence when the women departed for the drawing room, leaving the two men to talk over glasses of port. I felt Matt's absence keenly, however, when Lady Rycroft turned to me on the sofa. He could always be relied upon to rescue me in a social setting if need be. Tonight, I had to rely on Aunt Letitia, and I wasn't sure if she would dampen any small fires or add more fuel to them.

"India, dear, where did you have your credenza made?" Lady Rycroft asked.

The question caught me off guard. It was not what I expected. "I haven't changed the dining room furniture. What's in there now was already there when I moved in."

"What about the curtains in the drawing room? I know you changed those."

"From Peter Robinson in Oxford Street."

Her eyebrows shot up to the edge of her red turban. "Really?" She opened the drawer of the occasional table and pulled out a pencil and notepad. "And what about the dinner set?"

I sighed. Was this the entire reason for our invitation here tonight? So she could write down every shop I'd ever purchased from?

"India can't remember," Aunt Letitia said before I could respond.

194

Lady Rycroft's lips pinched. "What about your calling cards?"

"She can't remember that either." Aunt Letitia waved her tea cup in the air. "It was probably from that stationer in Oxford Street." She winked at me.

Lady Rycroft made a note. "And those earrings you're wearing tonight, India? They're new, aren't they?"

I fingered the gold and pearl earrings Matt had given me for Christmas.

Before I could tell her, Aunt Letitia said, "Those are from a jeweler on Oxford Street."

Lady Rycroft paused, pressing the pencil so hard into the page, the end broke. "You seem to do an awful lot of shopping on Oxford Street, India."

"She likes it. It has everything a young lady of taste and distinction requires."

Lady Rycroft's nostrils flared. "I was speaking to India."

"Aunt Letitia knows where I shop," I said. "After all, I shop at the places she recommends." I smiled. "She has very fine taste. Don't you agree?"

Lady Rycroft snapped the notepad closed and tossed it into the drawer along with the pencil. She slammed the drawer shut.

Aunt Letitia smiled into her teacup.

To my surprise, Charity giggled.

Her mother glared at her, but it had no effect. Charity suddenly rose and tugged on the bellpull. "Fetch me a glass of port," she ordered the butler when he entered.

He glanced at Lady Rycroft who gave a slight shake of her head. The butler bowed and left. He returned a few minutes later with a port glass on a silver tray which he offered to Charity.

She took the glass and sipped. Whatever was in that glass probably wasn't port, but she seemed unaware that her mother and the butler had conspired to dupe her.

C.J. ARCHER

Thankfully it wasn't long before Matt and Lord Rycroft joined us as I wasn't sure I could endure another conversation about shopping. Given the shortness of their time together in the dining room, their conversation had probably been as tortuous as ours.

Matt's gaze fell on Charity who sat with drooping eyelids, the empty port glass tilting at an angle as she held it. Her father plucked it from her fingers, rousing her from her daze.

What had been in the drink?

"And how is Lord Farnsworth?" Lady Rycroft asked, as if we'd just been discussing him.

"Davide is well," Aunt Letitia said carefully. "Why?"

"He seems like a thoroughly likeable character. Charity was quite taken with him at our party, weren't you, dear? It's a shame he had to leave early."

"It was an exhausting evening for everyone."

"We should do it again. Shall we say next Tuesday? Rycroft would like to meet him after Charity spoke so highly of him."

Charity made a snuffling noise but I wasn't sure if it was a snore or she disagreed with her mother.

"Next Tuesday," Lord Rycroft reiterated. "I can count on you to pass on my regards to him, can't I, Matthew?"

"I will certainly pass on your words, precisely as you spoke them."

"No, I meant—"

"I think it's time we left."

"But it's so early!" Lady Rycroft protested.

I indicated her daughter with her drowsy eyes and slack jaw. "Charity looks tired. It's not fair to keep her up."

"But I had hoped to speak to you alone, Matthew." She looked to her husband. "Just in case Rycroft didn't make everything clear."

"It was clear." Matt offered his arm to Aunt Letitia.

She took it and bade goodbye to her brother and sister-in-law, and patted Charity's shoulder as she passed. Charity's mouth fell open and she emitted a soft snore.

I thanked our host and hostess and followed them out. I managed to hold my tongue further until we were in the carriage and on our way. "So what did Lord Rycroft say when you were alone, Matt?"

It was Aunt Letitia who answered, not Matt. "Can you not guess? Davide was right. Tonight's dinner *was* about him."

"I'm to act as a go-between," Matt said. "My uncle asked me to put his offer to Farnsworth,"

"You mean offer of marriage?" I laughed. "That's ridiculous. Davide isn't interested in Charity. He made that quite clear when he all but ran from the room on the night of the party."

"That was before my uncle was involved." Matt's eyes were bright in the light of the lamp swinging in time to the gently rocking motion of the carriage. He was enjoying this. "He seems to think that turning this into a financial transaction will change Farnsworth's opinion of Charity."

"Depending on how generous the offer is, it would make a difference to the gentleman's opinion of the lady in many cases," Aunt Letitia said. "But Davide is not like most gentlemen, and Charity is the fruit that's been out in the sun too long—a difficult sell."

I looked at her in horror. "That's a little harsh."

"And yet true. My brother's offer of a generous dowry might work for an impoverished gentleman, but Davide is not that. How much did Richard offer?"

"A generous amount in the form of money and jewels," Matt said.

Aunt Letitia gasped. "He can't offer the Rycroft jewels! They're supposed to be passed down to the title holder. You are supposed to inherit them, Matthew."

"I told him he can do what he wants with them. I don't care if he gives them to a gentleman to encourage a marriage or gives them to Charity to ensure she has a comfortable life as a spinster."

"I suppose you're right. Better Charity has a comfortable living well into her old age than be a burden to you and India. So are you going to inform Davide?"

"Do you think I should? I can't decide if it's an insult to him or flattery."

"Knowing him, he would think the latter," I said.

"Then I'll tell him." He did not sound particularly thrilled with the notion. "Or perhaps it would be better coming from his closest friends."

"We'll do it," Aunt Letitia said before I could respond in the negative. She clapped her hands. "It will be most amusing."

"Unless he accepts the offer," I muttered.

* * *

I SENT a message to Lord Farnsworth the following morning inviting him to tea and he arrived at four instead of the stated three-thirty.

"I apologize for my tardiness, India," he said with a bow. "But you must blame Willie. She insisted on taking me out to lunch."

I glanced at the door but Willie did not follow him in.

"She remained at the club," he said.

"She was allowed into your gentleman's club?" Duke asked. "Ain't they for men only?"

He pressed a finger to his lips. "I told the manager she was my good friend, just turned twenty, and eager to experience the delights of his first foray to a London gentleman's club. I left her at the card table where she was fleecing Lords Ponsonby and Lockham. They were none the wiser."

Matt groaned. "I'll never show my face there again."

"Nonsense. Nobody knows she's related to you."

"But they may never let *you* back in," I said.

"Of course they will! They love me at White's, and she is a friend of mine. Or, rather, *he* is my friend. Don't worry, Glass, she resembled a man more than a woman when I'd finished with her." He hitched up his trouser legs and took a seat, quite oblivious to our open-mouthed stares. "Do you have any of those little cakes? The ones that are as light as air."

Aunt Letitia picked up the teapot and poured. "It's only seed cake today."

"That'll do."

I sliced the cake and handed him a piece on a plate. He regarded me with a curious smile on his face and a twinkle in his eyes.

"You have something exciting to tell me, don't you?" He indicated my cheeks. "You are pink with the effort of keeping it in, India."

"Do you recall that we were invited to dine with Lord and Lady Rycroft last night?"

"Ah, yes, now I know what you want with me today. You're going to tell me that Rycroft has placed a generous dowry on his wildcat of a daughter's head and wants me to take the bait."

"You have it in one, Davide."

"It's not the first time I've navigated the shark-infested waters of the matrimonial market. Nor will it be the last."

"So that's a refusal?" Matt asked.

"It is. Please let Rycroft down gently. I imagine it will disappoint your uncle and aunt. I hope they will eventually recover from the disappointment of rejection, although it will probably take time."

"He'll find another candidate soon enough when his generous offer becomes known."

"But none as fine as me."

Duke raised his teacup in salute. "Hear, hear."

Lord Farnsworth set his teacup down with a clatter and

stared at Duke. He wagged his finger at him. "I say, what about you? You're not married and not unpleasant to look at. Surely you need the dowry more than me, since you don't have your own house."

"Nothing less than a lord will do for them," Duke pointed out.

"But you're a duke!"

Duke sighed and returned to his tea.

"We've explained this to you," I said to Lord Farnsworth. "Duke is a name, not a title."

"You did? S'pose I mustn't have been listening properly. I've been told I have a dreadful attention span."

"Is that so?" Matt muttered.

Lord Farnsworth studied Duke from head to toe then back again, as if seeing him for the first time. "I did think it odd that you live here and not at your ducal residence. Why did your parents give you such a lofty name?"

Duke shrugged. "They just liked it, I reckon."

Lord Farnsworth clicked his tongue. "It ought to be illegal to name a child after a rank. It invokes confusion."

"Quite right," Aunt Letitia piped up. "Although Duke is far more of a gentleman than the Duke of Croxley. Horrid little man with a roaming eye that always falls on the young ladies."

The rest of the afternoon was a pleasant affair that lasted another hour before Willie arrived home. She was dressed in a well-cut suit instead of her usual cowboy outfit and her hair had been carefully pinned under so that it looked short. With her masculine walk and a deepening of her voice, I could see how she'd pass for a young man.

She stood in the doorway to the drawing room with a beaming smile and regarded us with glassy eyes. "You got to take me back there again, Farnsworth. I won a fortune. Those toffs are the worst poker players I've ever encountered, and I've played India."

THE SPY MASTER'S SCHEME

I bristled. "I'm not terrible."

"They didn't realize you were a woman?" Duke asked.

"Nope. They were too drunk, which is another good reason to play with them." She swayed a little and put her hand to the doorframe to steady herself. "The manager had an inkling, I reckon, but my generous tip ensured his silence. All in all, it's been a good day." She pushed off from the doorframe and entered the room, only to bump into Matt's chair. She apologized and fell into a vacant armchair. "Jasper'll laugh when I tell him." Her mouth clamped shut the moment she realized what she'd said, and her eyes dulled. She tried to remove her jacket, but her arm got caught and she ended up flailing about, knocking her hand on the chair. "God damned stupid clothes!"

Duke helped her remove it and folded it over his arm. "You all right, Willie?"

"Course I am," she muttered, crossing her arms over her chest. "I'm always all right, Duke, you know that. So what've you all been talking about without me?"

"Marriage," Lord Farnsworth said.

Willie's eyes suddenly widened. "Huh?"

"Lord Rycroft has offered me first pick of Charity's dowry if I take her off his hands."

"She ain't worth it."

"You didn't hear how much the dowry is," Duke said.

"It don't matter. He could offer me the moon and I wouldn't take it."

Duke opened his mouth to set her straight, but I caught his gaze and shook my head. I wanted her to ramble on about herself while she was under the influence of alcohol. Perhaps it was wicked, but it was the only way I'd get answers.

Willie closed her eyes again and yawned without covering her mouth. "It would take someone real special to get me to marry. Someone real special indeed."

"Can you think of anyone who is that special?" I asked.

Her answer was a soft snore. Darn. I'd been so close.

Bristow entered with a letter addressed to me, sealed with a crown insignia pressed into red wax.

I glanced at Matt. "It's from the home secretary, Henry Matthews."

Matt came to my side and rested a hand on my shoulder. "What does he want?"

I read out the relevant part of the letter. "'I request your presence in my office at ten o'clock.'"

"Why?" Aunt Letitia asked.

"He doesn't say."

"Will you go?" Duke asked.

Lord Farnsworth scoffed. "Of course she has to go. One doesn't refuse an invitation from the home secretary. Indeed, it's hardly an invitation at all. It's a command."

My gaze met Matt's and he squeezed my shoulder. "I'll come with you if you like," he said.

"Is he invited?" Lord Farnsworth asked.

I shook my head. "But he will come, because I won't attend without him."

* * *

THE FOLLOWING morning at ten we arrived at the grand Italianate building that housed the Home Office. It was more suited to be a palace than government offices, with its large entrance dominated by a wide, carpeted staircase, ornately painted ceiling and as many pieces of art as a gallery. Mr. Matthews' office was also large but it was more like what I expected a senior government official to occupy. The only artwork amid the thick-legged mahogany furniture was a portrait of the queen looking like a stern grandmother. A large window overlooking Horse Guards Road below let in an abundance of light.

Two men greeted us. The one who made the introductions

was Mr. Matthews, the home secretary, and the other was Mr. Le Grand, the man Sir Charles called the spy master. Despite both being middle aged with an air of authority about them, that's where the similarities ended.

Mr. Matthews was small and wiry, with a slight stoop and sharp gaze, whereas Mr. Le Grand stood like an unsmiling guard presiding over a dull meeting. He was handsome but not like Matt. Matt's good looks were obvious at first glance. Mr. Le Grand was more unassuming, and it took a moment before his features came together in a pleasing manner. He was tall but not domineering, slender but not thin, broad-shouldered but not angular. He looked as though he needed a good night's rest. Perhaps he was used to working at night, when wicked characters, ne'er do wells, and spies came out to play, and ten o'clock in the morning was too early.

"I was not expecting you, Mr. Glass," the home secretary began as we all sat.

"And yet I am here."

"I wanted him here," I said. "I hope you don't mind."

The home secretary smiled, but there was no warmth in it. "Of course not. I heard you were quite a force to be reckoned with on your own, however, and didn't require an escort."

"He's not my escort. He's my partner. We are a team."

"Whittaker needs to improve his character assessments if he failed to tell you that," Matt added. Although his tone was pleasant enough, it held a hint of steel.

Mr. Matthews shifted his weight, but Mr. Le Grand remained still, his eyelids at half-mast and his body relaxed. He sat near the window, not quite behind the desk but not in front of it with us, either. Perhaps he was there in an observational capacity only and had no intention of contributing to the meeting.

I wondered if he knew that Sir Charles had told us who he was.

Mr. Matthews turned to me, effectively ignoring Matt.

C.J. ARCHER

"You're probably wondering why you've been summoned here."

"I have quite a good idea," I said, "but I'd like to hear it from your lips."

"You are a unique individual, Mrs. Glass. A rare gem, as it were. Is it true you weren't aware of your magical ability until quite recently?"

"It is true. I'm a watch magician, but I assume you already knew that."

"Oh, you are much more than a watch magician. You've been called spell master by some, and the greatest magician of our time, by others. You come from magical stock on both sides of your family, but your ability surpasses anything your parents or grandparents could do." He paused, perhaps waiting for me to fill in the gaps.

I remained silent.

"You've been assisting Scotland Yard with several cases involving magic." He glanced at a piece of paper on his desk. "Detective Inspector Brockwell is your liaison with the Yard."

I nodded.

"May I thank you for your service to the crown on behalf of the nation, Mrs. Glass. Your assistance has proven to be invaluable in stopping crimes committed both against and by magicians. It's my understanding the country is safer because of you."

I narrowed my gaze. So much heady praise could only be leading in one direction. I didn't trust him. I didn't trust either of these men. They traded in secrets and sifted through lies, no doubt spreading some of their own when it suited them. If there was such a thing as an expert in lies, it would be these two men.

"I see you're impatient for me to get to the point," Mr. Matthews went on. "Very well." He leaned forward and clasped his hands on his desk. "We would like you to come and work for us."

I blinked hard. "You mean work for the government?"

"Yes."

I glanced at Mr. Le Grand, but his blank expression gave nothing away. "In what capacity?"

"Advisory, mostly. Now that magic is in the public domain, it must be regulated. As you're no doubt aware, there has been restlessness of late between magicians and normal people."

"Magicians *are* normal," I said tightly. "Those without magic are called artless."

He separated his thumbs before pressing them together again. "We would like you to give advice to the policy makers."

My heart tripped over itself. This was the opportunity I wanted; an opportunity to speak out against the guilds and their archaic system of issuing licenses to members only. It was an opportunity to change the way things had always been done, for the betterment of magicians all over the country, and to broker peace between artless and magician craftsmen.

"Would that be India's only role?" Matt asked. "Giving advice about magic to help form policy?"

Mr. Matthews tapped his thumbs together in a fast rhythm. "It will be an important part of her role."

Matt glanced at Mr. Le Grand. "Then why is he here?"

Mr. Matthews glanced over his shoulder at Mr. Le Grand. "He's here as an observer."

"There's no need for the spy master to observe a meeting in which you recruit an advisor." When Mr. Matthews didn't respond, Matt continued. "Since you seem reluctant to elaborate on India's role, I'll tell you why I think you really want her—for using spells already created and creating new ones."

Mr. Matthews sat back and settled his clasped hands over his stomach. His thumbs continued to tap away against each other.

Mr. Le Grand's drooping eyelids lifted, finally revealing the shrewd gaze he'd been trying to hide.

"Still no response, gentlemen?" Matt shook his head. "You can't possibly expect to recruit someone for a position when only half of the job description is given."

Mr. Matthews cleared his throat. "Yes. Well. There is a little more to it, of course. We wish to use your wife to help make Britain a powerful force on the international stage. While the British Empire already spreads around the globe, there are those who wish to see us fail. Your wife can single handedly protect our interests both here and abroad. Indeed, let's not underplay it—Mrs. Glass, you can change the course of history."

My heart sank further with every word until it settled in my stomach like a lump of ice. They did not want my advice. They wanted me to fly the carpet and drop bombs on their enemies.

"I think we should go," I said, standing. Matt rose too.

Mr. Matthews shot to his feet. "But we haven't begun negotiations!"

"Nor will we." Matt's voice was a low snarl that sent a chill through me. "Not until you realize my wife has honor, integrity and compassion. Not until you realize that she is *not* for sale, and certainly not going to create spells that will destroy for you—or for anyone." He jabbed a finger in Mr. Le Grand's direction. "If you had done your job properly, you would have known that, but instead you're wasting my wife's time."

Matt wheeled around, grabbed my hand, and together we strode toward the door.

"Destroy!" Mr. Matthews scoffed. "It's not destruction when it's one's enemies. You will be protecting your loved ones! Mrs. Glass, you will be the nation's savior if you do this, its heroine. If ever we are faced with an enemy invasion, *you* can save us."

I stopped as Matt opened the door and spun around to face the men. "Last time I read the newspapers, there was no mention of enemies at our shores. Indeed, *our* armed forces are the ones doing the invading. Good day, gentlemen. You know where to find me if you change your mind and wish me to assist with policy making only. But I will not be creating new spells, or using existing ones that can cause destruction. And, might I point out, there are no magicians capable of flying a carpet that can hold a bomb. Not even me." It was a lie, but I held Mr. Matthews' gaze and was proud of how convincing I sounded.

It was Mr. Le Grand who answered, however. "I'm disappointed, Mrs. Glass. This is a department that could do with a little more honor, integrity and compassion your husband credits you with. But you've made your stance clear, and we will not make this offer to you again. Goodbye."

I strode out with Matt at my side. Mr. Le Grand's words rang in my ears all the way home, not because I regretted my decision, but because there was an ominous ring to them that made me feel sick to my stomach.

CHAPTER 14

$\mathcal{W}$e called on Brockwell at Scotland Yard before heading home to apprise him of the situation. We also wanted to know if he'd suffered any consequences for confronting Sir Charles.

He was in a meeting when we arrived, however. We waited in the foyer and watched as policemen came and went, some in uniform, others in plain clothes. Perpetrators weren't brought in through the front door, but persons of dubious character passed us by as we sat on the chairs. Some were clearly prostitutes while others looked as though they'd yet to shake off the effects of the previous night's imbibing. They would be witnesses and victims, and friends of the arrested.

A woman who fell into all three categories made quite a scene as she tried to explain her predicament to the sergeant on the front desk. "Tell them!" she cried. "Tell them they arrested the wrong man!" She stabbed her finger into the counter surface, her face red with the effort of explaining. "He must be freed *now*!"

The sergeant put up his hands. "Look here, calm down!"

"I will not calm down! Not until my husband is freed. He

208

was simply trying to defend our property from the rioters. We are the victims in this situation! To be quite frank, that man deserved the beating he got after he broke our front window."

"This is a matter for your local constabulary, not Scotland Yard."

"They told me to come here! Are you telling me my husband isn't here? Then where is he?"

I rose to offer my assistance to a woman who must be a magician or magician's wife, but Matt placed a hand on my arm.

Brockwell chose that moment to appear in the doorway leading to the corridor. He signaled for us to join him in his office. "I have just come from a meeting with the commissioner," he said as he closed the door behind us.

"Have you been stood down?" Matt asked.

"Not yet. I've been given a warning. If I interfere in home office business again, I will be dismissed."

"But you didn't interfere," I pointed out. "You simply asked Sir Charles for clarification."

"While the confrontation with Whittaker was mentioned, it wasn't the commissioner's main issue. He was not pleased that I destroyed the carpet without his authority. In fact, he was livid. I tried to explain why I did it, but he refused to let me finish. Apparently my opinion doesn't matter," he bit off. "Only the opinion of his superiors count."

"They wanted that carpet," Matt agreed with a mutter.

"They will give up on the idea of flying it now," I assured Brockwell. "We have just come from the office of the home secretary, as it happens. I told Mr. Matthews and Mr. Le Grand that nobody could fly the carpet with any weight on it."

"And they believed you?"

"I think so."

Matt remained quiet.

"Will you dine with us tonight, Inspector?" I asked. "You

deserve some of Mrs. Potter's cooking after the morning you've had."

"It's probably best if I stay away."

"I suppose so. You don't want to be seen associating with us too much or the commissioner might think you're under our influence."

Brockwell cleared his throat. "It's not that." He picked up a stack of papers and shuffled them before slowly turning them over, perusing each one. "It's Willie."

"I'm sure she'd be happy to see you," I said carefully. "Perhaps you can even resolve the problem between you."

He picked up all the papers again and reshuffled them into a neat stack. "Did she tell you about it?"

"No."

"Then she's not ready to see me." He gave me a flat smile. "Thank you for the invitation, India, but it's best that I don't see her for a while."

I felt a little deflated as we headed home. The morning had been a disappointing one. The opportunity to advise policy makers had been within my grasp, only to have it snatched away. Indeed, it wasn't even an option, as it happened. They wanted me to do their dirty work, and dangled the carrot of advisory role in front of me as a lure. Matt had instantly seen through it, and I was glad he'd been with me.

Chronos arrived shortly after we arrived home and stayed for a light luncheon. He ate little, however, and looked somewhat uncomfortable afterward. He shifted in the chair, stretching his torso as he pressed a hand to his upper stomach

"Is everything all right?" I asked.

"It's just my indigestion again. So what happened this morning at your meeting with the home secretary?"

"How do you know about that?" Matt asked.

"Willie told me."

Willie suddenly stood and collected our plates. "No need

to summon Peter. I can take these to the kitchen."

Matt narrowed his gaze at her but she pretended not to notice, whistling as she left the dining room. Aunt Letitia followed her out.

I told Chronos how the meeting had unfolded. I prepared to defend my refusal to work with Mr. Matthews and Mr. Le Grand, but Chronos agreed with my decision.

"You can't trust these government types, India. Not where magic is concerned. They want to control magic—and therefore us—by dictating how it's used. If we let that happen, we are no longer a free nation of free citizens, we are pawns in their political games."

I blinked at him in surprise. "I always knew you were somewhat radical, but that is strong language, even for you."

"I'm proud of you, India. Proud of you for standing up for your rights and freedoms."

"That's not why I refused to work for them. I simply don't want to see my spells used to harm others. My magic is not a weapon. Nor am I."

He leaned forward and touched my cheek. His eyes shone as he smiled wistfully. "You are something of a radical too. You and I are not so different, after all."

My heart swelled and my eyes filled with tears. "I'm not radical. Just sensible."

His smile became lopsided. "Do you always have to have the last word?"

Willie returned before I could answer, brandishing a letter for Matt. "There ain't no return address on it."

He opened it and read. "It's from Mr. Matthews. He wants to meet me at White's for an informal conversation."

"Why you and not me?" I asked.

"He probably thinks Matt influences you," Chronos said. "He hopes to get Matt on side to convince you to change your mind. Little does he know."

"Idiot," Willie agreed.

Matt tossed the letter on the table. "I won't go. There's no point."

I wasn't so sure. "I'd like to know what he wants. On the other hand, you have been coming and going from the house a lot lately. I'd prefer it if you stayed home."

"I'll escort him to the club," Duke said. "Willie too. We'll make sure he's not exposed."

Willie slapped Matt on the shoulder. "I can come inside with you, if you want. They know me at White's now."

Chronos shook his head sadly. "Women at gentlemen's clubs? What is the world coming to?"

Matt agreed to meet Mr. Matthews, and I decided to call on Catherine at her shop for something to do. Woodall could deliver Matt to the club, take me to the St Martin's Street shop then drive Chronos home. Not wanting to disturb Bristow or Peter after our lunch finished, as they would be sitting down to their own luncheon in the servants' dining room, Matt was going to deliver the message to the coach house himself, but I insisted on doing it. Even in the mews, he was too exposed for my liking.

I rode in the carriage as Woodall drove to the front of the house. Matt and the others must have been watching for our arrival, because the front door opened before we'd come to a complete stop. Chronos joined me in the carriage first, while Duke and Willie escorted Matt down the steps.

A gunshot rang out.

Before the scream had left my lips, the flash of metal in the sunlight caught my eye. It was a knife, thrown by an unseen hand.

The movement spell sprang to mind, complete with the image of metal and the word Fabian used for it. Actual words failed me. My voice wouldn't work. I could not speak the entire spell in time to stop the blade from striking Matt. I could only think it.

The blade clattered onto the pavement before it struck him

and stayed there.

My body trembled as I stared at it. *I* did that, not by speaking the spell but simply by *thinking* about it. The thrill of my magical power was not what had me shaking all over, however. Something dreadful had occurred to me.

I now knew who was trying to kill Matt.

My heart shattered.

Matt had dropped to the ground the moment the gunshot rang out. He signaled that he was unhurt, but Duke pressed a hand and knee to his back, not letting him rise as he scanned the vicinity.

"Can you see who it was?" Chronos asked, squinting into the distance.

"There!" Willie pointed toward a figure sprinting away down the street. "After him, Woodall!"

She jumped onto the running board. Her hat flew off as the horses leapt forward but she did not try to catch it. She hung on with one hand and held her gun in the other.

I opened the window. "Don't kill him!"

"He deserves to be shot, India!" She aimed the gun.

"Put it down!"

She lowered the gun, but not because of my order. The figure had run into a lane too narrow for our carriage to turn into at speed. By the time Woodall managed it, the shooter was nowhere in sight.

Willie swore at the top of her lungs. "We'll never catch him!"

The sense of sickening dread that had filled me since my magic stopped the blade from striking Matt now threatened to overwhelm me. I gripped Willie's arm tighter as tears sprang to my eyes.

"Yes, we will. I know who it is. I know where he lives."

She turned to me, frowning. "Who?" both she and Chronos asked.

"Fabian."

CHAPTER 15

$\mathcal{I}$ had the devil of a time convincing Willie that returning home to Park Street was a better idea than driving to Fabian's house. Fortunately Woodall knew who to take orders from and drove back the way we'd come. We met Matt and Duke at the end of the long street, much to Duke's frustration.

"He wouldn't go back inside," he grumbled as we collected them both.

I touched Matt's face, his shoulders, and chest, searching for blood.

"I'm unharmed," he said. "The bullet missed and the knife fell short."

I threw my arms around him and buried my face in his throat. The warmth and strong pulse of blood in his veins helped steady my nerves, but I still felt ill. Yet again, I'd come so close to losing him.

And at the hand of someone I trusted, too.

"Tell him he's an idiot, India," Duke went on. "The shooter could have doubled back—"

"It was Charbonneau!" Willie blurted out.

I felt Matt tense.

Duke swore, quietly at first then again at the top of his lungs. He punched the padded door.

"Now that we know Matt's all right, can we tell Woodall to drive to Fabian's?" Willie asked me.

I drew away from Matt and nodded. I couldn't speak, not a single word. My throat was suddenly too tight.

Matt removed his glove and stroked his thumb over my cheek, wiping away a tear. "Are you sure?"

I hugged myself. "Yes. I sensed his magic. It was in the metal blade. I was able to overcome it, but there was resistance."

Duke removed the knife from his inside jacket pocket. I touched it but did not pick it up. The magical heat was so intense I felt it through my glove.

"What do you mean resistance?" Chronos asked. "You stopped his moving spell with your own?"

I closed my eyes and nodded.

Matt drew me against him and kissed the top of my head. He was alive, thank God, but he wouldn't be if Fabian had succeeded. I could hardly fathom it. I'd worked with him; I'd let him into my home; I'd helped him and liked him.

He'd betrayed me so completely I felt too shattered to focus.

"You had the opportunity to speak the spell?" Chronos asked, drawing my mind back to the incident. "I didn't hear you."

"I imagined the spell and pictured the blade diverting its course. I didn't need to say the words. The impression of it was so strong, so vivid, that it worked."

"Amazing," he said on a breath. "Your magic has grown powerful indeed."

I'd controlled Fabian's magic with the iron supports attached to the flying carpet but that was when his magic was aligned with mine by having the same purpose. This time was different. I had worked *against* Fabian's magic. My magic had overridden his—and I wasn't working with my natural element of watches; I'd been working with his. His *should* have been the stronger of the two.

"I'm not sure I could replicate it if I tried. It was an unconscious effort. I was running on instinct alone." And terror, I might have said. Terror at losing Matt.

He hugged me fiercely against his warm body, but with every passing second, I grew colder. Cold with anger. My unfocused daze was replaced with an icy fury as sharp as the blade Fabian wielded.

By the time we turned into Fabian's street, anger filled me completely. "He needs to pay for what he's put you through, Matt. He should be arrested. We'll capture him then take him to Scotland Yard."

Matt opened the window and ordered Woodall to drive on past the house and pull over at the end of the street.

"Why not confront him now?" I asked.

"Because if he was on foot, he won't have returned yet. We'll watch for him."

"I thought you were going to let him go free."

"No," he said ominously. "I want to speak to him as much as you do." He grasped my hand tightly.

I released a long breath and waited. Duke peered out one window and Willie watched from the other. I concentrated on breathing steadily, calming my nerves without dampening my anger. I wanted a clear head when I spoke to Fabian, but I wanted him to see how furious I was.

It was telling that none of us speculated about why Fabian had done it. We all knew. His motive was so clear to us now.

He wanted to make me a widow. He wanted to remove Matt so that he could swoop in and comfort me then marry me.

He didn't know me at all if he thought I'd ever marry again.

"There he is," Duke said. "Want me to tell Woodall to intercept him?"

"Wait until he's at the steps," Matt said. "We don't want him running off."

Duke gave Woodall instructions then a moment later, we rolled forward. The butler was just opening the front door as we pulled to a stop. We piled out of the carriage and stood at the base of the stairs, trapping Fabian.

At the butler's frown, Fabian turned around. He paled, but attempted a smile. "What a pleasant encounter. I was just out for a walk."

"You dropped your knife," Matt said in that chillingly idle tone he employed when he was furious. "Duke, would you mind returning it to Mr. Charbonneau?"

Duke tossed the knife. It clattered on the stone step mere inches from Fabian's feet.

Fabian swallowed hard. His gaze fixed on me.

The butler opened the door wider. "Sir!"

"It is all right. Go inside."

"Bring refreshments into the drawing room," Matt said to the butler. "We're staying for afternoon tea."

The butler waited for Fabian's nod and disappeared inside. Matt took the steps two at a time until he reached the same level as Fabian. Fabian jerked his head back and put up his hands in defense, expecting a punch, but Matt merely grabbed his arm and marched him inside.

We followed them into the drawing room. Matt shut the door and let Fabian go. Fabian blew out a shuddery breath only to draw it in sharply again when Duke stormed up to him. Fabian covered his head with his arms, but Duke merely shoved the Frenchman onto an armchair.

"Sit down and be grateful you're still alive," Duke growled. "Because everyone in this room wants you to pay for what you did."

Willie stood over Fabian and cracked her knuckles. "Some of us want you dead."

Fabian shrank into the chair, retreating as far from Duke and Willie as he could. I felt no inclination to order them to step back.

"You sent that letter asking me to meet Matthews at White's, didn't you?" Matt said.

Fabian swallowed and nodded. "I needed you to leave the house without India."

"My god," Chronos murmured. "You knew her magic was growing stronger. You knew she could stop your magic, but you didn't know she was in the carriage already."

I gasped as it all began to make sense. Chronos was right. "You knew I might use the spell to divert the knife that *you* directed with your magic. But *how* could you know I was capable of that?"

"I guessed," Fabian said on a rush of breath. You are growing more powerful, India. The books say this will happen."

"Books?"

"The authors of some very old texts say that some magic becomes more powerful the more it is used, and that spells do not have to be spoken, only thought." He tapped his forehead. "Only the most powerful can make thought spells work on elements that are not their natural one, however. *You* are one of those magicians, India. You can control more than your own magic. You can create spells. And now you grow strong with frequent use." He sat forward, his eyes gleaming.

Willie growled at him and he shrank back again, watching her warily.

"It was not personal," he went on. "I like you, Glass. You are a good man, and it would have pained me to end your life and see India mourn. But it was necessary for the greater good, the betterment of magic."

Chronos sat heavily on an armchair and rubbed his jaw with a trembling hand.

Matt's fists closed at his sides. He was very close to losing his self-control.

My self-control was not nearly so strong. I took a step closer and slapped Fabian's cheek. "You were willing to commit murder just so you could marry me and possess my magic!"

Fabian pressed his palms together, begging me or perhaps praying. Neither would work on me. My ire would not be quelled by sympathy, no matter what he had to say. There was nothing that could put right what he'd done. "Not possess your magic, or you," he said. "I would never try to control you or tell you what you can do with your magic. I did it for the *future* of magic." His eyes danced with what I now suspected was madness. How had I not seen it before? "Our children would be powerful, India. The combining of our lineages would lead a new generation into a bold future for magicians, one where wondrous spells could be created and admired."

"You're mad," I spat.

"No! My mind is very clear. The future is filled with possibilities, but only if we are together. If we have children together."

"I meant you're mad if you think I would ever marry you."

"In time, you would come to see—"

"Stop! You can attempt to justify your actions to yourself, but it won't work on me. You are an attempted murderer, Fabian, and I hate you. I loathe you with every fiber of my being."

I marched to the door and shouted for the butler. He was lurking not far away and came quickly. "Fetch Detective Inspector Brockwell from Scotland Yard. Take our carriage and tell him it's urgent."

He hurried off.

Matt came up behind me and settled a hand on my back. "Are you sure that's what you want to do?"

"Of course. He tried to kill you! Three times, no less." I glared past him at Fabian, cowering in the chair with Duke and Willie looming over him.

Matt expelled a deep breath and uncurled his fist. "They can't arrest him. There's not enough evidence."

"But we saw him."

He shook his head. "None of us saw him shoot or throw the knife. We only saw him running away."

I closed my eyes and pressed my thumb and finger against the lids. "So he'll go free."

"Unless Brockwell finds a witness, yes."

"Then what do we do about him?"

"Nothing."

"But what if he tries again?"

"He won't. His ultimate aim was for you to marry him, but even he can see that you'd never do that now, no matter how much he grovels."

I glowered at Fabian, a pitiful figure cowering in the chair, blinking at me with mournful eyes. "Not even if he came crawling to me on hands and knees."

Matt drew me into a hug and pressed his lips to my forehead. "It's over."

He was right, and Fabian knew it too. He would not attempt to kill Matt again. He knew there was no hope of us being together now.

Tears of relief spilled down my cheeks and onto Matt's chest, dampening his jacket. He held me fiercely, and gave me his handkerchief when the tears finally abated.

I dabbed at my eyes. "I don't think I'll ever trust a magician again. Between Fabian, Mrs. Trentham, Amelia Moreton and countless others, it's a corrupting influence that brings out the worst."

He touched my chin, gently drawing my gaze upward. His eyes softened. "There are many good magicians too. Gabe Seaford, Mirnov, Barratt and his brother. You. And it's not just magicians who are greedy for magic, it's the artless too. Look at Coyle, and even my Aunt Beatrice."

I gave him a lopsided smile. "You're not making me feel very good about the human race."

"Unfortunately in the business of criminal investigation, you will come across a disproportionate number of bad people. But the good outweigh the bad the world over, by a large margin. I've seen a lot more of the world than you, and you can trust me on that."

He kissed the top of my head again and took my hand. Together we sat on the sofa to wait for Brockwell. Fabian didn't move or attempt to, and remained silent, thankfully. I was in no mood to hear him attempt to deflect guilt.

My gaze settled on Chronos, sitting by the fireplace. He looked quite gray. I crouched alongside him. "Are you all right? You look unwell."

"I feel dreadful, but not ill. I feel..." He shook his head sadly. "I feel responsible."

"Why? Did you encourage Fabian on this path?"

His head jerked up. "No! Nothing like that. But I wanted you to marry him, or at least marry someone with strong magic like his. I never wanted you to wed Matt."

"I certainly recall you trying to discourage me." I patted his hand. "But you gave up and came to accept him."

"Thankfully he's rich."

I gave him a withering glare.

He attempted a laugh. "It was a joke. In all seriousness, you're right, and I did give up. I like him. I like him a lot, and I know he's right for you. But I can't help shaking the feeling that Fabian and I are not dissimilar. We are both excited by magic and its possibilities. We both want to shore up the future with strong magical lineages. We are both focused on a better future for magicians."

I sighed and glanced at Fabian again. He couldn't hear us, but he watched through narrowed slits, perhaps wondering what we were talking about. "All of that is true, but with one key difference. You love me more than you love magic. Fabian never once considered my wishes. They were always secondary to his plans."

He touched my jaw and gave me a grim smile. "You are the best granddaughter an old man could wish for. I don't deserve you or your forgiveness."

I kissed his cheek. "You do deserve it."

When Brockwell finally arrived with two constables, we told him what had happened while the constables stood outside. Fabian remained silent, his gaze averted, as we explained that he'd confessed.

Brockwell removed his hat and scratched his head. "I can hardly believe it."

"I do *not* confess," Fabian finally said. "I have not done these crimes they accuse me of."

Brockwell sighed as he continued scratching. After a moment, he called in his constables and ordered them to arrest Fabian. "He's an iron magician," he informed them. "He can wield it to his advantage, so use your truncheons if necessary and watch him closely."

"I will not use my magic," Fabian said with his chin tilted forward. "But I did not do these crimes either. You have no proof."

Brockwell and Matt exchanged glances. Brockwell knew what he had to do, but Matt had already conceded that Fabian would be let go.

The constables pulled him to his feet but didn't bother with handcuffs.

"Wait," Duke said. "Before you go, I have something to say." He swung his fist and punched Fabian's jaw.

Fabian stumbled and would have fallen if the constables hadn't caught him.

Duke dusted off his hands. "You can take him now, unless Willie wants a turn."

Brockwell stepped between them before Willie could accept the offer. "I think it's best if we refrain from physical violence. It gives the police force a bad reputation."

Willie stabbed a finger in Fabian's direction. "You're lucky. If I catch you near Matt again, or India, your luck will run out. I guarantee it."

Fabian rubbed his jaw then walked toward the door unaided. The constables and Brockwell followed.

"Put him in a cell with a window too small for him to crawl through," Matt called after the inspector.

"All of our holding cells are like that."

"And have men guard him at all times. He can mold the sliver from an iron bar into the shape of a key."

Brockwell simply tossed a wave as he disappeared down the stairs.

I retrieved my reticule from the sofa where I'd left it. "No prison can hold him."

"It won't matter for long," Matt said. "They'll have to let him go if they can't find a witness."

"We have to hope that he realizes he'll never have me now and won't try anything again after he's released."

Willie patted the handle of the gun thrust down her waist band. Duke came to stand beside her, his right hand curled into a fist again. Together they strode out and glared at Fabian until the police carriage drove off.

* * *

THE FOLLOWING day at fifteen minutes past four, Brockwell informed us in person that he'd released Fabian due to a lack of evidence. While the news was expected, it was still disappointing.

"He did not try to escape," Brockwell reported as he joined Matt and me in the sitting room. "I'm not sure my men could have stopped him if he tried to strike them with flying iron bars."

"That is a relief," I said.

"For what it's worth, I think the time in the holding cell made him reflect upon what he'd done. He might even be remorseful, although admitting that would implicate himself so he would never say so to me."

"What makes you think he's remorseful?" Matt asked.

"That's what Willie told me after I let her out of the cell."

Matt stared at him. "Willie was in there?"

"And Duke and Cyclops." Brockwell frowned. "You didn't know?"

"No. India?"

"I didn't know either," I said. "When they told us they were heading out last night, I thought they were going to a pub or gambling den. Are you saying they asked to see Fabian and you let them into his cell? Inspector, that could have been rather dangerous."

"Only for Charbonneau."

I couldn't admonish him, since I had stayed awake most of the night thinking of accidents I wished would befall Fabian. "Is he all right?"

"Physically, he was the same as when I locked him up. Emotionally, he seemed shaken. I suspect they threatened him with forms of torture if he were to set a foot wrong again. I imagine Willie was particularly medieval in her descriptions." He chuckled softly.

Perhaps he and Willie had talked through their problem after she finished with Fabian. Perhaps she'd felt such immense relief afterward that she decided their relationship was more important to her than their argument.

I shook off the thoughts. There were more important

things to worry about than their romantic problems. "Would you care to join us for afternoon tea, Inspector?"

He put up his hands and backed away to the door. "Not today."

"Willie isn't home," I assured him. I did not tell him that I expected her to return shortly from her walk with Aunt Letitia and Duke.

"Even so, it's best if we have as little to do with each other as possible for a while."

I opened my mouth to protest, but Matt got in first. "Very wise, Brockwell. Willie doesn't like to be pushed in a particular direction."

"No one is pushing her," I said.

"That's not the way she'll see it."

Brockwell agreed with him.

As Brockwell left, another visitor arrived. Professor Nash sat on the edge of the chair and fidgeted with the brim of his hat. Bristow brought in tea, but the professor put down the cup as soon as I handed it to him. We knew what upset him, but we gave him time to broach the topic when he was ready.

He finally relinquished his poor hat, pushed the spectacles up his nose and told us what was on his mind. "I received a letter from Mr. Charbonneau today saying he was not interested in pursuing our research any further."

"Did he say why?" Matt asked.

"Not in the letter. He simply wished me well. Naturally I went to his house to ask him directly. At first his butler said he was not at home, but then Mr. Charbonneau himself appeared at the door and invited me inside." He touched the bridge of his spectacles again even though they had not slipped down. "He then informed me that he no longer had the heart for magical research. I pressed him further, suggesting that he ought to speak to you, Mrs. Glass, and that's when he told me he was no longer welcome in your home. I asked why and he told me the most extraordinary story." He glanced between Matt and me. "Dear God. It's true, isn't it? He tried to kill Mr. Glass."

I nodded. "On three separate occasions."

Professor Nash pressed a hand to his heart. "This is shocking. So very shocking. To think, he was your friend. He has been a friend to me, too."

"I'm surprised he admitted his crimes to you," Matt said.

The professor finally picked up his teacup. "He didn't. Not quite. He claimed you had accused him of attempted murder but the police couldn't find evidence so he was released. I didn't ask for further information, and he didn't offer any. But I know you both as thorough investigators, and also his good friend, so I was quite sure you wouldn't accuse him if you weren't certain." He blew on the tea only to set the cup back in the saucer. "I also know how desperate he was to strengthen his magical lineage. That's why he did it, isn't it? To make you a widow, Mrs. Glass, and hope you would go on to marry him and bear his children?"

I winced. It still pained me to think about it, and probably would for some time. I was yet to fall pregnant with Matt, so it was a testament to Fabian's desperation that he would put so much hope into my ability to conceive.

"There's nothing for it, now," Professor Nash went on. "He must leave England."

"Did he say he would?" Matt asked.

"He didn't mention it. Indeed, our meeting was very brief. I felt too awkward to stay long in his presence." He sighed. "I imagine I'll never see him again."

"Will you continue your research without him?" I asked.

"Of course. It began without him and it will continue without him. It will just move at a slower pace again. Perhaps Oscar Barratt can help me, now that he has nothing better to do after the release of his book."

"He's working for the *Gazette* again," I said. "But do ask him. He might want to work alongside you in his spare time."

"He'll be too busy with the wedding coming up."

"His engagement to Louisa has ended." I didn't want to tell him that Oscar had ended it but was telling everyone that Louisa did. Although I knew it was the gentlemanly thing to do, I didn't think it fair. She didn't deserve such consideration.

But the professor seemed disinterested in the particulars. Indeed, he looked worried by the news. "Oh dear. That is unfortunate. Most unfortunate indeed."

"Why?" Matt asked.

Professor Nash studied his tea with a frown. "Because she is rather smitten with Charbonneau." He sounded distant and had a faraway look in his eyes, as if working through a problem in his head.

"And why is that unfortunate?" I asked.

He pushed his spectacles up his nose and regarded me. "She came to me some days ago and asked me to put in a good word with Charbonneau. I thought it very forward of her, but I chalked it up to the young ladies these days having modern sensibilities. I told her I would speak to him, but of course I didn't. That is beside the point. The point is, when she spoke about Charbonneau, she brightened like an electric light. Indeed, to describe her as smitten with him is not quite accurate. Obsessed would be a better word. When Charbonneau is cut off from his friends here because of his actions, he might turn to her for sympathy and comfort. She will stand by him."

"Why would that be a problem?" I asked.

"Because together they would be quite a force. They are both wealthy, and he is magically powerful. Both are mad for magic. I don't quite know what that combination would look like, but I can't shake a sense of foreboding about them colluding."

A sense of foreboding settled into the pit of my stomach

too. I glanced at Matt for reassurance, and he offered it to me in the form of a small smile.

"It won't happen the way you think," he told Nash. "You're forgetting that Charbonneau isn't interested in Louisa for a wife. She's artless. He wants the mother of his children to be a magician. She can knock on his door all she likes, he won't let her in."

The professor smiled weakly. "I hope you're right."

As did I.

But the sense of foreboding would not go away. Fabian's situation had changed overnight. He might no longer think as he once did. If Louisa was the only friend he had left in the city, he could turn to her, and together they could form a new scheme that ensured magic remained powerful into the future.

$\mathcal{I}$t was an evening when I was glad our friends liked to visit unannounced and stay for dinner. I needed the distraction, but even more importantly, I needed to be surrounded by people I loved and trusted. We convinced Professor Nash to return at eight and invited Catherine too. She arrived just five minutes before Chronos and Lord Farnsworth, who seemed to assume they had a standing invitation.

Mrs. Potter always prepared enough for unexpected guests and we sat down to a hearty feast. The dining room soon filled with the sounds of our friends and family enjoying their food and one another's company. My heart swelled.

As the final course's plates were cleared away, I caught Matt watching me from the opposite end of the table. He smiled warmly and raised his eyebrows in question. I nodded and his smile widened.

The ladies retired to the drawing room after dinner, although Willie stayed with the men in the dining room because, as she put it, she'd rather drink port and talk about horses and gambling than sip tea and discuss fashion and wedding arrangements.

As far as our party was concerned, she was right about the topic of conversation. Although they'd not set a date or received her family's blessing, Catherine was eager to tell Aunt Letitia and me about her plans for her wedding day.

"I didn't realize Cyclops had asked you," Aunt Letitia said, sounding put out that she hadn't been told.

"He hasn't. Not properly. But we have an understanding, and as soon as Nate asks my father, we'll set a date."

"And when will he ask your father?"

She glanced toward the door. "He's waiting for the right moment. Hopefully that moment will be soon."

"Oh?" I asked. "Are your parents starting to accept him?"

She shook her head. "They like him, but they're still saying my life will be difficult if I marry him, and they don't want that for me."

Aunt Letitia clasped her hand. "I offered before and you didn't want my help, but I'll ask again. Do you want me to speak to them?"

Catherine smiled. "No, thank you, Miss Glass, but all will be well very soon. You'll see." She glanced at the door again as voices drifted up to us from the entrance hall.

Footsteps pounded on the stairs, accompanied by Bristow ordering someone to wait.

I stood, as did Catherine, ready to face the forceful newcomer.

Gareth Mason burst into the drawing room, and I sat back down with relief.

Catherine's youngest brother was little more than sixteen years old, and hadn't fully grown into his long limbs yet. He was all angles with a mop of blonde hair that fell into his eyes as he removed his cap. He scrunched it in both hands as he bit his lower lip.

Catherine rushed to him. "What is it? What's the matter?"

"Pardon my intrusion, Mrs. Glass, Miss Glass, but I need to speak to my sister."

More footsteps approached the drawing room, but it was only Matt and the others come to see what the commotion was about.

Cyclops pushed his way through. "Gareth! What are you doing here?"

"I'm in a bit of trouble. Can you help me?"

"What sort of trouble?"

"My friends wanted me to join them on a nighttime... excursion, and I refused."

"What sort of excursion?" Matt asked.

"They want to go to the cemetery and...look around."

Catherine clicked her tongue. "You mean get drunk and deface property. Honestly, Gareth."

He put up his hands in surrender. "I told you, I refused. You know Ma doesn't like me going out at night. But this time my friends are being real insistent. They say they'll beat me if I don't go." He nibbled his lip again. "I'm scared, Cath."

Despite his big eyes and forlorn look, she had no sympathy for him. She reminded me of her mother as she thrust her hand on her hip. "Those boys are always getting you into trouble. When are you going to learn to stay away from them?"

His gaze narrowed. "Probably now."

She huffed out a breath. "We'll notify the police."

"No! They'll know it was me who told on them! They'll beat me senseless, Cath!" He turned to Cyclops. "What should I do?"

"You can tell me where to find them," he said. "I'll have a word with them."

Gareth blew out a breath and his body relaxed. "Would you? That would help. They'd listen to you. Can you come now?"

"Of course."

"Me and Duke will come too," Willie said.

"No!" When we all looked at Gareth, he added, "I think

just Cyclops. Too many and they'll react the wrong way. They'll think they're being ambushed. I don't want to make enemies of them more than I already have."

"I don't know," Willie hedged.

Cyclops clapped her on the shoulder. "I'll be fine. They're just a few local lads, and I'll do my best impression of a cutthroat pirate. They'll be quaking in their boots when I finish with them."

Willie reluctantly agreed to let him go alone, but she complained about it for some time after Cyclops and Gareth left. I think she was more frustrated at being left out than worried about their safety.

"That was rather a to-do," Lord Farnsworth said as he sat beside Aunt Letitia. "Are you all right, dear lady?"

"Yes, of course," she said with a nonchalant shrug of her shoulder. "Dramatic interruptions are commonplace in this household. I'm rather used to them."

I resumed my seat beside Catherine on the other sofa and clasped her hand. "They'll be all right."

She gave me a comforting smile. "I know. I am sorry for Gareth's interruption. It's been a pleasant evening up until now."

"And it shall be again," Aunt Letitia said. "Cyclops will see that those thugs leave your brother alone. They'll be too terrified to put a foot wrong once he's finished with them."

Willie frowned at the door. "Wish I'd gone with them. Ain't nothing scarier than a woman dressed like a man wielding a gun."

"Amen," Chronos muttered.

Cyclops arrived home an hour later looking satisfied with himself. He accepted a glass of brandy from Duke and took a seat. We all waited for him to speak, but it took Willie kicking his ankle for him to notice us staring.

"All is well," he said. "Gareth is safely home, and his so-called friends have promised to leave him alone."

"What did you have to do to them to get them to promise that?" Willie asked.

"A few well-chosen words did the trick."

She scoffed. "Words? That's not much fun."

He smiled at Catherine and she smiled back.

"Did my parents see him come home?" she asked.

His smile vanished, replaced by a small wince. "They did, sorry. I wanted him to be quiet, but he made a real ruckus when he let himself in. They came downstairs to see what was going on. I think we woke them up."

"How did they react?"

"They were worried at first when they saw me, but Gareth told them what happened." He laughed softly and shook his head. "He made me sound like a hero saving him from a life threatening situation. That boy can act better than anyone I've seen on stage."

"No," she said quickly. "No, he can't. He must have been more worried than he let on when he was here, that's all. Thank you, Nate. I do appreciate you going to his rescue."

He tried to contain his shy smile, which only made him look sweet. Catherine looked as though she wanted to kiss him right in front of everyone, but she remembered where she was and refrained.

Aunt Letitia rose and pretended to read the ladies' magazine opened at the page of wedding dress designs that Catherine had set down when Gareth arrived. Instead of returning to her seat, she stopped beside Catherine and whispered, "Perhaps now would be the right moment for him to ask your father."

* * *

AN INVITATION CAME the following day from Mrs. Delancey, asking Matt and me to join her and the rest of the collector's club for an evening of "magical entertainment."

"What do you suppose that means?" I asked him as he read the invitation in his study.

"Perhaps she plans to have a fairground magician perform sleight-of-hand tricks."

"Very amusing."

He tossed the card on his desk. "It would be more entertaining than the usual lectures. At least for me."

"You don't have to go."

"I want to go. I want to see what they think about Charbonneau now."

"Do you think they'll know about it yet?"

"They are a close-knit group with some well-informed people among their membership. They'll know."

Collector's club meetings were always fraught affairs, and I often didn't want to attend. But I found that I agreed with Matt about this one—I was curious to see what they thought of Fabian now.

Matt was also right about them knowing. The sudden cessation of all conversation upon our entry was a clear sign that we were the evening's main topic of gossip so far. Mrs. Delancey recovered first, inviting us into her drawing room with warm smiles and a friendly greeting.

"You haven't brought your interesting little cousin, Mr. Glass," she said, peering past us.

"I didn't think Willie was invited," he said.

"That doesn't always stop her though, does it?"

The group was smaller than usual. Mrs. Delancey had clearly invited only specific members, not the entire club. This wasn't going to be a usual meeting or lecture then. Indeed, I suspected it had been hastily put together to discuss Fabian's betrayal and to see my reaction.

Going by Louisa's dark expression, she was taking Fabian's side, as Professor Nash suspected she would. The professor himself was with her. Going by his red face and heavyset brow, they'd been having a heated exchange, although I couldn't imagine the quiet professor winning against the forthright Louisa.

Oscar was not present, but Lord Coyle was, along with Hope and Sir Charles Whittaker. I thought Sir Charles had a nerve showing up when he was not a collector. Most likely few others in attendance knew that, however, and he wanted to maintain his disguise.

I sidled closer to Matt, suddenly feeling surrounded by people I didn't like. The professor was the friendliest face, until Lord Farnsworth breezed in, all swagger and toothy smiles.

"Why the long faces?" he asked with blustery innocence.

The professor shushed him and whispered something in his ear.

"Oh, *that*." Lord Farnsworth waved a hand in the air. "Terrible business, just terrible, but we must all look on the bright side."

The professor frowned which caused his glasses to slip down his nose. "There's a bright side?"

"Of course! Glass isn't dead!" He started a round of applause, and Mr. and Mrs. Delancey and the professor joined in. Even Sir Charles clapped, but I suspected that was to keep up his ruse of affable gentleman of leisure.

"Stop it!" Louisa snapped. She even stomped her foot on the floor. "Stop this at once. It's cruel to celebrate the smearing of a good man's name."

"I say, Louisa, steady on. Why are you taking his side?"

"Because he didn't do it."

"He did," I told her through a tight jaw. "He admitted as much to us but refused to repeat his confession to the police."

Louisa's eyes flashed. "This is an abomination. Fabian is one of the most powerful magicians in the world. His magic is strong, his lineage ancient. We cannot blame him for wanting to strengthen it."

"Would you forgive so easily if he tried to kill someone you loved?"

"Of course."

Lord Farnsworth leaned closer to me and whispered, "She doesn't love anyone."

Louisa's nostrils flared and she stormed up to me. "Fabian may not be innocent, but he shouldn't be derided. Everyone deserves a second chance, and I'm going to extend that courtesy to him, even if no one else will." Her gaze darted around the room at the faces staring back, finally settling on Lord Coyle. "What about you? You covet pieces of Fabian's iron for your collection. Would you abandon him now when he needs your influence the most?"

Lord Coyle covered the head of his walking stick with both hands. "My dear, I have no interest in Mr. Charbonneau's affairs, criminal or otherwise. He is free to sell me pieces of magic iron or not. That won't change."

Louisa tossed her head and strode out of the room.

Mrs. Delancey raced after her, calling for a footman to notify Louisa's coachman that his mistress was leaving.

Mr. Delancey came up to us and greeted Matt with a handshake and me with a bow. "I'm not sure Louisa will get another invite after that little tantrum. I thought she was particularly engaged to that ink magician fellow, the one who wrote the book on magic."

"She was," I said. "But not anymore."

"Well, well. Ordinarily I'd sympathize with the chap for having his heart broken, but I think he escaped the noose with that one."

"I don't think his heart was engaged in the first place."

He moved off only to be replaced by Professor Nash. His face was still flushed and his brow creased. "Her support for Charbonneau was more public than I expected it to be, but love can make one act rashly, so I'm told."

"You think she loves him?" I asked, genuinely curious.

"I don't know."

"She's in love with his magic," Matt said.

Mrs. Delancey returned, a hard smile on her face in an attempt to smooth over the social disaster Louisa had caused. The evening turned as excruciating as her smile from that point. The entertainment she'd promised turned out to be Mrs. Delancey showing us her magical objects yet again, and telling us how she'd acquired them.

Lord Coyle broke away from the group during Mrs. Delancey's speech about her set of magical silver forks. He walked off without a word to his wife. When she realized he was no longer by her side, Hope picked up her skirts and raced after him. At the door, he glanced back at Matt and me and jerked his head for us to follow.

I thought we shouldn't do as commanded, but Matt wanted to know what Lord Coyle wanted. We slipped away and joined Lord and Lady Coyle in the small chamber off the drawing room. His walking stick leaned against a table and a cigar was wedged between his thick lips. He struck a match and lit it.

"I don't think our hostess would like you smoking in this room," Hope said.

He puffed three times on the cigar, sending smoke billowing around him. "I hear you rejected an offer to work for the home office."

I managed to keep my features schooled despite my surprise, but Hope did not.

She blinked rapidly at me. "Why do the home office want to employ India?"

"Come now, my dear, try to use that brain of yours for something other than spending my money. I know you have one. Marriage to me cannot have dulled your intelligence already."

It was as if he'd slapped her. She stepped back and

seemed to recoil at the same time, her face wincing as if in pain.

Matt took pity on her and explained. "The home secretary wants India to drop bombs from flying magic carpets in wartime."

Hope gasped. "But how did they know you can do that, India?" Even as she said it, she turned to her husband. "*You* told them, didn't you? That's why you met with Sir Charles. You told him we saw India flying off on a carpet with the iron magician, and Sir Charles told his superiors."

Lord Coyle removed his cigar from his mouth and pointed it at his wife. "There, you see. That's the intelligent woman I married."

"Are you finished?" Matt snapped. "India and I have a talk we want to listen to."

Lord Coyle grabbed his walking stick and leaned into it. "I wanted to thank India for rejecting the home secretary's offer. If not for her rejection, I doubt Mr. Matthews would have offered the same position to me."

"You're working for the government?" I blurted out.

He smiled as he bit down on the cigar. "I gave Sir Charles the information about you flying off on a carpet on the condition he credit me as the source. It seems he kept his promise, and after you rejected the job, Mr. Matthews came to me."

"You are hardly a replacement for India," Hope said with a sneer.

"Of course, of course. Nothing is as good as a powerful magician to fly the carpet. But I have other skills that India could have provided but chose not to—I can act as a liaison between the government and magicians; I have a lot of sway with the community."

"Through blackmail and intimidation," I bit off.

He gave me a rueful smile. "I have ideas too. Lots of ideas as to how magic can be harnessed for the good of the British Empire. In this, I am probably more valuable than you, as my interests align with the government's in many ways."

The floor suddenly felt unsteady beneath my feet and the air left my lungs. *This* was what Lord Coyle wanted all along —power and influence at the highest level. He was not interested in money, nor did he care about being influential among the collector's club members. He didn't even particularly care about magical lineages or the future of magic. He wanted to direct national policy and wield power on a global scale, and he saw his knowledge about magic, and his ability to manipulate magicians as a means to obtaining it.

Lord Coyle's phlegmy chuckle rattled in his chest. "I see this has come as a shock to both of you. I'm sure once that wears off you'll realize that magic can play a role in furthering the interests of this great nation of ours."

"Not without me, it won't." My words became lost as the door burst open and Sir Charles stormed inside.

With his teeth bared and his eyes glittering like hard stones, I finally felt as though I was seeing the real Sir Charles Whittaker. There was nothing of the elegant gentleman about him now. He was an angry snake, poised to strike as he confronted Lord Coyle. With their faces inches apart, he spat, "You used me."

"It was a mutual exchange of information," Lord Coyle said idly. "We both benefited."

"You stole my idea."

"What idea?" Matt asked darkly.

Sir Charles seemed not to have heard him. He was focused on Lord Coyle, like a wild animal on its pray—or its predator.

Lord Coyle continued to smile around his cigar, unperturbed. "The idea about dropping bombs from flying carpet on our enemies factories and bases."

I stared wide-eyed at Sir Charles. "That was your idea?"

Sir Charles's nostrils flared, and he finally tore his gaze away from Coyle. "He told me about seeing you fly the carpet, and I informed my superiors. I thought it could be used in wartime to drop bombs. I didn't take that suggestion to my superiors at the time but held it back on his advice. Then he swooped in and told them, and he let them think it was his idea."

Lord Coyle smacked his walking stick into Sir Charles's shin. "Move aside. My wife and I are leaving."

Sir Charles's lips pinched so hard they turned white, but he moved out of the way.

"I'd like to stay a little longer," Hope said. She seemed to rally after looking quite stunned throughout the confrontation.

Lord Coyle limped off. "I'll send the carriage back for you."

Sir Charles marched up to the closed door and put a hand against it, blocking Lord Coyle's exit. "You owe me for stealing my idea."

Lord Coyle grunted. "It's payment for the information I gave you about the flying carpet. Without me, you would not have anything valuable to offer Le Grand. I saved your job for you." He raised his walking stick and smacked it hard against Sir Charles's leg.

Sir Charles groaned and clutched his shin. "I know things about you, Coyle," he snarled. "I know what you've done."

Lord Coyle opened the door and limped out.

A strained silence filled the room. Mrs. Delancey's cultured, girlish voice broke off mid-sentence as she protested Lord Coyle's early departure. The other club members stared at us.

Matt placed a hand lightly on the back of neck. "Are you all right?"

"He now has even more power than before," I whispered.

"It means nothing without you. The magicians he manipulates can do very little on their own. Certainly nothing of use to the home office."

I looked to Sir Charles for confirmation, but he wasn't listening. He limped out of the room too and rejoined the group of club members as Mrs. Delancey continued her talk.

"Hope?" Matt said. "Would you like to sit?"

With a hand at her throat, she stared after the gentlemen. "This is not what I wanted," she muttered. "It's not what I wanted at all."

It may not be the sort of marriage she'd hoped for, when she accepted Lord Coyle's proposal, but she couldn't have expected it to be a bed of roses, either. With her husband's power growing, she must realize that she would become more influential too.

I found it hard to believe she didn't want that.

* * *

WITH MATT'S PRODIGIOUS MEMORY, he was able to recite the meeting almost word for word for Cyclops, Willie and Duke. They joined us in the dining room for breakfast after rising at a reasonable hour, despite going out together the previous night. But while Willie had left with one of the barmaids, and Duke decided to call on his paramour, Widow Rotherhide, Cyclops had returned home.

Given Willie and Duke hadn't slept as much, it was unsurprising they seemed somewhat unfocused this morning, yawning as they listened to Matt. Cyclops was as sharp as ever.

"What do you think Whittaker meant when he told Coyle he knows what he's done?" he asked.

"That's what I'd like to know," Matt said.

Their gazes connected. "I have the day off," Cyclops told him.

Matt picked up his coffee cup and rose. "Let me refill this and we'll go. I want to catch him before he goes out."

Willie wrinkled her nose. "Who?"

Duke yawned. "Coyle, I think."

"Idiots," Cyclops muttered.

"He means Sir Charles," I said. "And I'm coming too."

All five of us went, with Willie electing to ride alongside Woodall on the driver's seat. She hoped the cold air would wake her up. Duke should have ridden with them. He yawned all the way.

The landlady answered the door when Matt knocked. When she saw us, she sighed. "You lot again. He's not in."

"When will he be back?" Matt asked.

"I don't know. I haven't seen him this morning, and I didn't hear him go out. He left his breakfast tray untouched, too." She clicked her tongue. "Such a waste of food."

"If you didn't see or hear him, how do you know he left?"

"He wouldn't still be in his room at this hour. It's almost ten. He must have gone out for breakfast."

"Has he ever gone out to breakfast before and forgotten to tell you not to bring up a tray?" I asked.

Her eyes narrowed. "Now that you mention it, no. He's always considerate like that." For someone who was paid by Mr. Le Grand to spy on Sir Charles, she was not very efficient.

"Mind if I take a look in his rooms?" Matt asked.

She hesitated before stepping aside. "I wouldn't usually do this, but something doesn't feel right." She hurried off into the gloomy corridor. "I'll fetch the spare key."

Matt knocked on Sir Charles's door at the top of the landing while we waited for the landlady. There was no answer. The landlady joined us and unlocked the door.

"It's just me, Sir Charles," she said loudly as she entered the parlor. "We were just worried—" She covered her mouth with both hands and smothered her scream.

I rushed past her, along with Matt, only to stop short upon seeing the gruesome sight of Sir Charles's dead eyes staring back at us from where he sat sprawled in an armchair, his throat cut.

CHAPTER 17

J managed to steer the landlady back downstairs to the kitchen where I made her a cup of tea from the pot warming on the stove. She was still shaking, her face pale. Although she'd spied on Sir Charles for Mr. Le Grand, she was clearly not a professional agent. She'd probably accepted the task for a little extra money.

I returned upstairs once she was settled. Duke had gone to Scotland Yard to fetch Brockwell, while Willie, Cyclops and Matt inspected the body and Sir Charles's rooms. I avoided looking directly at him. I'd already seen his cut throat and bloodied clothes and didn't wish to see them again.

Matt handed me a piece of paper. "We found this on the table beside his glass of brandy. The knife is on the floor."

I read the two lines on Sir Charles's personalized stationery, written in all capitals, then glanced quickly at the knife, lying on the floor between the round occasional table and the chair.

"It must have slipped from his fingers," I said.

"Or it was placed there by his killer."

"You don't think this suicide note was written by him?" The note stated that he was ending his life because he felt deep regret that Mr. Pyke almost died after the failed carpet experiment. He blamed himself for forcing the magician to fly it.

"I'm keeping an open mind, but he didn't display any remorse over Pyke when we confronted him."

"Perhaps if Pyke had died, he might have."

"But Pyke didn't die. There's also the handwriting itself that makes me skeptical that he wrote it. Willie is looking for samples of his writing now, but block capital is the typography of choice for someone attempting to hide their own style."

Willie was sitting at the desk by the window, sifting through pieces of paper. "There ain't too many with his own handwriting on them. They're mostly letters from others, receipts and orders." She waved a sheet of paper. "This here is a half-written letter to his mother."

Matt took it from her and we compared the capitals to the suicide note. The letter was written in cursive, however. "It's impossible," I said with a shake of my head.

Matt returned to the body to inspect the wound, so I joined Cyclops in the bedchamber. We searched high and low, underneath tables and the bed, inside the cupboard and storage boxes, in the light fitting, a vase, and a gun case. While I checked inside shoes, Cyclops inspected Sir Charles's more intimate clothing items, including the seams, as well as the shaving brush, toothbrush, and other grooming items. He even dug his fingers through the jar of Macassar Oil for hidden objects or correspondence. We found nothing of interest. I thought it unusual not to find communications from Mr. Le Grand, and said so.

"Whittaker would have been under orders to destroy any messages he received," Cyclops pointed out.

"But wouldn't he have kept notes? Like Coyle does in his notebook."

Cyclops tapped his forehead. "Someone in his line of work

keeps that information up here. They don't write it down. If he had left important documents lying about, Coyle would have taken them after he killed Whittaker."

"You're subscribing to the theory that Coyle murdered him?"

"Did Whittaker strike you as someone to commit suicide because he felt responsible for another man's injury?"

I sat on the bed with a sigh. "I didn't know him well enough to say one way or another."

We continued our search but found nothing of importance by the time Brockwell arrived with Duke and three constables. He took in the scene with his usual slow, deliberate manner, before his gaze finally settled on Willie.

She perched on the window sill, her arms crossed over her chest, staring down at the street below. She responded with brisk indifference when he greeted her, but did not look directly at him.

He cleared his throat and bent to inspect the body. Now that I'd had time to steel myself, I too studied Sir Charles. The deep wound on the right side of his throat was positioned where a right-handed man would stab himself. He must have discarded his evening tailcoat as soon as he arrived home and laid it across the back of the sofa. It was clean. Blood had soaked through his once pristine white necktie, waistcoat and shirt and spilled onto the chair cushion and even onto the floor where the knife had been found. There was so much of it, but it was dry now.

I turned away once again as my stomach lurched.

Matt touched my hand. "This won't take long. Do you want to wait in the kitchen?"

I shook my head as the inspector stood. "A knife in the neck is not the first choice for suicides," he said. "There are a lot of other methods that are easier and quicker."

"Maybe it was the most convenient method," Cyclops said. "It doesn't require much planning. It must have been a spur of the moment decision and he wanted to get it over with before he changed his mind. That's if it were suicide."

Brockwell arched his brow first at Cyclops then Matt. Matt handed him the suicide note and indicated the knife. He waited for Brockwell to finish reading then told him his theory that Sir Charles was murdered.

"By whom and why?" Brockwell asked.

"By Coyle, because Whittaker threatened him last night at a collector's club meeting. Whittaker was furious with Coyle for stealing his idea about magic and using it to muscle his way into the home secretary's good graces. He told Coyle he knew secrets about him, something he'd done."

Brockwell twisted his mouth to the side as he scratched his sideburns. They were looking particularly long and unkempt today, even for him. I glanced at Willie to see if she at least regarded the inspector wistfully, but she was still staring out of the window.

Brockwell picked up the knife and squinted at the handle and blade.

"It's a kitchen knife," Matt said. "It's not the sort of blade found in a gentleman's rented accommodations or the sort a burglar carries on his person."

"Have you asked the landlady if any are missing?"

"Not yet."

"Cyclops, take one of my men with you and get her to take a stock of her knives. Have a look around while you're down there."

The inspector insisted on searching the parlor and bedroom himself while they were gone. Matt and Duke joined him, but I stood with Willie and leaned one shoulder against the window frame.

"Are you all right?" I asked.

"Course I am. I've seen dead men before."

"I mean with Brockwell here."

She rolled her eyes. "He's here to do his job, not see me."

"Do you want him to come and see you?"

She shrugged.

"If you do, you should let him know. Perhaps you should call on him to show him you're still interested."

She gave me a withering glare. "He doesn't want to see me. Not anymore."

"What's happened between you?" She merely shrugged again so I grabbed her shoulders and gave her a little shake. "Tell me!"

Brockwell returned, notepad in one hand and pencil in the other. "Excuse me, ladies." He cleared his throat. "May I have a word with you, India? Will you give me a statement of your version of events last night, please, specifically regarding the conversation between Whittaker and Lord Coyle."

"You're going to treat Coyle as a suspect?"

"Perhaps." He indicated I should sit then proceeded to write down my account. He then asked Matt to do the same.

Brockwell was just flipping the notebook closed when Cyclops and the constable returned. They reported that a knife matching the one found on the floor was indeed missing from the kitchen.

"Not only that, the back door was unlocked," Cyclops said. "The landlady is convinced she locked it, as she does every night along with the front door. The killer could have picked the lock, taken a knife as he passed through the kitchen, then left the same way."

Brockwell nodded. "Thank you, Cyclops, I'll go downstairs and take her statement now. The rest of you should leave. India is looking a little peaky."

"I'm all right, but I do think we should go. There's nothing more to do here."

The journey home was a somber one. I suspected Willie was still sulking, but the rest of us were mulling over what we'd seen as well as the events of the previous night. The more I thought about it, the more convinced I was that Matt and Cyclops were right, and Lord Coyle had killed Sir Charles because he threatened him. Or perhaps simply because he no longer had a use for him. Coyle had, after all, used Sir Charles to gather information and gain a position of power in the government. With that goal achieved, Sir Charles was no longer an asset, he was a liability. By threatening him last night, Sir Charles had sealed his own fate.

Suspecting Lord Coyle had done it was one thing, but having him arrested for murder was another altogether. Lord Coyle wouldn't have broken into the house himself and thrust the knife into Sir Charles's neck with his own hand. He had accomplices for that. Accomplices he paid well to keep quiet.

But paid accomplices weren't particularly loyal. They could be bought or coerced into telling the truth. We had to trust that Brockwell would find Coyle's men and exert enough pressure to turn them against their employer.

Matt couldn't settle to anything after we arrived home. He complained that he had no business matters that required his attention, nor did any of the books in our library appeal to him, and the newspapers were full of "sensationalist" stories that didn't hold his interest. He even suggested we go shopping together for something to do. Considering Matt liked shopping as much as most men, I knew he must be desperate to take his mind off the death of Sir Charles.

"Why don't we just go for a walk around Hyde Park instead," I said.

After two hours, we returned home feeling invigorated and somewhat less frustrated. I didn't think the feeling would last long, however, and worried Matt would soon head off to Scotland Yard to learn what progress Brockwell had made in his investigation.

Not long after hanging up our hats and coats, we had a visitor. Hope entered the drawing room like a fierce storm dressed head to toe in steel gray. Her expression was just as ominous with severely drawn brows and a set jaw.

"How delightful to see you," Aunt Letitia said without much sincerity. "Has somebody died? A distant relative of your husband's perhaps?"

Hope shook her head as if to clear it. "What?"

Aunt Letitia eyed Hope up and down. "You're dressed in half-mourning."

"Nobody died." She turned away from her aunt, presenting her with her profile.

Aunt Letitia stiffened at the slight.

"Why didn't you do something, Matt?" Hope's voice was part whine, part accusation. "I told you so you would act, yet you did nothing!"

Matt had stood upon Hope's entry and since she had not yet sat down, he remained standing too. Her accusation seemed to catch him off guard, but only for a moment. "Will you join us for tea? Bristow, another cup for Lady Coyle, please."

The butler bowed out as Hope sat, somewhat reluctantly.

"I'm not here for tea," she bit off. "I'm here to find out why you did nothing after I gave you the information."

Matt looked to me, but I shrugged, not sure what she meant either. "What information?" he asked.

"I informed you that my husband met with Sir Charles Whittaker in secret in the garden square, and now he's dead."

Aunt Letitia gasped. "Lord Coyle is dead?"

Hope clicked her tongue. "No, Sir Charles is. Do keep up."

"Are you implying you think your husband had something to do with Sir Charles's death?" Matt asked.

Hope's fingers entwined together in her lap. "I don't know. It's possible. But if you'd done something with the information I'd given you, perhaps he we wouldn't be in this predicament."

Now I understood why she'd told us about that meeting.

We had suspected at the time she had a motive, but couldn't fathom what it would be. It now seemed she had wanted us to inform Scotland Yard, or perhaps someone higher, and put an end to such meetings. It seemed she knew her husband was up to something with Sir Charles and that worried her.

"You mean the predicament of Sir Charles's death?" I clarified.

She flicked her wrist, dismissing my suggestion. "I mean the predicament we're now faced with my husband gaining a position in government. Do you know how powerful that makes him? He was not above the law before, but now he is."

"No one is above the law," Matt said.

She scoffed. "Don't be so naïve. You know better than anyone how the world works, how it favors men like my husband." She pressed her fingers to her forehead as if trying to suppress a headache. She looked rather pale now that the flush of anger had left her cheeks.

Bristow returned carrying a tray with a cup and saucer. I poured the tea and handed the cup to Hope. She immediately placed it back on the table, untouched.

She fixed a glare onto Matt. "I tried to foil my husband's plans by telling you about him meeting Sir Charles. Why didn't you do something with the information?"

"If you wanted me to do something, you should have told me so."

She made a scoffing sound again.

"What did you want me to do?" he asked.

"I don't know. Perhaps warn Sir Charles to be careful what information he passed on because my husband cannot be trusted. Or warn the home secretary that one of his spies was not keeping information to himself. If Sir Charles had been dismissed, he would never have given my husband the idea about dropping bombs from flying carpets."

"Coyle is clever, calculating and forward thinking," Matt

said. "He would have come up with the idea on his own sooner or later."

Her lips pinched with her refusal to concede the point.

"Why do you want to stop your husband anyway?" I asked. "The more power he has, the more power you have."

She bristled. "You think I don't know what my husband is like? You think I am not aware of the way he could abuse his power? Some think I'm entirely avaricious, but I can assure you, riches and respect are enough to satisfy me. Marriage to Coyle has given me both. I don't want more and I don't want him becoming more powerful than he already is."

That was what she meant in the Delanceys antechamber when she said it's not what she wanted. She didn't want her husband to become even more powerful. She didn't want to live a life where she feared him.

I suddenly sat forward. "We'll protect you, Hope. You don't have to stay with him. Divorce might be out of the question, but you don't have to live in that house one moment longer than necessary."

She shot to her feet and glared at me down the length of her nose. "Don't be absurd. How will that look?"

Her biting retort rendered me speechless.

Matt, however, remained composed. "Does it matter?" he asked.

"People will think me weak, pathetic. Thank you for your offer, but it's not one I will accept."

"Hope is right." Aunt Letitia surprised us all by speaking. I thought she'd failed to follow the conversation. "She made her bed, now she must lie in it."

Hope gave her aunt a stiff nod then strode out of the room. I hastily followed to ensure Bristow was there to see her off and, as usual, he was ahead of me and already waiting for her in the entrance hall at the base of the staircase.

I returned to the drawing room and sat with a sigh. "Why

do I feel as though I've just faced a champion fighter in the ring?"

"Because conversations with Hope are bruising," Aunt Letitia said. "Particularly of late. I miss the clever but naïve girl she used to be."

"Marriage to Coyle has forced her to grow up quickly, I suspect." I turned to Matt, sitting with a thoughtful expression. "Should we be worried about her?"

"I don't know," he said. "But I'm going to worry regardless."

* * *

BEFORE DETECTIVE INSPECTOR BROCKWELL ARRIVED, I worried that Matt would go in search of him. He was desperate for an update on the investigation, and my attempts to distract him failed miserably. Thankfully Brockwell timed it perfectly, arriving just before the dinner gong sounded.

We all welcomed him into the drawing room with enthusiasm. All except Willie, that is. She didn't do anything rude, like get up and leave, but she refused to even look at him when he made a particular point of looking at her when he greeted us.

The entire household was there, as well as Lord Farnsworth, Catherine, Chronos, and even Oscar. Brockwell's arrival made our party feel complete. Everyone had been apprised of the murder, and we'd taken advantage of Aunt Letitia being in her room dressing for dinner to discuss it. All were of the opinion that Lord Coyle was certainly a suspect, and probably the guilty party.

"Will you join us for dinner?" I asked the inspector when he settled in a chair.

"No, thank you, India, I'm just passing by to give you some news about the investigation into Whittaker's murder. I prefer not to stay, if that's all right with you."

"Of course."

Having no further instruction, Bristow bowed out and closed the door.

"What's happened?" Matt asked.

Brockwell sighed. "The investigation has been closed. I was directed to rule it a suicide. There'll be no coronial inquest."

"Who directed you?"

"Commissioner Munro himself."

Duke swore under his breath. "Matt can speak to him tomorrow and try to get it overturned."

Brockwell shook his head. "It won't do any good. I suspect he was following orders given by his superior." The commissioner's superior was the home secretary himself. "With a suicide note found at the scene, it's not an unreasonable conclusion to come to."

"It is unreasonable when there are doubts," Oscar said.

"You didn't let me finish. It's not an unreasonable conclusion to come to when the two main suspects are an earl who now works for the home office, and spy master Le Grand."

"Blimey," Lord Farnsworth muttered. "You think the government sanctioned Whittaker's murder?"

Brockwell shrugged. "We can speculate all we want. The verdict of suicide won't be altered."

Matt had remained silent up until now, but he nodded at this. He knew it was hopeless. He'd known all along that Brockwell's hands would be tied in this investigation and that the truth might be buried. That didn't mean it couldn't be dug up, but Scotland Yard wouldn't be wielding the spade.

While Matt looked somewhat resigned, Brockwell seemed disappointed and frustrated. Poor man. He would have spent most of the day on the investigation only to have it quashed.

"Thank you for coming here to tell us," I said. "Are you sure you won't join us for dinner?"

"Do stay," Lord Farnsworth urged. "After all, we have

things to celebrate. Glass's life is no longer in danger, for one thing." He clapped lightly in Matt's direction. When no one else joined in, he added, "Let me see... I know! My horse Midnight Blue is in fine form for the spring races. And there were no protests by the artless today."

"Yes there were," Cyclops said.

"Really? Where?"

"Lambeth and Islington."

"I don't go near either of those places." He frowned hard as he thought. "Let me see, there must be more good news." He snapped his fingers. "Willie didn't get thrown out of White's last night, despite a rumor that she has breasts."

Duke laughed. "Who started that rumor?"

Lord Farnsworth deflated beneath Willie's sharp glare. "I was bored. I wanted to see what would happen," he muttered.

Brockwell cleared his throat. "I'm very happy for everyone's good fortune. But I think it's best that I leave now."

Lord Farnsworth sighed as he appealed to me. "I tried, India, but it's hopeless."

I tugged on the bellpull for Bristow and the butler arrived and saw Brockwell out.

Lord Farnsworth, Duke and Cyclops all turned to Willie with stern glares. She tilted her chin and looked away.

"I have some good news, as it happens," Catherine announced. "I was going to tell you later, Nate, but I might as well do it now. My mother has asked you to dine with us tomorrow night."

"I don't understand," he said carefully.

She grinned. "She wants to thank you for scaring off that gang that Gareth has been tangled up with."

"They're not really a gang. Just a group of youths in high spirits with too much time on their hands."

"I know, but don't tell my parents. They've been so worried about him these last few weeks. But after Gareth told them how you protected him and threatened those youths if they came near him again, my parents think you're wonderful."

"But I didn't do anything."

Duke clapped Cyclops on the shoulder. "Don't argue. Accept it. This is what you wanted."

Cyclops's smile started slow but quickly widened. "All right. Thank them for the invitation. I accept."

Later, after dinner had finished and Aunt Letitia retired, I sat alone with Catherine in the drawing room while we waited for the men and Willie to join us. Peter the footman poured each of us a glass of brandy at the drinks trolley. The men couldn't be allowed to keep all the vices to themselves.

"I feel as though we should be smoking cigars," Catherine said with a laugh as she accepted the glass from Peter.

"Aunt Letitia would have a fit if you did. She loathes it when someone smokes in here." I waited for Peter to bow out before turning to my friend. "You colluded with Gareth, didn't you?"

Catherine fluttered her pale lashes and shrugged a shoulder. "Whatever do you mean, India?"

"Your sly smile is giving you away. I know you orchestrated this gang of youths to bully Gareth then asked Cyclops to step in and diffuse the situation. Gareth was obviously in on it."

"Don't tell Nate. He'd be embarrassed." She settled into the chair and swirled the liquid around her glass. "You're right in that Gareth helped me with the scheme, as did his friends. I had to pay them, of course, but Gareth did it for free. He can be sweet, sometimes. I know he idolizes Nate, so he wants to see him accepted by our parents too. You should have heard my mother go on and on about how fortunate he was that Nate stepped in, how capable he is, and how he's got a big future ahead of him in the police force." Her smiled widened. "My plan worked better than I expected."

I must have had too much wine at dinner because I giggled at the image of Mrs. Mason now begging Cyclops to marry Catherine. I rarely giggled these days, but I felt at ease now with Matt's life no longer in danger. And while Sir Charles's demise was a terrible business, it didn't directly affect our household. I felt much lighter of heart than I had in some weeks.

Willie entered, only to stop short upon seeing us both giggling. She made a face as if revolted. "I hoped for some civilized conversation in here."

"Are the men not being civilized?" I asked.

"They keep pestering me about what went wrong between me and Brockwell. Even Matt."

I patted the cushion beside me on the sofa. Once she was seated, I turned to her. "What did go wrong?"

She shot to her feet again and strode to the door. But I was ready for her attempted escape, and raced past her. I blocked the exit. "I won't let you pass until you tell me."

She tilted her head to the side and arched her brows. "You know I can easily move you."

"I don't see how. I'm bigger than you and quite possibly stronger."

She gave a derisive snort.

"I'm sure if you had a weapon, you could threaten me, but you're unarmed."

Catherine joined us and placed her arm around Willie's waist. "Come and sit down and tell us all about it. Perhaps we can help you solve the problem."

Willie let herself be steered back to the sofa. She sat with Catherine on one side and me on the other. Before she knew what was happening, we'd each grasped one of her hands so she couldn't easily escape.

She sighed deeply. "Jasper asked me to marry him."

I stared at her then exchanged glances with Catherine. "And you don't want to get married," I said flatly.

"I refused him. I told him I ain't never marrying, despite what the Romany woman said. I don't want a man to change me. I don't want anything to change. I like my life the way it is, without a husband in it."

"But do you want the inspector in it?" Catherine asked.

Willie looked down at the floor and nodded again.

"Sometimes we have to make sacrifices, or we'll lose the ones we love."

Willie pulled a face. "It ain't love. We're just good friends."

"You and Duke are good friends," I told her firmly. "You and Lord Farnsworth are good friends. You don't want to be intimate with either of them, do you?" I knew I'd got through to her when she didn't toss a rude retort back at me. "Let me put it another way. Would you be this upset if Duke decided to return to America without you?"

"I'd be upset, but I'd be happy for him if that's what he wanted."

"There, you see? There's your answer."

"I don't remember asking a question."

"Your question is, what do you do now?" I said. "Do you tell Brockwell you want to be with him but without any change from the status quo, and therefore risk losing him forever because he wants more?"

"Or do you give marriage some serious consideration?" Catherine finished.

Willie searched our faces, perhaps looking for the answer. But it wasn't something we could decide for her. She had to do it on her own.

"I need another drink," she said, rising.

The men joined us and Lord Farnsworth headed directly for Willie standing at the drinks trolley. He whispered something in her ear.

"Did you solve her problems?" Matt asked as he sidled up to me.

"Not entirely, but I believe we did a better job at helping

her decide what to do than you men." I leaned into him and rested my head on his shoulder. "What do you think they're talking about?"

He followed my gaze to Willie and Farnsworth, heads bent together conspiratorially. "They're probably discussing which gambling den to visit tonight."

"He's making her laugh."

"I think she's laughing at him, not with him."

"Either way, he's good to have around if he can cheer her up."

Matt nodded at Catherine and Cyclops, talking quietly in the corner. "They look happy. It seems Catherine's little ruse worked."

I pulled away to look at him properly. "You know about that?"

"I guessed, as did Cyclops."

I smiled. "I hope he doesn't let on that he knows. She'll be disappointed she didn't orchestrate a secret coup."

"She did orchestrate one, and she should be pleased with herself for coming up with the idea. The important thing is, Mr. and Mrs. Mason aren't aware it was a ruse and they're now willing to accept Cyclops into their family."

"And into their hearts, soon enough. He has a way of winning people over."

Matt gently touched my chin. "You seem very content tonight, India."

"That's because I am. Look around. Except for Willie, everyone is happy, and her situation is not all that dire, really. To have a good man want to marry her is not the end of the world."

He laughed softly, his breath feathering my hair. "It is to her, but I know what you mean." He kissed the top of my head. "I hate to dampen your good mood, but what about Charbonneau? You were fond of him."

"I'm disappointed in him. Deeply so. Angry too. But I

won't think about him anymore. I refuse to dwell on him a moment longer. He doesn't deserve it." I touched Matt's cheek, tracing the divot of his dimple with my fingertip. "He has been stopped, and you are well. That's all that matters."

His arm tightened around my waist. "He won't harm us or our loved ones again. I'll make sure of it. Coyle too. I promise you."

He couldn't make such a promise, but I appreciated it nevertheless.

I looked around at our little group of family and friends. Farnsworth was doing his best to take Willie's mind off her dilemma, while Duke and Oscar were deep in conversation. Cyclops and Catherine spoke quietly in the corner, their fingers lightly touching, and Chronos had fallen asleep on the sofa, his head tipped back and mouth open. Although Aunt Letitia and Brockwell were absent, they were there in spirit.

I didn't need anything more than this. With Matt at my side and our friends and family for company, I had more than enough to fill my heart.

Matt must have thought so too, because he kissed me thoroughly without a care that everyone could see.

Available from 1st March 2022:
THE GOLDSMITH'S CONSPIRACY
The 13th and final Glass and Steele novel

GET A FREE SHORT STORY

I wrote a short story for the Glass and Steele series that is set before THE WATCHMAKER'S DAUGHTER. Titled THE TRAITOR'S GAMBLE it features Matt and his friends in the Wild West town of Broken Creek. It contains spoilers from THE WATCHMAKER'S DAUGHTER, so you must read that first. The best part is, the short story is FREE, but only to my newsletter subscribers. So subscribe now via my website if you haven't already.

A MESSAGE FROM THE AUTHOR

I hope you enjoyed reading THE SPY MASTER'S SCHEME as much as I enjoyed writing it. As an independent author, getting the word out about my book is vital to its success, so if you liked this book please consider telling your friends and writing a review at the store where you purchased it. If you would like to be contacted when I release a new book, subscribe to my newsletter at http://cjarcher.com/contact-cj/ newsletter/. You will only be contacted when I have a new book out.

ALSO BY C.J. ARCHER

SERIES WITH 2 OR MORE BOOKS

Cleopatra Fox Mysteries

After The Rift

Glass and Steele

The Ministry of Curiosities Series

The Emily Chambers Spirit Medium Trilogy

The 1st Freak House Trilogy

The 2nd Freak House Trilogy

The 3rd Freak House Trilogy

The Assassins Guild Series

Lord Hawkesbury's Players Series

Witch Born

SINGLE TITLES NOT IN A SERIES

Courting His Countess

Surrender

Redemption

The Mercenary's Price

ABOUT THE AUTHOR

C.J. Archer has loved history and books for as long as she can remember and feels fortunate that she found a way to combine the two. She spent her early childhood in the dramatic beauty of outback Queensland, Australia, but now lives in suburban Melbourne with her husband, two children and a mischievous black & white cat named Coco.

Subscribe to C.J.'s newsletter through her website to be notified when she releases a new book, as well as get access to exclusive content and subscriber-only giveaways. Her website also contains up to date details on all her books: http://cjarcher.com She loves to hear from readers. You can contact her through email cj@cjarcher.com or follow her on social media to get the latest updates on her books:

CPSIA information can be obtained
at www.ICGtesting.com
Printed in the USA
LVHW091929200821
695510LV00001B/3